HELLO,
HOLLYWOOD!

Books by Janice Thompson

WEDDINGS BY BELLA

Fools Rush In
Swinging on a Star
It Had to Be You

BACKSTAGE PASS

Stars Collide
Hello, Hollywood!

HELLO, HOLLYWOOD!

A NOVEL

Janice Thompson

Revell

a division of Baker Publishing Group
Grand Rapids, Michigan

© 2011 by Janice Thompson

Published by Revell
a division of Baker Publishing Group
P.O. Box 6287, Grand Rapids, MI 49516-6287
www.revellbooks.com

Printed in the United States of America

Library of Congress Cataloging-in-Publication Data
Thompson, Janice A.
    Hello, Hollywood! : a novel / Janice Thompson.
        p.   cm. — (Backstage pass ; bk. 2)
    ISBN 978-0-8007-3346-9 (pbk.)
    1. Women television writers—Fiction. 2. Hollywood (Los Angeles, Calif.)—
Fiction. I. Title.
PS3620.H6824H45 2011
813'.6—dc22   2011015426

Published in association with MacGregor Literary Agency.

11 12 13 14 15 16 17   7 6 5 4 3 2 1

To my dog-sitter, Heather, who used incredible restraint and did not duct-tape my dogs to the ceiling while I was away.

1

What's My Line?

"Tell me what you think about this idea." I turned to face my fellow writers, my imagination shifting into overdrive as a clever scene unfolded in my head. "Angie and Jack are in a hut in the Amazon. They're wrapping up their honeymoon—maybe packing their bags or something—when an unexpected monsoon hits. Within minutes they're trapped inside the hut, water rising around them." I rubbed my hands together, unable to contain my excitement as I shared the best part. "Only, it's not *really* a monsoon, and they're not *really* in a hut."

"Huh?" Bob, the youngest in our band of writers, looked up from his spot on the sofa, his laptop nearly sliding to the floor. He scrambled to catch it, then steadied it on his knees. "What do you mean?"

Taking the empty chair next to the sofa, I laid out the rest of the idea. "I mean the whole thing has only been a dream.

In reality, Angie is sound asleep in the bathtub in their Los Angeles apartment, and the water has overflowed. The scene takes place a month after she and Jack have returned from their honeymoon. She's dozed off reminiscing about what a great time they had in the Amazon. Then she wakes up to find the bathroom flooded. Great, right?"

From his spot at the desk, Paul groaned, his thick black brows furrowing. "Athena, again with the Amazon thing? We closed out the last episode with that shtick. We've finally got the show's ratings back up, and we need to keep them there. Rehashing a previously used story is a death sentence for a sitcom." He rose and stretched, then leaned down and attempted to touch his toes—his usual routine after several hours of unproductive powwowing. When he stood upright, his cheeks were flushed.

"Yeah, network execs pay us to come up with new, fresh material every episode." Bob reached for his coffee cup and took a swig, splashing some on the edge of the laptop. He used the tail of his shirt to clean it off. "Not the same old, same old."

"But that's just it," I argued. "This will be fresh. I'm talking about a flashback scene. It'll be a great way to transition the viewers from one episode to the next. We left them hanging, you know. They'll expect us to pick up where we left off."

Besides, guys, this is a great idea. Swallow your pride and admit that a female writer can come up with something brilliant every now and again. I reached for a piece of baklava from the tray on the desk and took a bite of the honey-encrusted goodness, grateful for the excuse not to speak. My gaze shifted to the piano on the far side of the room. I could almost hear the Amazon theme music playing now. Maybe before the day was out I could actually compose something usable for the episode.

"I was thinking we could start this episode with Jack and

Angie on an airplane flying back from their honeymoon." Bob put his cup down on the coffee table, his eyes taking on that familiar glazed-over look that so often accompanied one of his more far-fetched ideas. "Maybe a couple of the animals from the rain forest are on the plane in the seat behind them. The monkey and the . . ." He scratched his head. "What did we use again?"

"A macaw," I reminded him, mouth still full.

"Right. The macaw." He typed a few notes into his computer, then looked back up at me. "So, we give the animals dialogue. What do you think?"

"Talking animals?" Paul did not look convinced. He took a few steps in our direction, plopped down on the sofa, and gave Bob a "you've got to be kidding" look.

"Or . . ." Bob backspaced with a rapid *click, click, click*, erasing the words he'd typed onto the screen. "Maybe we give the animals thought bubbles or something like that. They can be talking about how happy they are to be coming to Los Angeles with the newly married couple. Then we can use the macaw and the monkey all season long as props."

Paul shook his head as he leaned over to look at Bob's laptop screen. "Look, I know we're supposed to keep this show funny and all, but talking animals? We might as well be writing for Pixar or Disney. I don't know about the two of you, but I signed on to do a weekly sitcom involving real people, not some animated show with talking monkeys and ducks."

"Macaws," I corrected after licking my sticky fingers. "A macaw is not a duck."

"Technically it's a parrot," Bob added. "But if you want to nix that idea, I'm okay with it. Now that I think about it, it sounds pretty stupid." He shrugged. "But hey, you know my motto."

"Throw all of your ideas out on the table, even the really dumb ones." We quoted his favorite mantra in unison.

And boy, was that talking animals idea a dumb one.

I released a slow breath, feeling the pressure of the situation. We had until five o'clock today to come up with a rib-tickling episode that our producer would put his stamp of approval on. Otherwise we might not have a show next week. And if *Stars Collide* didn't air . . . I shuddered, thinking about it. We would air, even if it killed us.

From the looks of things, it might.

Paul rose and paced the tiny office, his nervous movements presenting yet another distraction. Suddenly he turned our way with a gleam in his eye. "Ooh, here's an idea. Jack and Angie are talent scouts, right? They have one of the top agencies in L.A. with the most gifted up-and-coming young stars. Why not take advantage of that? If we want to keep this episode fresh, let's incorporate the kids. It's been weeks since we've really showcased our younger cast members. We're overdue."

"What do you have in mind?" I asked, my curiosity piqued. Writing for the kids was always a blast. Maybe Paul was on to something.

His soft blue eyes sparkled. "Remember that old *Dick Van Dyke* episode? The one where they were on a hunt for child stars to appear on *The Alan Brady Show*? Every parent in the neighborhood showed up without warning so their kids could audition." Paul pulled out the piano bench and took a seat, his face now beaming.

"Priceless," I said, unable to keep a grin from erupting. "One of my favorites. So, what are you thinking? Variety show?"

"Sure, why not? We have enough young talent in the *Stars Collide* cast to pull off a variety show–type episode." Paul chuckled and slapped his knee. "I can see it now. We'll showcase the talent of the kids. Songs. Dances. Drama bits. You name it. The children will get a kick out of it, and all of those stage moms will be thrilled. What do you think?"

"I love it." Clasping my hands together, I thought about the possibilities. This would buy us another week, and the audience would eat it up. I hoped.

Just then the door to our office eased open, and Rex Henderson stuck his head inside. The elderly man had served us well over the past several months in his new role as producer, and I had nothing but respect for him. He took a look around the room, his eyes widening. "You've changed the furniture in here." His gaze narrowed. "Is that a new sofa? Looks like something I owned in the sixties."

"Yep." I pointed to the divan. "Got it at a garage sale." I rose, excited to share my vision for the room. "We set everything up just like the office set on the old *Dick Van Dyke Show*."

Rex's eyes widened again. "Oh?"

"Yes, see where we've put the rest of the furniture?" I motioned to the chair I'd been sitting in, then gestured to the desk across the room. "Pretty clever, eh? Even have an old typewriter like the one they used in the show. And, of course, we kept the piano right where it was, so we can be inspired by music whenever we like. I think it's the perfect space for a weekly sitcom team."

"How's it working out for you?" Rex asked. "Helping the creative flow?" He took a few steps in my direction, the wisps of soft white hair atop his head looking a bit unruly. His eyes narrowed as he took in the tray of baklava. I motioned for him to take a piece, which he did.

"Oh, well, you know . . . We just brought in the new furniture yesterday," I said. "Haven't really had time to see the long-term effects." *Hopefully it will work.*

He plopped down onto the divan and bit into the pastry, a look of pure satisfaction settling over him. Good. If I couldn't win him with my witty writing, maybe my baklava would do the trick.

After eating every bite and licking the honey from his

fingers, Rex glanced my way, and I knew we were ready to get down to business once again.

"Where do we stand with this week's episode?" he asked. "Come up with something to wow me yet?"

"Actually, we have." I smiled, praying he would like the idea we'd been mulling over. "We're thinking of a variety show episode, showcasing the talents of the kids."

"Variety show?" Rex appeared to be thinking about the idea. "What's the theme?"

"A welcome-home extravaganza for Jack and Angie," I said, hoping the guys would play along. "When they get home from their honeymoon, they find that their clients—the kids they represent—have prepared a show to celebrate." Another thought occurred to me, so I voiced it aloud before it slipped away into the great abyss of unspoken ideas. "Maybe the whole variety show could be jungle themed, if you don't think we've overdone the Amazon angle." I gave him a pensive look. "What do you think?"

"Might be a good transitional piece, to remind the viewers where Jack and Angie have been on their honeymoon."

I knew it! We're not done with that Amazon bit yet.

Rex glanced at the clock on the wall. "But you'd better lock this thing up tight. Give serious thought to each of the cast members. Come up with a specific song or dance they can do, then tie it all together with some sort of believable thread. The kids can't just be putting on a show for the sake of putting on a show. The viewers will never buy that. You need a story too. So get with it."

Bob saluted and I groaned inwardly, praying Rex wouldn't see it as a sign of disrespect. Bob tended to be a little sarcastic at times. Hopefully today he would guard his tongue.

"Oh, and by the way," Rex said, his gaze drifting once again to the tray of baklava, "network execs have been talking about bringing in a fourth writer. I think it's a great idea myself."

"A fourth writer?" we all echoed.

I felt my pulse rate increase as I thought about what he'd said. "Who?" I finally managed. "And why?"

He shrugged. "This is a pivotal season for the show. After years of keeping our hero and heroine apart, we've now brought them together as a married couple. The sense of anticipation is gone, and our advertisers are afraid the show is going to slip in the ratings if we don't keep things fresh. So a new creative voice will add a whole new dimension. That's the idea, anyway. But nothing has been finalized, so don't get yourselves too worked up."

Ugh. Like that's possible.

"Oh, and speaking of advertisers . . . could you guys possibly work in a scene where someone is brushing their teeth? We've been asked to do another product placement—Sparkle toothpaste."

I groaned. How many times over the past several months had we been asked to sneak products into a scene? Forcing a smile, I nodded. Surely we could come up with something creative. Maybe a singing, tooth-brushing macaw scene.

Rex rose, giving the divan another glance, then headed to the door. I followed him, my heart working overtime as I contemplated his comment about adding a new writer. Would he—or she—end up replacing one of us? A shiver ran down my spine as I thought about the possibilities. Beads of sweat popped out on my brow as I watched my future in the industry slipping through my fingers.

Stay calm. Don't get worked up when you don't even know what's happening.

"We'll have something on your desk by five o'clock," I promised him. "And you'll love it. Everyone will love it. It's going to be great."

Smile, Athena. He'll think you really believe that. I flashed an Academy Award–worthy grin, holding it to the count of three. Perfect.

"That's why you were named head writer, Athena." He gave me a gentle pat on the back. "You know what it takes to get the job done."

I felt the edges of my lips turn down as a wave of insecurity washed over me. Nothing like a little pressure in front of my fellow workers. And male workers, at that.

Rex disappeared into the hallway and I closed the door behind him, bracing myself for Paul and Bob's reaction to Rex's parting words. I knew they hated the constant reminder that I'd been named head writer. Who could blame them?

I glanced at Paul, who had shifted to a slumped-over position at the piano bench. He muttered something indistinguishable under his breath. Probably better that I couldn't hear it. Bob paced the room, his pursed lips cluing me in to the fact that he hadn't taken Rex's words well.

How could I fix this? I needed these guys—more than they knew. Over the past few weeks I'd battled more than a few inner struggles related to my writing skills. I certainly couldn't write this week's script by myself.

"Listen," I said, looking back and forth between my two good friends. "He doesn't mean anything with all of that head writer stuff. Everyone knows you two are the real talent. I'm just . . ." *Washed up. A has-been. Wondering if they'll hire me as a waitress at Mel's Diner once you guys figure out I'm a fraud.*

I decided to drop it. No point in voicing my insecurities. It wouldn't boost their confidence to know I'd lost my comedic zing. It might scare them, in fact. I knew it scared me.

"I'll bet they're not really looking at bringing in a new writer," I said. "It's probably just some sort of incentive to keep us on our toes. You know how they are. Always offering incentives." I forced a smile.

"Well, this one's working." Paul rose and began another round of toe touches, puffing out short breaths. He walked to the dartboard, obviously ready to take out his frustrations. Bob joined him. Over the next five minutes, I watched the guys toss darts with keen precision. This was nothing new. They often resorted to throwing sharp objects when upset.

Bob fingered a dart in his hand and looked my way. "Whoever scores the highest gets to choose the theme of this week's show."

"No way. We're choosing our shows by playing darts now?" I asked.

"Yep. Want to join us?"

"I stink at darts. Besides, isn't that kind of like gambling? I'm not a gambler. No way."

They both looked at me like I was crazy.

"Don't be ridiculous. Give it a try." Bob handed me a dart. I threw it at the wall and missed the board altogether. It poked a hole in my purse.

"Ugh. I paid a fortune for that purse." I wriggled the dart out of the leather and tried again, this time hitting the coat rack. "Don't think I could hit the broad side of a barn," I said. "So obviously I don't get to choose this week's theme."

"You're the head writer, Athena," Paul said. "You always get to pick."

I turned slowly, drawing in a deep breath. *Tell me he did not just say that.*

For a moment no one in the room spoke a word. Bob plopped back down on the sofa and grabbed his laptop. "Okay, I'll give this episode my best shot. But you both know I probably won't be with the show much longer, especially if they're bringing in someone else. Once my screenplay sells, I'm out of here, and I won't look back."

He mumbled something about how he would be his own head writer when the movie was picked up, and I did my best not to take it personally. How could I, with so many other thoughts tumbling around in my head? Instead, I offered a nod and said, "That would be great, Bob."

"It's just a matter of time." He fidgeted with the cover on his laptop. "My agent is shopping the screenplay to George Clooney's people even as we speak. George has his own production company now, you know. It's going to happen soon. I can feel it in my bones."

"Right." I didn't want to discourage Bob, but that screenplay of his had been shopped to every major production company in Hollywood over the past three years, and no one seemed to be biting. While I hated to say his Amish vampire story was dead in the water, I couldn't help but wonder.

Dead in the water. Hmm.

Those words gave me a great idea for a song-and-dance number a couple of the kids could do, one with a colorful Amazon-themed backdrop. Bob would surely go along with the idea if I told him we could dress up some of the boys and girls as monkeys and macaws and give them great choreography.

Yes, that would work. I could actually see it all now. Everyone would be happy. But what songs could we use?

Half a dozen jungle-themed tunes ran through my head, and I began to hum one after the other. Bob and Paul both stared at me, gazes narrowing. They could tell I was up to something, no doubt.

Within seconds, I was seated at the piano, pounding out "The Lion Sleeps Tonight" and a host of other familiar tunes. Oh, what fun!

Bob took the spot next to me on the bench, laptop in hand, as I poured out a plan of action between songs. Thankfully, he and Paul played along, adding all sorts of funny bits. In fact, at one point we laughed so hard I could barely catch my breath. It felt good to be back in the zone again. Very good.

And it felt even better to know I'd regained the respect of my fellow writers. Having them on my team meant every-thing to me.

The words "Tell me what you think about this idea" bounced across the room dozens of times over the next couple of hours as we ping-ponged back and forth, idea upon idea, laugh upon laugh. By the time Bob typed, "The End," my con-fidence had been fully restored and all of the baklava eaten. Somehow we'd even managed to squeeze in a toothpaste bit.

Squeeze. Toothpaste. Ha!

Who needed a new writer? Why, we were a great team. A laugh a minute. And I'd actually led the way, offering most of the gags.

Thank goodness. Maybe my funny bone wasn't broken. Maybe it just needed a little TLC. And maybe . . . just maybe . . . I wouldn't have to find a job as a waitress after all.

2

Family Affair

On Saturday morning I pushed open the door to my parents' sandwich shop, the tantalizing smells of lamb, cumin, and garlic greeting me. Mmm. I'd always loved a gyro in the making. Apparently so did the customers, who pressed through the door on a regular basis for my parents' now-famous foods. Super-Gyros offered sandwiches and desserts but also carried a variety of Greek and other Middle Eastern fare—everything from fresh hummus to pita bread to imported cheeses and kalamata olives. Yum. And what other restaurant in Van Nuys sported a sign with a superhero eating a foot-long sandwich? Classic. My mother often bragged about that sign, which her parents had designed years before.

"Athena-bean." My father took a few steps my way, his Super-Gyros apron clean and starched. Thirty-seven years of marriage with my mama and she still kept his aprons looking like they'd been professionally laundered. "How's my girl today?"

"Good." *Except for that crazy dream I had last night, where I was floating down the Amazon on a sixties divan, eating baklava.*

He pulled me into his arms and squeezed me so tight I could barely breathe. Not that I minded this routine. No, I'd come to count on it. My father loved me unconditionally and showed me every chance he got. Fortunately, I was the sort of girl who loved being loved. In fact, I never grew tired of spending time with my family. Some people might find that odd at my age, but not me.

I glanced up at his twinkling eyes, then took in his thinning salt-and-pepper hair, noticing something different. "Hey, you got a haircut."

"Yes. Your mama . . . she made me." He pointed to the lower half of his face. "Made me trim the beard too. What do you think?"

"Looks nice. Very respectable."

"Thank you." He ran his fingers over his thick but tidy mustache and down to his graying beard. Not many men could get away with a mustache like that, but on my father it looked grand. More than grand, really. He looked like he belonged in a magazine for Greek tourism.

"Want an early lunch?" he asked, pointing to the array of meats and cheeses. "Just got a delivery of the most beautiful tomatoes I've ever seen. Very fresh." He reached behind the counter and came out with a box of deep red Romas that took my breath away.

"Tempting, but I don't think so. Kat is meeting me and we're having a girls' day. Pedicure and the whole bit." I smiled just thinking about it. How long had it been since I'd had a relaxing day with a friend? "We're probably going out to lunch for Italian food after. Dying for fettuccine with Alfredo sauce."

"Italian." He sighed as if I'd somehow betrayed the family with my craving for pasta. "I see." He pushed the box of tomatoes out of sight.

"It's okay, Babbas." I grinned. "If I know Kat, she'll buy a gyro or two to take home to her hubby afterward. Scott loves our food. He sings your praises all the time, and so does she."

His eyes sparkled. "That Kat is such a good friend to my girl . . . and to our family. She brings us lots of business. It's good to have a star in your corner."

"Yes." My heart warmed as I thought about my best friend. Playing the role of Angie in *Stars Collide* had propelled her to superstar status. Why she'd chosen to hang around a nobody like me remained a mystery. Still, I appreciated the fact that she never seemed to notice I was a nobody. And she occasionally joked that she always knew what was coming next in her life, since I scripted her lines. I always got a laugh out of that one.

Not that I felt like laughing right now. Thinking of Kat reminded me of the pressures of my job. What a week!

Leaning against the counter, I sighed. "I could use some R & R. To be honest, I wanted to spend all day sleeping after the week I've had. Kat had to talk me into getting out of bed."

"Are they giving you a hard time at the studio?" My father's bushy brows furrowed in concern. "I'll come up there and give them a piece of my mind, if so. No one messes with the daughter of Alex Pappas." He stiffened his stance, his broad shoulders suddenly more intimidating.

I smiled. "Nah, they're not too rough on me." *Trust me, I'm rough enough on myself.*

"Good." He ran his fingers over his mustache. "But you know what they say in the old country: 'A person can be as sweet as honey or as heavy as steel.'" He gave me a pensive look, one I attempted to interpret. For whatever reason, I couldn't figure it out.

"Huh?"

"There are two ways to go about handling an attack, sweet girl—the heavy-handed approach or the sweet-as-honey approach. It's your choice. I prefer the tough approach. Your mama . . ." He gestured with a tilt of his head to my mother, who worked on the other side of the counter. "She's sweeter than the honey on those pastries she's baking."

My mother flashed a bright smile. "Thank you, Alex. I'll take that as a compliment. And besides, I like it that you're tough. One of us needs to be. I'm an old softie." She pointed to her rounded midsection and laughed. "In more ways than one."

"Just don't want to see anyone upsetting my girl," my father said. "If they do, I come after them like a papa bear protecting his cubs. Understand?"

"Yes." I shifted my gaze to the counter, where a customer stood waiting to order. "We'll go easy on 'em this time, Babbas. It'll be okay." He turned to wait on the man with a hundred-dollar bill in his hand. Big spender. We liked those at Super-Gyros.

I'd just started to take a step toward my mother when my older sister's toddlers raced my way, squealing with delight. "Aunt Athena!" Three-year-old Mia leaped into my arms, all giggles and smiles. I cuddled her against my shoulder, her dark curls bobbing up and down in excitement as she squirmed. Oh, what a beauty queen she was. And how my heart sprang to life every time I held her in my arms.

"How's my big girl today?" I asked after giving her a dozen little kisses on her cheeks.

Her lips curled down in a pout. "Mama says no candy. Can I please, Aunt Athena?"

"If Mama says no, it's a no." I leaned down and whispered, "But I'll bet you can change her mind if you behave."

"I will! I be good girl!" She gave me a mischievous grin.

"Me too!" little Becca said, clinging to my thigh. "I be

good!" The two-year-old looked up at me with a smile so sweet it melted my heart. I would have given her candy right there on the spot if she'd been mine. Unfortunately, her mother would've killed me.

"Thank you, girls. Now go play with Mary and Trina." I shooed them toward the room in the back, where my two teenage cousins waited to babysit them.

"When will you marry and give them more little ones to play with, Athena-bean?" My father crossed his arms over his chest and gave me a stern look once his customer had left.

"Aw, Babbas." I groaned. "Again with the getting married stuff? Give me time."

"I like to tease you, that's all," he said. "You can stay single as long as you like. Break every man's heart if you wish. It's fine with me."

"Break every man's heart. Humph." I groaned inwardly this time. In order to break a man's heart, I'd have to get to know him first. Right now, the only guys I knew were Bob and Paul, and they were scarcely husband material. Bob was married to his screenplay, and Paul . . . well, after his third divorce, he'd given up on the idea of marriage altogether. Or so he said. Not that he was my type. No, I hadn't exactly found my type yet. Not since the breakup of a lifetime four years ago, anyway. Ack. No point in going there today.

"You break their hearts"—my father's voice lowered to a whisper—"and I'll take care of breaking their necks." His face turned red and the veins in his neck began to throb. Never a good sign. "The next man who hurts you like that"—he muttered something in Greek—"will see my wrath firsthand."

"Alex, not in front of the customers." My mother looked my way and shook her head, her thinly plucked brows elevating at his word choices, even if most of the others in the shop didn't have the proper translation. "Our customers might not speak Greek," she whispered, "but the Lord does."

My father rolled his eyes. "I feel sure even the Lord himself would find a few choice things to say about that so-called man who hurt my daughter." Off he went again, proclaiming his disdain for the man who'd broken my heart by ditching me just weeks before our wedding. Nothing like a little public humiliation.

"Athena, come," Mama called out. "I need you."

Sure she did. I could tell a diversion when I saw one. I took a few steps in her direction, grateful for the reprieve.

"Try the loukoumades," Mama said. "I think this is my best batch so far. So sweet and delicious, just like me!" She laughed and I couldn't help but join in. My mother didn't usually sing her own praises, but she wasn't above a bit of comedy when the situation called for it. Hmm. Maybe that's where I'd gotten my flair for the comedic.

She held out the plate of loukoumades, and I sighed with delight. I'd never turned down the little golden puffs of good-ness before, and I wasn't about to start now. Making my way behind the counter, I reached for the plate of golf ball–sized fritters and popped one in my mouth, savoring the gooey honey and cinnamon topping. Yum. A second bite revealed another tasty treat.

"Love the extra walnuts," I said after licking my fingers clean. "Perfect." I reached for another, gobbling it down.

"Save some for the customers." Mama slapped my hand and I feigned offense.

"I only had two!"

"Still, you don't need the calories," she said. "Do you want to turn out like me?" She began to rant—in Greek, of course—about how many pounds she'd put on this past month alone. I stifled a grin and said nothing, as always.

"Leave Athena alone," my sister said as she passed by with a tray of cheeses in hand. "She's thin as a rail. She could stand to put on a few pounds." Larisa turned my way and sighed. "Must feel lonely being the only skinny one left in the family."

Skinny? She thought 138 pounds at five-four was skinny? And had the girl seen my thighs? They were covered in cellulite.

I refused to comment on the grounds that it might incriminate, well, any one of us. Mama, God bless her, was short in stature and had passed "pleasantly plump" about fifty pounds back. Still, her beautiful brown eyes and gorgeous olive skin made up for any other imperfections. And who could argue with the woman's cooking? As for my sister, who cared if she hadn't taken off a few additional pounds since baby number three's arrival? These things took time. I happened to love my family members just as they were—chubby or not.

"I've finished up the rice pudding," Mama said, interrupting my thoughts. "Want to help me with the baklava? Aunt Melina was supposed to be here an hour ago, but her liver is acting up again."

"Ah." This wasn't the first we'd heard about my aunt's liver condition. I suspected it had a little something to do with the ouzo she used to wash down the chocolate koulourakia cookies after dinner each night. Just one more thing we never talked about in the Pappas family—my aunt's drinking problem. One thing about our close-knit group—we loved both the sinner and the saint. No family member was outside the reach of our circle of love and trust. Still, I had to wonder how long Melina could go on drowning her sorrows. Made me a little sad, really.

My sister's words startled me back to attention. "No one makes the phyllo dough like you do, Athena. Our baklava is the best in town because of you." Her smile warmed my heart as she placed the tray of cheeses on the counter and turned back toward the children.

I settled in beside my mother to work, my eyes and ears

wide open for things I could use as comedic bits in an upcoming episode. Half the stories I came up with for the show came from my own family. Not that anyone had to know that. So far no one in the family had figured it out. Well, my brother Niko, but he hardly counted. These days he spent more time than anyone else giving me fodder, especially now that he'd taken up professional wrestling on the side. He passed by and gave me a wink, which I returned.

The clanging of the bell above the door alerted us to the fact that someone else had arrived. The mailman. Odd. He usually left the mail in the drop box outside.

"Certified letter for Thera Pappas," the fellow said, pausing to wipe the sweat from his brow. "From Greece."

"For me?" Mama paled and clasped her hands to her chest. She whispered up a prayer, asking the Lord for his mercies. "The last time I got a letter from home, the news was bad," she whispered. "My poor aunt Athena had gone to be with Jesus."

"Humph." My father wrinkled his nose. "More likely the old girl is playing chess with the devil right now, and beating him."

"Hey now, I'm her namesake," I reminded my father. "Be careful what you say about her."

"Why your mama wanted to name you after that old—" He rolled his eyes and muttered something under his breath in Greek. Hmm. Maybe the circle of love and trust didn't extend to everyone in the family after all. Looked like my father had a bias against this particular aunt. Must be more to the story than I knew.

"For your information, our little Athena-bean was named after the virgin patron saint of Athens," Mama said. "It just happened to be my aunt's name as well. Nothing I could do about that."

Lovely. I wasn't sure which made me more nervous—being named after a virgin saint or the aunt everyone hated.

Mama signed for the letter and held it to her chest for a moment, her eyes closed. My father took the opportunity to extend the welcome mat to the postman, offering him a free gyro and a cup of Greek coffee. Within a minute, the frazzled fellow was seated at one of the little tables in the corner, a contented look on his face.

"Mama, come. Sit." I ushered her to a small table, away from the growing crowd in the shop. She took a seat on the tiny wooden chair, her ample frame causing the chair to creak. Extending my hand, I offered to open the envelope for her.

"Would you?" she asked, her hands shaking. "With so many relatives left in the old country, I'm a nervous wreck at times like these. Heaven only knows what kind of news this letter holds." Mama's lips began to move, and I could tell she was praying. Her eyes fluttered closed, and she drew her hands to her chest. "Read it, Athena. I can take it, whatever it is."

"If it's bad, you would have received a call," I reminded her. "One of the cousins would have phoned you, for sure." Never one to show much patience, I yanked open the flap on the envelope.

My mother's eyes popped open, and suddenly she was all business again. "Careful!" She gestured dramatically with her hands. "Don't tear the stamps. I like to keep them for old times' sake." She went off on a tangent about how precious the stamps from the old country were to her, what significance they held.

"Okay, okay." I did my best to avoid the large, colorful stamps as I pulled out the letter. It appeared to be several pages thick. Unfolding it, I took a look at the handwritten message . . . all in Greek. Hmm. I could speak the language. Mostly. But reading it was another thing altogether. Unlike most good Greek girls, I hadn't gone to Greek school as a kid. What I'd learned about the language had come directly from my parents and other relatives.

"I'd recognize that handwriting anywhere." Mama reached for the letter with a trembling hand. "Mean-Athena." She shivered and clutched the note to her chest, then whispered, "She torments me even from the grave."

"Maybe not," I said. "Read it."

Mama's eyes scanned the note, and the hard expression softened a bit as she turned the page. By the time she finished reading, my mother had tears in her eyes. "Oh, praise the Lord. The old girl must've softened near the end. It's a miracle."

"Really?"

"Yes." Mama sniffled. "This is a wonderful letter." She passed it my way, pointing to a certain line near the bottom of the second page. "And look. She's sending me a gift."

"From heaven?" I asked.

"No." Mama giggled. "It's obviously something she arranged before she died." I watched as my mother skimmed the final page, then folded the letter and put it back in its envelope. She dabbed her eyes. "This is God's grace and mercy on our household," she said in Greek. "He revisits us with kindness to repay all of the evil Athena bestowed during my childhood. God rest her soul."

Okay. I couldn't hold back any longer. I had to know. "What was the deal with Aunt Athena not liking you, anyway? What was her problem?"

Mama's eyes brimmed over. "When my parents came to America to open this shop, they didn't have money for all of us to travel, so they left me with Aunt Athena. I was just eleven at the time and still in school, so it made sense to leave me behind, I suppose. It was only for a season, and people did that all the time back then. It was perfectly normal."

"Why would that make her despise you?" I asked.

Mama shrugged. "My father always said the man she loved didn't care for the idea of a child in the mix. He left her not too long after she took me in. I think she blamed me for the breakup. Maybe he would've stuck around if not for me. I guess we'll never know. But I've always felt guilty for something I had no control over."

"Unrequited love." I sighed, knowing all too well what *that* felt like. Still, how could my aunt turn against my mother? "You were just a child at the time. And you weren't going to be there forever. Only until your parents could afford to bring you to the States. Right?"

"Yes, but I always felt bad that—"

Unfortunately, Mama never made it any further into the conversation. I heard someone call out, "Athena!" and I looked up to discover my best friend, Kat, had arrived. So had her elderly grandmother, Lenora Worth Henderson, who sported a rhinestone-studded ball gown. Not unusual for the eccentric seventy-something, but a little out of place at Super-Gyros.

Mama's eyes grew wide and I whispered, "I'll explain later."

"Hope you don't mind that I'm coming along, Athena," Lenora called out in her singsong voice. "It's been simply ages since I had my nails done." She held out a shaky, wrinkled hand to show off her bare nails. "The last time, Doris and I went together. Oh, we had such a wonderful time."

"Doris?" my mother asked.

"Doris Day, of course," Lenora said. "She's making movies now, you know." Off she went on a tangent, talking about Doris Day's supposed upcoming movie with Rock Hudson, one that was bound to delight viewers.

Mama's eyes grew wider, and she whispered into my ear, "Hope she doesn't scare the customers."

I did notice a few people looking Lenora's way. A couple seemed to recognize her—she was a regular on *Stars Collide*, after all—but a few just looked puzzled. I would've taken them aside to explain, but how did one go about explaining Lenora Worth Henderson, anyway? *Aging Hollywood star. Beginning stages of Alzheimer's. Married to Rex Henderson, our show's producer.* My smile never wavered as Lenora carried on about her friendship with Doris Day. By the time she finished the story, she had us all—family and customers—believing Doris and Rock had just wrapped up filming on *Pillow Talk.*

"Remarkable," my mother said, looking as if she bought every word. "I predict it's going to be a big hit." She gave me a little wink, and I nodded in agreement.

"Oh, I hope so! Doris deserves it. She's a lovely lady, and has such great morals too. Quite an example for the young people of today." Lenora giggled and turned to Kat. "Well, girlie, we'd better get this show on the road. I promised Lucy and Desi that Rex and I would swing by their house tonight for appetizers. Desi makes the most wonderful gazpacho soup. You've never tasted anything like it. Very Cuban." Off she went on another tangent, giving us details about the meal she planned to share with Lucille Ball and Desi Arnaz.

"Sounds wonderful," my mother said, still playing along. "You'll have to get the recipe so we can carry it in the store." I almost bought the convincing smile that followed.

Thank you, Mama, for being so good to her. Not everyone would have taken the time to treat Lenora with such care, but my mother, God bless her, had a knack.

"Exquisite idea." Lenora clasped her hands together and looked around Super-Gyros. "What a lovely setting you have for a romance here," she said, turning to me with a playful wink. "I always say there's nothing more powerful than good food to spawn a romance."

"Amen to that," my mother and sister echoed.

I wasn't sure how I felt about the words *spawn, food,* and *romance* being used in the same sentence. Made me a little queasy. So did the stares from all of the married folks. They seemed to be boring holes through me as the word *romance* was spoken. *Okay, people. Enough already. I'll fall in love again. Someday. With someone who isn't a jerk. In the meantime, please trust that God has everything in my life under control.*

"Athena says she's happy single." My father approached and drew me into his arms, then planted a kiss on my forehead. "So leave her be, everyone."

I'd never seen a group of people deflate so quickly.

He leaned over and whispered "*Gnothi seauton*" into my ear. I knew the English translation—"Know yourself"—but had a feeling he was trying to share something a little more than that. With a hoarse whisper, my father conveyed his real meaning. "Just be yourself, Athena. Don't worry about what others think. When you stand before God, he won't be asking for the opinions of those around you."

I nodded and gave him a kiss on the cheek. We said our goodbyes and headed to the door. As we did, Kat drew near and whispered, "What's with that 'Athena is happy single' line? Are you telling me you wouldn't jump at the chance to fall in love? I don't believe that for a moment."

"Oh, well, I . . ." I couldn't seem to finish my sentence because, in that very moment, the handsomest man I'd ever seen brushed past me in the doorway, interrupting my thoughts. He was tall, dark, and definitely superhero material, right down to the broad shoulders and confident stride.

For a moment our eyes met and we both paused. Well, I paused. I think maybe he stopped because I stepped on his foot. Regardless, he hesitated long enough for me to get another look at those rich brown eyes and that hint of a dimple on the left side of his gorgeous lips. He raked a hand through those thick dark waves and flashed a smile so bright it nearly blinded me. Okay, maybe it was the glare coming from the reflection of the sun against the glass pane in the door, but still . . .

"I'm so sorry." I pulled my foot back.

"No problem." His smooth voice captivated me at once. So did the dimples, now clearly visible.

Wow. Maybe I would have to reconsider my stance on men. Or better yet . . . figure out some way to write this modern-day Adonis into my life story. Not that I was actually the one writing my life story, of course. *Snap out of it, Athena. Focus.*

"Come along, pretty girls!" Lenora's voice rang out, and she gave me a little nudge. "We've got places to go, people to see."

"O-okay." Honestly, the only person I wanted to see was my story's potential hero, but he'd just disappeared into the mob of people inside my parents' store. With life—and Lenora—pressing me forward, any romantic scenes I might've written slipped right out of my head. Oh well. There would be plenty of time to pencil in a hero later. I hoped. In the meantime, I'd stick with the line that I didn't need a man in my life. Everyone seemed to be buying it, anyway.

Well, everyone but Kat. She gave me a look that said, "I saw that, Athena," before stepping through the door. Yep, she was definitely on to me. Oh well. What were best friends for, if not to see into your heart?

I flashed a smile and dove into a senseless conversation, first about the weather, then about Lenora's beautiful pink convertible parked at the curb. Kat continued to give me that "I'm not buying it" look, but I did my best to ignore her.

After climbing into the backseat, I turned once more toward the shop and released a lingering sigh as I realized something—or someone—wonderful might have just slipped through my fingers.

So long, Adonis. Great meeting you . . . even if it was only for a moment.

3

Howdy Doody

On Monday morning I arrived at the studio with my arms loaded. Mama had insisted upon sending goodies from the shop, as always. Not that I minded. Bob and Paul had taken to calling Monday Feed the Starving Writers Day. Bringing the food made for a lovely way to kick off the week, and it also gave my parents the opportunity to pass off unsold products to hungry souls in need. Not that Bob and Paul were in need, necessarily, but they did always seem to be hungry.

I found the office door wide open. Stepping inside, I made my usual Monday morning proclamation: "I come bearing gifts!" Then I waved the bags so they could see just how much I loved them.

I did love them, of course. They were crazy and had stinky-boy feet, and they drove me nuts at times, but we were family. And family events always focused on food. Well, at least my family events.

"Mmm. Thought you'd never get here." Bob rose from the sofa, placed his laptop on the coffee table, and headed my way. "What did you bring this time, Athena? Sandwiches? And more of those olives, I hope. They're great."

"And that Greek salad I love?" Paul asked, reaching for the bags. "The one with the feta cheese and red onions? Hope you didn't forget that."

"Yep. Got it all." Passing off the bags, I felt like the weight of the world had been lifted. "We've got a busy week ahead of us, guys. I need you to be well fed and happy."

"Busier than usual?" Bob's brow wrinkled as he placed a bag on the coffee table and began to dig inside. He came out with a jar of kalamatas, which he promptly opened. "What's up?" He popped an olive in his mouth. Then a second. "Something happen we need to know about?" he said with a full mouth.

"Have you heard something from the man upstairs?" Paul asked, the creases between his eyes deepening.

"Man upstairs?" I had to wonder if Paul had finally had that religious experience I'd been praying for.

He pointed up to the ceiling. "Rex just moved into the office above ours this morning, remember?"

"Ah." I wanted to laugh at the image that presented, but I found myself distracted. The funny stuff would have to wait until after I shared the latest news with the guys. I reached to close the door, in case any of the cast or crew happened by, then turned to face the guys head-on. "We have a lot to talk about. I spent Saturday with Kat."

"Oh?" Bob glanced my way and shrugged. "What's up?"

"Well, she shared a few things with me. Personal stuff. I asked if she minded if I told you guys and she said no."

"Spill the beans, Athena," Paul said.

"She said that Rex is going through a really anxious spell

right now. So much so that she's worried about his blood pressure."

"What's he so anxious about?" Paul asked as he unloaded the bag with the large salad container. "The show?"

"Yes. Ratings have slipped a little."

"Again?" Paul groaned.

"Yes. He's worked up about Lenora too. The doctor had to up her Alzheimer's meds. So according to Kat, Rex is feeling pretty frazzled right now." I released a slow breath, determined to make the most of this rough situation. "I think we need to give him the best possible script this week. He loved the variety show bit in the last script, but we've got to do better than that. Got to move the plot along. Maybe do something daring."

"Daring, huh?" Paul sank into a chair and opened the salad container. He reached for an onion and popped it in his mouth.

"I thought of something that will help us get inspired," I said. "We should watch some old *Dick Van Dyke* episodes."

"Great idea," Bob said. "I know my favorite, but what's yours?"

I thought about that for a moment before answering. There were so many to choose from, after all.

"I love that one where Rob finds out Laura lied to him about her age when they got married. Classic. By the end of it, you found yourself rooting for both of them. That's the goal, really, to pull the viewers into the story and somehow get them to empathize with both the hero and the heroine. If you can do that, you've got a great show on your hands."

"My favorite is that one where Laura thinks her romance with Rob is fading, so she dyes her hair blonde." Paul slapped his knee. "Did you see that one?"

"Of course," Bob said. "And what about the walnut one? Was there ever a better one than that? No way."

We all started laughing at the memory of Rob Petrie opening his coat closet and being swallowed alive by thousands of walnuts.

"Talk about a great show. It not only lasted for countless seasons, it's still being enjoyed today," I said. "That's what we're looking for with *Stars Collide*—something that will stand the test of time."

"I've got the perfect idea," Bob said with a twinkle in his eye. "Been thinking about it a while. You're gonna love it, and I really think it will help the show go down in history."

"Oh?" Paul and I both said. I was always interested in a great idea.

Bob popped another olive in his mouth, then spoke around it. "Jack and Angie should have a baby."

"How can they have a baby?" I argued as I dropped into my usual spot on the chair next to the sofa. "They've only been married a couple of months. It's too soon for her to have a baby."

"No, I mean they find out they're going to have a baby," he said. "I know it hasn't been long since the honeymoon ended, but adding a baby to the mix ups the ante on several levels, and that's what we need right now. Tension. Conflict."

"Good point. Good stories are built on conflict," Paul chimed in from the chair behind the desk. He took a bite of the salad—using his fingers, naturally—and a look of pure bliss settled over him. I rose and handed him a fork, which he took with a grunt. If the guy was going to gulp down a Greek salad for breakfast, he needed to do it with a utensil, at the very least.

"Babies add a *lot* of conflict to our lives." Bob spoke the words as if he'd experienced this firsthand.

"Well, yes," I managed. "But . . ." *A baby?*

"If we introduce the pregnancy near the beginning of the season, we could rush things along and she could actually have the baby before the season ends."

"You really have given this some thought."

"Yep. I think it's a great idea. And can you even imagine the fun we could have when we get to that scene where she's ready to have the baby? It could be hysterical."

Obviously you've never had a baby.

I thought about his idea as I settled back into my chair. It might work, but how would Kat take the news that she'd have to spend this season wearing a faux baby bump under her clothes? And how would the viewers respond to the news that the couple had transitioned from "just married" to "married with children" in such a short time? Would they buy it?

I didn't have much time to think through my concerns. With the ideas ping-ponging back and forth between the two guys, I felt like I'd been caught up in the middle of a Pac-Man game gone berserk. Someone needed to stop this train of thought before we completely derailed the show.

"Guys, I—"

"Oh, what about this," Paul interrupted, his eyes widening. "We can set up the 'Angie's Having a Baby' episode just like the old *I Love Lucy* one, where Lucy tried a hundred different ways to tell Ricky she was expecting. Remember? Something always went wrong."

"Yes, but—"

"In the end, she went to the Copa Cabana and gave him the news in the middle of his performance." Paul wiped his mouth on the edge of his sleeve. "That was one of the highest-rated episodes in television history, by the way. Maybe we can match it. Really push the ratings up for our show in the process. Our sponsors would love that." He began to carry on about the sponsors, but he lost me after a couple of minutes.

"There's no Copa Cabana in our sitcom," I said. "So I don't follow."

Paul rolled his eyes. "You're missing the point. Angie's news about the pregnancy just needs to be revealed in a public setting. That's all I meant. Someplace where Jack is caught off guard. Comedy is always better when the characters—and the viewers—are caught off guard."

"Well, I know, but—"

"Great idea." Bob rose and began to pace the room, olive jar in hand. "Let's think it through. Maybe they're in a restaurant—Cuban, so the viewers will make the connection—and the bandleader sings 'We're Having a Baby,' the song that Ricky sang to Lucy when he got the news." Bob swallowed another kalamata whole.

"Ooo, better idea," Paul said. "The children they represent through the talent agency can all be there, hiding in the wings. They can sing the song to Jack."

I shook my head. "How will Jack know the song is a message to him from Angie? Besides, it's too creepy to imagine a group of children singing 'We're Having a Baby.'" A shiver ran down my spine at the very idea.

Paul sighed. "Okay, fine."

Bob pursed his lips for a moment. "Maybe Angie can give Jack the news—minus the kids—and then the bandleader calls him up to the stage to sing the song."

"Who do we get to play the bandleader?" I asked, almost caught up in the idea. "It's got to be someone who can look, act, and sing like Desi Arnaz if we stand a shot at pulling this off."

Not that I think we can pull this off, just for the record. But I'll play along if it will make you two happy.

Bob snapped his fingers. "I know! George Lopez."

"George Lopez the comedian?" I asked. "Does he sing?"

"Who cares?" Bob said. "He'll only have to sing a line or two, then he'll call Jack up onto the stage to finish the song. He's going to be perfect."

"I'm still not sure about this," I said. "Besides, if we use a recorded song, we'll have to pay royalties. That's problematic."

"We use recorded music all the time." Paul gave me a pensive look. "Besides, advertisers pay for all that stuff. So what's the big deal?"

"You don't like this idea, Athena?" Bob asked.

I shrugged, unsure of how I felt right now. With so much coming at me so fast, maybe I just needed time to process it. If we threw Angie into a pregnancy, it would change absolutely everything about the dynamics of the show. Did we want to do that? All to bring the ratings up? Would it even work, or would it backfire on us?

"I think we need to slow down a minute," I said after thinking things through. "I'm not sure the time is right to add a pregnancy this season. It's not settling well with me, and I'll bet it won't go over well with Rex either." I could only imagine the look on his face if we tried to pass on this news to him. We could very well throw him into a panic. Then again, he was the one who'd pushed to get Angie and Jack hitched last season. Maybe he'd love this idea.

"Have some olives." Bob passed the jar my way. "Nothing like a kalamata to break down your defenses so we can talk you into this."

I rolled my eyes.

"What?" He feigned innocence. "It's a brilliant idea, Athena. Admit it. Solves so many problems and increases our opportunity ten times over. Maybe a hundred."

The two guys rambled on and on about Kat—er, Angie's—baby. A boy. Somewhere along the way Bob started calling him "Little Ricky."

I sat in my chair, mouth closed, completely zoned out. I somehow managed to finish off the jar of olives—well, all but one—along with three cookies. Okay, four. But who would notice? The guys were off in sitcom land, rewriting the old black-and-white television shows from days gone by. Me? I just wanted to keep this modern-day show alive. And I wasn't sure that impregnating the sitcom's female lead was the way to go about it. Not that I had any better ideas.

At some point Bob took a seat on the sofa next to me and kicked off his shoes. His stinky, sock-covered feet landed on the coffee table just inches from where I sat. From the look—and smell—of things, those socks hadn't been changed in a couple of days. Disgusting. Who could think with that sort of distraction?

I squeezed my eyes shut, ready to focus on a plan of action, one we could all live with. Strange, I could only see Kat—er, Angie—with a baby bump. She would kill me if we went through with this. And no telling what Lenora would do. In her current state of mind, she would probably think Kat was really pregnant. Did we want to stir up that kind of drama? My mind reeled as I contemplated the complications this plot twist could cause.

"Athena? You still with us?" Paul drew near and knelt at my side. "You haven't said anything for the last several minutes."

Thank goodness I didn't have to answer. The phone rang, startling me. I picked it up and recognized Rex's voice.

"Athena, I'm headed down to your office in a few minutes," he said. "Lots going on, so we need to talk. Gather the troops."

"Talk? About what?" My heart began to race.

"Big news from network execs," he said. "It's important that we get some things settled, okay?"

"O-okay." I hung up the phone, more unnerved than ever.

"Who was that?" Bob asked.

I managed only three words: "The man upstairs." My thoughts gravitated to our sitcom characters, Angie and Jack. What sort of parents would they be? Would they offer their children the ideal home environment, like my mom and dad had, or would they argue and fight over every little thing?

Athena, are you actually thinking about this pregnancy angle?

Hmm. Maybe I was. In fact, the more I thought about it, the greater the appeal. Like the guys said, it would add conflict to the show and would give us a really cool way to wrap up the season when the time came. Boy, could we add a lot of humor. And the possibilities for conflict were everywhere, especially if the pregnancy caused Angie to have to step back from her workload.

Within minutes, Paul and Bob had me talked into the nutty idea. I could almost hear my father's voice in my head now: *You know what Aristotle said, Athena-bean. "No one ever creates anything great without a dash of madness."* Right now I felt plenty mad. In a wacky, creative sort of way. And why not? This might turn out to be a lot of fun. Or it might just be the end of my career, but at least I'd go out with a smile on my face.

"When did Rex say he was coming?" Paul asked.

"Any time now. Why?"

"Because . . ." Bob quirked a brow, then reached into the toy box behind the desk—the one he'd lovingly named the Muse. He came out with a soccer ball, which he passed my way. "Put this on."

"Excuse me?"

"Stick it under your shirt. That's how we'll tell Rex about the pregnancy idea. He'll get a kick out of it." Bob snorted. "Get it? A *kick* out of it?" He pointed to the soccer ball, then doubled over in laughter.

"Oh no you don't." I shook my head and pressed the ball back into his hands. "Not gonna do it. You can't make me. There's got to be a better way to break the news."

"You're such a girl." Paul groaned as he looked on. "Why don't females ever just go along with things? Why do they always have to argue?"

40

I started to respond but decided it would probably come out sounding like an argument, so I capped it. Bob tossed the ball my way, startling me. I caught it midair and sighed. Okay, I would play along. They'd never let me hear the end of it if I didn't.

I turned away from the guys and wriggled the soccer ball up under my new white blouse. As I did, that sick, squeamish, "you're gonna regret this" feeling washed over me. Still, I couldn't chicken out now, could I? Not after what Paul had said about females.

With the ball situated, I turned back to face the guys and shrugged. "Okay, so what do you think?"

Paul looked at me, a little bug-eyed, but said nothing at first. He finally managed a weak, "Wow."

"You look like the real deal, Athena," Bob added, his voice now lowered to a whisper. "Ironic."

"Ironic? What do you mean?"

"Kind of Virgin Mary–like," Bob said.

"Virgin Mary?" I asked. "Did we have to go there?"

"Well, didn't you tell me once that Athena was the virgin patron of Athens?" Bob scratched his head and gave me a closer look. "Just seems weird to see her in the family way."

"This was your idea, remember?" I stared down at my baby bump, ready to snatch it out and forget the whole thing. "This is ridiculous. I'm not going through with it. There's got to be some other way to break the news to Rex without publicly humiliating myself. Let's skip this."

"No, wait. We'll all do it, then you won't be alone." Bob grabbed a basketball, which he shoved under his T-shirt. Then he tossed a football to Paul, who attempted to do the same. His belly ended up looking pretty lopsided, but that didn't really matter. He just made a joke out of it, one that brought a much-needed smile to my face. Within seconds, we were all doubled over in laughter. In fact, I got so carried away that

I had to hang onto my belly to keep my soccer baby from falling out.

I reached for the olive jar and popped the final olive into my mouth just as a rap sounded at the door. Before we could open it, it swung wide and Rex stepped through.

Bob belted out, "We're having a baby, my baby and me," with Paul chiming in on the last couple of words.

I would have joined them, but the words lodged in my throat as I caught a glimpse of the man standing directly behind Rex in the doorway.

Tall. Dark, wavy hair. Perfectly sculpted face.

Adonis.

4

Two and a Half Men

There are those moments in life when you wish you could just dive under the covers and hide. As I stood with soccer belly extended, facing the handsomest man the Lord had ever placed on Planet Earth, I had the craziest desire to do just that. Fortunately—or unfortunately—I never had the opportunity.

Rex looked my way with a fatherly gaze, his eyes narrowing as he took in my midsection. Then he looked back and forth between Bob and Paul, the worry lines between his eyes growing exponentially. For a moment he said nothing. Well, with his voice, anyway.

"I can't leave you kids alone for a minute, can I?" he said at last. "What are you cooking up in here?"

"Follow the clues, Rex." Bob waddled across the room, hands cupped around his shirt-covered basketball to emphasize his faux pregnancy. "Do you get it? Can you solve the mystery?"

Rex's gaze narrowed further, and he raked his hand through wisps of thinning white hair. "You're all in need of psychiatric help?"

Paul snorted. "We've always known that. Try again."

Bob punched Paul in the arm, and his basketball baby came rolling out. I would have mentioned it, but I couldn't seem to stop looking at Adonis, who now leaned against the doorjamb, his face lit with a half smile as he quietly observed the goings-on. The handsome stranger shifted his gaze to me. For a moment our eyes locked. Bluebirds sang. The earth stopped spinning. My heart shifted into overdrive.

Then his gaze gravitated to my belly. Ack! I shook off my daydream, realizing what an idiot I must look like. Still, how could I get the soccer ball out without making a bigger spectacle of myself? I'd wedged it in there pretty tight.

By now, Paul had removed the football from under his shirt, leaving me the only expectant writer in the room. Lovely. The virgin patron of Athens, all alone in her ninth month of pregnancy.

Rex looked my way. "Athena? Something you want to tell me?"

"Um, well . . ." *Think, Athena. Be quick on your feet.* I mustered up all the courage within me and began to sing in melodramatic fashion: "We're having a baby . . ."

"My baby and me!" Bob and Paul chimed in.

We all paused and stared at Rex, who still looked dumbfounded. Clearly, he didn't get it.

At this point, Adonis spoke his first words. "You're . . . you're having a baby?"

"Not me personally," I said, feeling a rush of warmth to my face. "Angie's having a baby. This season. If Rex likes the idea, I mean."

"Angie's having a baby?" Adonis continued to stare, and

I suddenly felt as if he could see all the way down into my soul. Weird.

"Yes, we want to write a pregnancy revelation into the next episode." I did my best to look self-assured as I turned back to Rex, looking directly into his eyes. "What do you think?"

Adonis's voice interrupted my thoughts. "We're going to have to talk about that one, now aren't we?"

What happened next was like a scene from *The Twilight Zone*. Everything shifted to slow motion. Bob turned, mouth hanging, to face Adonis. He said something, but it came out sounding like a muddy, "Wa, wa, wa."

Adonis responded by narrowing his gaze. Paul coughed—an exaggerated, lengthy cough. And I . . . well, I found myself having one of those weird out-of-body experiences that so often accompany panic attacks. Heat washed over me, and I reached for a bottle of water, ready to get back to reality.

Did that guy just say what I thought he said?

I turned to face him, completely befuddled by his brazen words. Who did this fellow think he was, chiming in on our script writing?

Rex chuckled, which lifted the mood in the room, if only for a second. "Guess the cat's out of the bag." He paused and cleared his throat. "I brought Stephen down here to make introductions."

Stephen? Well, that answered one question. Handsome had a name. Other than Adonis, anyway. And he clearly had something to do with the decision making of the show. But what? Did he represent one of our sponsors, perhaps? If so, he'd better be prepared for a battle.

Rex smiled and patted the stranger on the back as if they were old friends. "He's going to join the writing team, as of tomorrow. Stephen's got some great ideas regarding this season's first few episodes. I think you're going to love them . . . and him."

Every bit of enthusiasm about the upcoming episode slithered out of the room at Rex's announcement. I found myself wondering if perhaps I'd misunderstood.

"W-what?" I managed.

"I'm so glad to be here," Adonis said. He extended his hand. I took it, noticing at once his firm grip. I'd always loved a man with a firm grip. However, I had to wonder if this particular man had a grip on something far bigger than my hand. My job, for instance. Did he plan to weasel his way in and take my position as head writer?

Rex gave me an odd look, and I realized I still hadn't said anything. Neither had Adonis released his hold on my hand. I wanted to pull it away, but something kept me hanging on.

"Welcome . . ." What did he say his name was again?

"Stephen. Stephen Cosse."

"Welcome, Stephen. Nice to meet you. I'm Athena Pappas."

If you're here to take my job, think again. I'm not going anywhere, mister. Four seasons I've been with this show. Four seasons. Try that on for size.

"I've heard a lot about you, Athena."

"O-oh?" I could only imagine.

Stephen flashed a winning smile, then turned toward Bob, who grunted out his name and tossed his basketball back in the toy box. He returned to the divan and pulled his laptop onto his knees.

Paul introduced himself, then settled behind his desk, where he dove into his salad. Without the fork. For once I didn't care. Let him make a bad first impression. What did it matter?

Rex took a couple of steps in my direction. "I don't want to discount what you've planned for this week's episode, Athena. Are you serious about this baby idea? If so, we need to talk. I know we mentioned it a while back, but nothing was set in stone."

At the word *baby*, I went into a panic. I still looked nine months pregnant.

"Oh, well, I—" I turned and wriggled the ball out of my shirt, my thoughts a jumbled mess. How dare Rex spring a new writer on us without telling us first? Okay, so maybe he'd mentioned the possibility of network executives bringing in someone new, but to actually do it without consulting me, the show's head writer? Talk about insulting. "We're pretty serious about the idea," I managed at last, gripping the ball as if my life depended on it. "But nothing's written in stone yet."

Give us an hour or two and it will be.

"That's good," Stephen said, offering his first hint of a smile. "Because the show is at a crossroads, and I'm not sure the time is right to go there yet. Maybe in a few weeks, but not yet. I guess we can talk about all of that later, though. We're going to be spending a lot of time together and coming up with some great ideas as a team."

"Humph." Paul looked up from his salad, then snatched a piece of near-wilted lettuce and popped it into his mouth, his gaze shifting to the piano.

From his spot on the divan, Bob muttered something indistinguishable. I did my best to ignore him. If Adonis—er, Stephen—was here to stay, we should make the best of things.

Rex placed his hand on my arm, redirecting my thoughts. "Athena, I'm going to take Stephen around and introduce him to the cast and crew. Want to come with?"

I plastered on a smile and nodded. "Sure. Love to." Actually, I did want to see the look on Kat's face when she met this fellow firsthand. Would she recognize him from Saturday?

I gave him another look, setting his physicality to memory. Tall. Probably six-four. And handsome didn't even begin to describe it. The guy looked like something off a *GQ* cover, only better. Another glance at that perfectly sculpted jawline convinced me he was definitely better than a *GQ* cover. And here he stood—in my office!

Just as quickly, my mind-set changed. He might be handsome, but I wouldn't let my guard down. I couldn't afford to.

Jana from our wardrobe department was going to flip. She'd already managed to fall in love with every guy on the crew over the past three years. Of course, none of her relationships stuck, but still. She'd probably love to get her hooks into this one. And what about Nora, our hair and makeup girl? Likely she would fall in love with Stephen's jet-black hair. Thick. Wavy. Perfectly styled.

Focus, Athena. Don't let the enemy trap you in his snare.

I followed Rex and Stephen out the door and down the long hallway toward the studio. Once there, we found Kat and Scott rehearsing their lines with our show's director, Tia Morales. Bob had taken to calling her Tia the Terror due to her brusque personality. How would our tough-as-nails captain take the news of the addition to our *Stars Collide* family?

It didn't take me long to find out. Tia turned toward us, her dark eyes widening in surprise as she caught a glimpse of Stephen. Usually one to speak her mind, she barely managed two sensible words as introductions were made. Great. He'd managed to knock her off her feet with only a glance.

Then again, he'd left a similar first impression on me.

"Wardrobe fit, everyone."

I turned as Jana's voice rang out. She entered the room with an armload of costumes, stopping cold as soon as she saw Stephen. Her jaw dropped and she lost her grip on the costume pieces. Stephen managed to catch them as they fell, sweeping in like a white knight on a steed.

Go ahead, look like a hero. Just wait till they see you're here to snag more than wardrobe pieces. You've come to steal my job. Then see what kind of reception you're going to get.

"Th-thank you." Jana's eyelashes fluttered as she regained

her hold on the items, and her cheeks turned the prettiest shade of cotton-candy pink. Nothing like a little girlish flirting to make a boy sit up and take notice.

"Of course." He flashed a winning smile, showing off his pearly whites.

For a moment it kind of felt like I'd tripped and landed between the covers of some cheesy romance novel. One with a great cover model, sure, but with just enough stupidity in the story to make you wonder why you'd wasted your money. The kind of book you usually ended up throwing against a wall.

Funny. I felt like throwing something against a wall right now. Where was this week's script when I needed it?

By now, half the cast and crew had gathered around. Rex clapped his hands to get their attention. "*Stars Collide* family, please welcome our newest member, Stephen Cosse. Stephen's just moved to L.A. from Vegas and is going to be joining the writing department. We're fortunate to have someone of his caliber."

"Ooo, you're a writer." Jana came closer, her eyelashes now batting so rapidly she looked like a helicopter coming in for a landing. "Want to pencil me into your script?" She clamped a hand over her mouth, her cheeks flaming red. "I can't believe I said that."

I couldn't either. Still, Stephen didn't seem bothered by her words. He continued to grin—that goofy, cockeyed grin—as more people joined our circle.

"Stephen's got several years of experience as a comedy writer, so be prepared to laugh a lot when he's around." Rex patted him on the back and offered an encouraging smile. "If anyone can bring a smile to your face, he can."

So far I wasn't laughing. Couldn't find much to laugh about on my way to the unemployment office.

"Tell us all about yourself, Stephen." Jana's eyes looked

as if they might pop out of her head. "Since we're going to be working together and all."

He shrugged. "Not much to tell. I've been working in Vegas for the past three years as a stand-up comedian. Worked a lot of the casinos and hotels. That sort of thing."

Wait a minute. You're a comedian? I thought you were a writer.

I never got to pose the question. Jana let out a squeal. "Oh, I know you! You did an HBO special, right?" When he nodded, she hollered, "I saw that. It was hysterical!" She dove into a lengthy chat about how he'd made her laugh so hard she cried.

Hmm. I hadn't seen any HBO special, so I felt pretty clueless. Still, if the guy had his own show on a major cable channel, he must not be too shabby, right? Fear wriggled its way up my spine as I contemplated the possibility that he might actually be well-known.

Thankfully, the conversation shifted. Stephen's next words caught my attention. "I have a daughter, Brooke," he said. "She's not exactly a comedienne. I see more potential for drama than comedy with her."

Every woman in the room appeared to deflate at this news. So, he had a daughter. Must be a wife in the wings. Still, no wedding band. Odd.

Not that I really cared. At this point, the only thing I wanted to do was boot this guy right out the door so I could go back to writing in peace. After spending a few more minutes staring at that handsome face, anyway. It wasn't every day we had someone this gorgeous come through.

"Brooke is eleven," Stephen added, then shrugged. "Well, almost twelve. She reminds me of that nearly every day now. Acts like she's going on twenty, though, which is kind of weird. Most of the women I know try to act like they're younger than they really are, but not this kid."

"Hey now," Lenora said, "age is nothing to be ashamed of." As she smiled, the crinkles around her eyes deepened.

"My thoughts exactly," Stephen said. "And it's funny you brought that up. I've been thinking about adding more seniors to the cast."

We'll talk about that. As a team. In the meantime, please stop making announcements without checking with me first. Have I mentioned that I'm the head writer of this show?

At the news about the addition of seniors, Lenora's smile broadened. "Well, I like that idea. I surely do. You'll give me more playmates."

At this point, Scott and Kat engaged Stephen in a lively conversation about the direction of the show, honing in on what he'd just said. I shot daggers with my eyes at my best friend, who didn't seem to notice my angst. In fact, the only time she looked my way, she mouthed the words, "Wow, he's so cute!" then made some sort of quirky back-and-forth gesture, indicating we'd make a great couple.

Oh no you don't, girlfriend. I'm not dating the enemy. It's against my policy.

Not that I really had a policy, but still. There was that whole issue of the guy who'd broken my heart years ago. A girl couldn't be too careful when she'd already been sliced 'n' diced by a handsome man she'd once thought to be trustworthy.

Kat pulled me off to the side, a suspicious grin on her face. "He's the new writer?" she whispered. "Girl, this is a gift from the heavens. Don't let it pass you by."

"Stop it, Kat," I whispered back. "He's my co-worker, not my love interest."

"Well, if I got the chance to write this script, I'd scribble him in as the Romeo to your Juliet. No doubt about it. Have you seen his eyes?"

"You're asking me to fall in love with someone because of his eyes?"

"Not because of. But physical attraction is important. Aren't you attracted to him at all?"

Um, yeah. I'd have to be blind not to be.

"He's okay." I bit my lip to keep from saying anything else and tried to look nonchalant. "Nothing to write home about."

"Okay?" She laughed. "Nothing to write home about? You need to check your temperature, girlie. I think maybe you're not well. Or maybe you're just not awake yet."

"I'm wide awake and fully in control of my senses." *Mostly.*

"Then I hope your spiritual antenna is up, because my gut tells me we've got a winner here. He's going to turn out to be something really special, and I don't want you to miss it. Or, rather, miss him. Don't let this train pass you by."

"You can tell all of that just by looking at him?"

She nodded. "Yep. Call it discernment. Call it a hunch. This is a great guy."

"You're crazy."

"Maybe, but you can mark my words. We've got a keeper here, and you'd better snatch him up before Nora or Jana get to work on him. You know how they are. They're probably already making plans."

"They can have him. Trust me."

When Tia called the others to return to work, I took a few steps in Stephen's direction. For the first time, I found myself alone with him. Not that he seemed to notice. No, he appeared to be overly fascinated by the camera setup. Perfect time to get some answers. Might as well dive right in.

I tried to keep my voice steady as I spoke. "So, I think I heard you say that you're a comedian, not a writer. Did I hear that correctly?"

He turned away from the cameras and looked me in the eye. "Oh, I should have clarified. I've always come up with my own material, but I've never written for a television sitcom before. This will be my first show like this."

"Hmm."

"Well, that's not completely true, I guess." He shrugged. "We recorded a live comedy show for HBO last year, but that's about it. Nothing like what you're doing here."

I turned to Rex, giving him my best "what were you thinking?" look. Not that he noticed. He'd shifted his attention to Tia and the rest of the cast and crew.

I muttered one of my mother's favorite phrases. In Greek, of course. These undercover remarks often brought a sense of relief and calm. And besides, if I said it in Greek, no one would be any the wiser.

Stephen looked my way when I finished, his face lighting up. "Sophocles."

"Excuse me?"

"What you just said. 'Much wisdom often goes with fewest words.' It originated with Sophocles. Still love hearing it in Greek, by the way. Takes me back. Every time I hear it, it reminds me of a Scripture my grandmother taught me as a kid."

"O-oh?" He translated Greek philosophers and quoted the Bible? If my mother ever met this guy, she'd offer him our sandwich shop as a dowry.

"You know the Scripture I'm talking about, right?" Stephen's expression grew more serious. "Even a fool is thought wise if he keeps silent, and discerning if he holds his tongue."

Ack. I could only hope he wasn't making a personal reference.

"So, let me get this right." I reached to touch his arm, noticing for the first time the rock-solid biceps. *Focus, Athena.* "You're . . . you're Greek?"

"And proud of it."

"That explains why you showed up at my parents' place the other day."

"Your parents' place?" He shook his head, clearly confused. "What place?"

"They run a little sandwich shop in Van Nuys called Super-Gyros. We met when I was leaving the store."

"Wait a minute." He nodded. "I think I do remember. We passed each other in the doorway, right?"

"Yes."

A knowing look came into his eyes. "You stepped on my foot."

"See how unforgettable that move was?"

"True. You've got me there." He flashed a smile so bright his teeth sparkled. Reminded me of something I'd seen once in a toothpaste commercial. "How could I forget our first meeting? You broke my big toe."

"W-what?"

"Kidding." He laughed. "You're in the business of first impressions, I guess. That soccer-ball pregnancy takes the cake."

"Yeah, well, I do my best." What else could I say, really?

"Speaking of the sandwich shop, Rex and I are talking about going back on Saturday. Hope it works out." He gave me a curious look. "Will you be there? I'm just not sure it would be the same if you didn't stomp on my foot as I enter. I won't truly feel welcome unless you do."

"Very funny." Maybe the guy did have a sense of humor after all. So he was a little on the sarcastic side. I'd heard worse. "I usually help out on Saturdays. My parents are pretty swamped on the weekends, so I lend a hand. From what they tell me, I'm the phyllo dough expert."

"Me too." The intensity in his eyes threw me a little. "I make a mean baklava."

"Me too." *And please stop comparing your baking skills to mine. You have no idea who you're messing with here, mister.*

That white-toothed smile dazzled me once more. "We'll have to have a contest one day."

"Perfect." *Sucker.*

"We'll see who comes out on top."

Ugh. That last line reminded me that he'd come to take my job. Well, potentially, anyway. If I didn't watch my back, he might very well land on top. And I might end up in the poorhouse.

Well, not exactly the poorhouse. My parents wouldn't kick me to the curb if I lost my job. Likely they'd throw a party. Kill the fatted calf and all that. They'd been trying to get me to work in the shop for years.

Still, I didn't know what I'd do if I lost the ability to write for *Stars Collide*. Would it leave me wondering if I'd ever catch another break in this town? Cause me to reconsider my calling as a writer?

Hopefully I wouldn't have to find out anytime soon.

5

The $64,000 Question

I barely slept a wink over the next several nights. If network executives felt the show needed a fourth writer, there must be some reason. Didn't they trust us? Were our jobs in jeopardy? What would I do if I lost my place as head writer? These and a thousand other questions slithered through my mind as my imagination kicked into overdrive.

Just as quickly my thoughts drifted back to Adonis. Stephen. He might be the enemy, but I couldn't seem to find his pitchfork and horns no matter how hard I looked. How could I possibly see past those gorgeous eyes and dark hair to remember he'd come to take my job? All I wanted to do was be swept away by that dazzling smile and that piercing gaze. And what about those broad shoulders? Who could miss those?

Slow down, Athena. You don't know that he's come to take your job. Could be he's just as nervous as you. This is his first sitcom gig, after all.

What was up with that, anyway? Who hired a virtual unknown for a sitcom that was number four in the ratings? Were these people crazy? They seemed to be willing to gamble with the show's future like Vegas high rollers.

On Friday night, I reached for my laptop, pulling it into bed with me. After signing onto the internet, I typed Stephen's name into the search engine, along with the word *comedian*. My heart skipped a beat when I saw that over 420 websites came up. No way. I scrolled through several and had a fast but thorough introduction to the life and times of Stephen Cosse, renowned comic. Wow. Looked like the guy had quite a following, including a fan club and a Facebook fan page. And apparently that HBO special was a huge deal among comedians and comedy lovers alike. Crazy. How come I'd never heard of him?

Easy. I'd never been to Vegas. And who had time to watch HBO when I spent my days writing sitcom scripts? I lived, ate, and breathed *Stars Collide*. Anything that happened outside Studio B was a mystery to me.

You need a life, Athena!

I shut down the laptop and leaned back against the pillows. When my eyes finally drifted shut, the image of Stephen's chiseled features took center stage in my imagination. I envisioned him as a romance cover model, long dark hair blowing in the breeze. Okay, short dark hair blowing in the breeze caused by the fan some poor props guy was holding just a few feet away, while the cameraman snapped the photos.

Though I knew very little about his background or upbringing—short of what he'd told us at the studio—I could almost picture him riding in a boat down the Amazon, fighting off snakes and other wild creatures.

Shake it off, Athena. Go to sleep.

Only one problem—I couldn't sleep. At midnight I took an over-the-counter sleeping pill. It produced zero results. At

1:10 I sat up in bed and turned on the lamp. If I couldn't get past this, I might as well think it through logically. So what if *Stars Collide* had a fourth writer? So what if it happened to be another guy? I'd survived this long surrounded by males in the industry, hadn't I? What difference would one more messy, food-consuming, stinky-footed male writer make in the grand scheme of things? Who cared that he'd had a special on HBO? These days, practically anyone could get a special on TV, right?

By 1:45 my stomach was tied up in knots. I began to wonder if perhaps I had an ulcer. By 2:30 I'd mapped out an alternative plan for my life: I'd work at my parents' store, making baklava. Not exactly what I went to college for, but who cared? Working in a sandwich shop wasn't the end of the world, right? With so many people out of jobs these days, I'd be fortunate to have the income. And maybe my parents wouldn't think I was a slouch if I earned my keep by working in the shop. Of course, my mother would grumble that I hadn't married and given her grandchildren yet, but I would jump that hurdle when I came to it. Hey, I could always adopt.

By 3:15 I'd talked myself out of the sandwich shop idea. Really, if I was as good at making phyllo dough as everyone said, why not open my own bakery? *Sweets by Athena.* No, too plain. *Delectable Delicacies by Athena.* Nah. Too long and complicated. Maybe I would come up with something later, after I rented that empty building just a few doors down from Super-Gyros and set up shop making pastries—Greek and otherwise.

Only one problem. I didn't really know how to make anything that wasn't Greek.

Okay then. I'd do a Greek pastry shop, specializing in the sweets I knew and loved. Maybe Mama could help me. No, she was too busy at the sandwich shop. Hmm. Maybe my sister? Or Aunt Melina. She was always looking for something to do. Of course, she was usually a little on the tipsy side, so no telling what the bakery goods would turn out like. Likely she'd load up the cupcakes with rum and sell them to customers by the dozen. The ones she didn't eat, anyway.

At 4:20 I got up to go to the bathroom, then returned to my room and paced. What was the point in calling myself a Christian if I didn't trust God with the finer points of my life? What a hypocrite I'd become. Maybe I just needed to pray about all of this. Give it to him. Or try to.

Moments later, I crawled back into the bed, propped up my pillows, and lit into a prayer session, bending the Almighty's ear in my direction. He already knew my fears, of course, but I reminded him anyway, just in case he'd forgotten. And surely he realized I needed an income, right? I couldn't go on living with my parents forever. Well, I could, but my child-hood bedroom had passed its expiration date years ago. A twenty-eight-year-old woman didn't need to start each day by looking at Strawberry Shortcake bedsheets and wallpaper. And the little hand-painted dresser had been cute in the early nineties, but no one had furniture like that anymore. Well, no one in their late twenties.

My thoughts shifted to my fellow writers, and I prayed for them. Well, two of them, anyway. I couldn't bring myself to pray for Stephen just yet.

Hmm. I suddenly faced a crazy temptation. Maybe I should pray that his writing skills would turn out to be lousy so that Rex would send him packing.

Nah. That would just be wrong.

Right?

By five in the morning, I'd finally fallen asleep. I dreamed that I was at the World Cup, playing soccer with the ball I'd kept hidden in my shirt. I'd just prepped myself to kick the black-and-white ball into the goal when a member of the opposing team—one who looked suspiciously like Adonis—

tackled me and knocked me to the ground, then kicked the ball in a different direction. Just as quickly, the ball morphed into a baby, which he scooped up and passed off to me. I, in turn, handed it to Kat, who looked dumbfounded as the cooing infant began to cry. Still, she held on tight, eventually singing the little one a lullaby. Very, very odd.

I awoke at eight, feeling like I'd been run over by a Mack truck in the night. One glance in the mirror made me wish I had. Were those really my eyes? Who had bags like that at my age? And what was up with the drool marks on the right side of my lips? They'd crusted over in a faint little dribble. Gross. The wrinkle marks on my cheek weren't so bad, but the red streaks in my eyes made me look like I'd spent the night mourning the loss of a loved one.

No, even grief couldn't make me look this bad.

Mama stuck her head in my door to tell me she was leaving for the shop. After taking one look at me, she promptly declared that I must be ill.

"Go back to bed, Athena. You need the rest. Poor girl." She began to speak in Greek. Something about how no man would find me attractive in my current condition. Lovely.

I offered up my best argument. "No, I want to help. You need me."

She pointed to my eyes, a look of horror on her face. "Not *that* bad."

"I'll look better after I take a shower and put on some makeup. Don't worry."

She clucked her tongue and disappeared into the hallway, muttering something in Greek about how life shouldn't be this hard for a twenty-eight-year-old who still lived at home with her mother. About how she'd hoped for a better life for me. I chose to ignore her comments. I turned on the shower, letting it run until the bathroom filled with steam.

I'd hoped the hot shower would awaken me, but it nearly

proved to be my undoing instead. Apparently the heat of the water and my lack of sleep were a poor combination. I found myself feeling worse than ever. Woozy, even. What a mess.

I staggered out of the shower, forgetting to rinse the conditioner out of my hair, which meant I had to get back in. Good grief.

Snap out of it, Athena. Just be normal.

I managed to dress, though I ended up with two shoes that didn't match. After straightening out that fiasco, I headed to the car and drove to Super-Gyros, ready to put last night's craziness behind me. With each new day came new blessings. Right?

Moments later, I joined the rest of my family behind the counter. The familiar scent of peppers, onions, and spices almost roused me from my daze. Almost. At least I felt at home at the shop. I was among my own people, people who didn't care if I could make them laugh or not.

Aunt Melina sat in the play area with the kids, her trusty coffee mug at her side. I knew it didn't really contain coffee. Well, not much. She often flavored her real beverage of choice with a bit of coffee. Probably to disguise the truth. I had to wonder how long she could go on hiding her real issues from the world. Did she even want help, or had she grown content in her pain?

I went to work on the phyllo dough, remembering my middle-of-the-night ponderings. Maybe that bakery idea wasn't such a bad one after all. I'd try to sneak away after the lunch crowd left to check out the empty space on the other end of the strip mall. Maybe I'd even take Mama with me. See what she thought about the idea. Surely she'd have a lot of advice about baking. And she certainly knew the ins and outs of running a business.

Oh, who was I kidding? I couldn't bake baklava for a living. God had called me to write, and write I must. Hadn't every writer who'd ever pounded the keys gone through something like this? Surely my insecurities were ill-founded. Yes, of course they were. Why, in a day or two, I'd be over this. Hopefully.

Hey, here's an idea. Who says I have to write sitcoms? I can always get work at the newspaper. Put out a few magazine articles. Well, sure. Newspapers are always looking for writers.

But what if I ended up writing for one of those gossip magazines? My fiction-telling skills were good . . . but not that good. Besides, my conscience wouldn't allow me to exaggerate the truth. Unless . . .

An idea took hold, one I couldn't ignore. Maybe I could write a book. Yeah, I could write a book. A murder mystery about a Las Vegas comic who turned up missing after moving to L.A.

Nah. The publishers would never buy it. Too predictable.

What was up with these neurotic notions rolling through my brain? Hadn't I spent the wee hours of the night praying about all of this? Hadn't I given my worries to God? He probably wouldn't take kindly to my current train of thought or the fact that I still seemed to be in fix-it mode.

Lord, help me. I'm trying to take my hands off. Really.

"You okay, Athena-bean?" My father looked my way, his eyes narrowed to slits. "You . . . well, you don't look like yourself today."

Ugh. I'd hoped a pound and a half of makeup would've disguised that fact.

"I'm okay, Babbas." A tiny sigh escaped, one I hoped he wouldn't notice. "Just a few problems at the office."

"Again?" My father took a couple of steps in my direction. "They treat my daughter badly?"

"No, not really. I just . . ." I felt the sting of tears. "I'm just not sure about my job security anymore. What happens if they boot me out the door? Then what?"

"Ah. Is that all?" He slipped me into a warm embrace. "It's okay, Athena-bean. You can come work for Babbas. All the gyros you can eat and good company too." He flashed a toothy smile. "And we have a great dental program."

Great. Just what I'd always hoped for. A great dental program. With all the pastries I planned to consume to drown my woes, I'd probably need it.

"We'll talk later, Babbas," I said, then gave him a little kiss on the cheek. One thing about my father, he sure knew how to make a girl forget about her troubles. I'd found him to be the perfect counterbalance to the guys at the office, who loved nothing more than pointing them out.

Elbow-deep in phyllo dough, I shifted gears, determined to put my worries behind me. Off in the distance, the bell above the door clanged, and I looked up as an elderly man entered, shoulders stooped. His soft, wrinkled skin reminded me of a pug puppy, and the pale blue-gray eyes spoke of weariness. *Wow. He'd make a great character in a sketch.* I filed away his physical attributes for use in a future episode. If I kept my job, anyway. Right now I'd better not be making any plans for the future, just in case.

The man straightened a bit, brushed the rain from his jacket, and sighed. "They told me it never rains in Southern California." I recognized the accent at once. Greek. Thick yet shaky. "They were wrong."

Mama smiled in his direction. "Sorry about the weather, but welcome to Super-Gyros. What can I get for you? Are you hungry? If so, we have the best gyros in the state. And if you like coffees, ours are wonderful, simply wonderful."

He stared at her as if seeing an apparition. "Thera. Little Thera." His voice trembled. For that matter, so did his hands as he extended them in her direction. "You don't remember me, child?"

"Remember you?" Mama stared at him for a moment, a

blank expression on her face. I drew near. So did my sister. And my sister's children. And Babbas. After a few moments, the man said something to my mother in Greek. I barely made out his words through his tears. His name, maybe?

"M-milo Consapolis?" Mama's eyes widened and she took a step backward. "Aunt Athena's Milo?" Mama began to rant in Greek, her emotions now in full swing.

"One and the same." He extended his hand once again, now speaking only in Greek. "Though if memory serves me correctly, your aunt broke my heart when you were quite young, so you can hardly call me Athena's Milo."

"She broke your heart?" Mama shook her head. "But she always said . . ."

"That I left because she took you in?"

"Yes." Mama's voice broke and tears filled her eyes.

Milo shook his head. "Nothing could be farther from the truth. I was perfectly agreeable with the idea of marrying Athena and taking you into my home as my own child until your parents could send for you. That was never a problem."

Mama nearly collapsed against the countertop at this news. "Then why did she say that?"

"You know of her legal struggles, right?"

"Legal struggles?" Mama shook her head. "No."

"When her mother died, the family estate was left to Athena under the condition that it remain in the family name. She was in her late thirties at the time and had never married. Likely her mother thought she would remain unattached. Athena's attorney advised her not to marry if she wanted to keep the home." He shrugged. "I'm sure there were ways around it, but her fear kept her from finding out, so she remained single." The pain in his eyes reflected his feelings about that.

"I had no idea." Mama swiped her eyes with the back of her hand.

Milo nodded, still looking wounded. "Athena had so many

internal struggles. In my heart, I believe she thought I would eventually leave her, just like her papa abandoned her as a little girl. You know?" He took Mama's hand. "Thera, I know that she loved you, in spite of the way things looked, and I felt you had a right to know."

"You've come all the way here—to California—to tell me this?" Mama wiped away a tear and sniffled. "I can't believe it. God bless you for that."

"Well, I came for another reason too." Milo shifted back to English. "I received a call from Athena's attorney the week after she passed away with specific instructions to bring you a gift. One she wished you to have."

"A gift?" Now my mother's tears began in earnest. "Yes, I received the letter. I knew some sort of inheritance was on its way. Oh, that poor, dear woman. How I misjudged her over the years! This just goes to show you that no one is beyond God's reach. He has worked a miracle by softening my heart toward her, even if it is too late."

Milo winked, the soft wrinkles around his eyes becoming more pronounced. "You wait. I bring him in."

"Him?" Mama's face paled, and she fanned herself with a napkin. "Oh, heaven help us. Don't tell me Mean-Athena had a son no one knew about. I don't think I could take another shock."

"Not a son . . . exactly." Milo's expression shifted, but I couldn't quite read it. What was this guy up to?

Moments later he returned with a crate in hand. A dog crate. He set it on the ground and nudged it along with a push. "Pappas family, I give you Zeus, Athena's only child. He's a Greek Domestic Dog."

Milo opened the door to the strangest-looking dog I'd ever seen. The little mongrel bounded out of the crate, heading straight for the cheese display. Once there, he leaped up on the table, pouncing on the plate of feta samples. Next he headed to the meat aisle, where he attacked a package of salami and chewed through the plastic. Then he set his eyes on me.

Uh-oh. I formed a cross with my index fingers as if to ward off the evil spirit dwelling inside the beast, then took giant steps backward as he lunged my way.

Aunt Melina went a little crazy at this point. She spit three times—as was her custom whenever she encountered demon spirits—and muttered, "Ftou, ftou, ftou!"

It didn't work. The dog leaped up, knocking over my cup of coffee, which spilled all over my white blouse. My foot landed in a wet spot on the floor and I went sprawling. The ornery mutt took this as a sign that I wanted to play. He jumped me—literally—licking my face, my ears, my hair, and my hands. I found myself pinned to the ground, the smell of doggy breath nearly causing me to hurl.

"Get away from me, you mangy mutt," I hollered. "What do you think you're doing?" I clamped my eyes shut, willing the dog away. Still, the licking continued, though Milo did his best to pull the dog away. Disgusting!

A decidedly male voice rang out, merging with the other sights, sounds, and smells. "Athena, if you're gonna run with the big dogs, you're gonna have to move faster than that."

I looked up, my gaze landing on Adonis. Er, Stephen. Perfect. Couldn't have planned this any better if I'd tried. Rex and Lenora stood behind him. I noticed that Lenora wore a glittering white gown and carried a scepter. Well, at least I thought it was a scepter. She'd obviously made it out of tinfoil. It took me a minute to figure out her costume, but I finally got it. Glenda, the good witch.

Apparently the sequins in her gown interested the dog too. He bolted her direction, yapping to beat the band. Stephen intervened, grabbing the dog by the collar and yanking him back. His voice remained low but steady. Firm. "Don't even think about it."

In that moment, I wished Lenora could wave her magic wand and send Toto—er, Zeus—right back to Kansas. Or Greece. Whatever.

Mama, never one to miss an opportunity to marry me off to any available candidate, set her eye on Stephen. "Who do we have here?"

"Stephen Cosse. I work with—" He never got to finish the sentence because the dog jumped up and licked him in the face.

My brother appeared from the back room, concern registering in his eyes as he saw Zeus. "Someone want to explain why we have a dog in the shop? Do we want the health department to shut us down?" His gaze shifted to Lenora in her shimmering getup, then back to the dog. No telling which one brought more confusion.

"This is Zeus!" Milo proclaimed. "Your inheritance from the motherland."

"We inherited a dog?" Niko took a few steps in our direction and extended his hand to help me up. Thank goodness.

"Not just *any* dog," I said, brushing off my pants legs. "A *Greek* dog."

The cantankerous canine turned and offered a low growl, as if willing my brother to stay put. Never one to be outdone, Niko reached for the broom and began to wave it in the dog's face, which caused the longest—and loudest—yapping spree I'd ever witnessed outside of watching *The Dog Whisperer*. Seriously? What kind of dog could keep on barking that long and not eventually end up with vocal strain?

At this point, Milo handed Mama a note. She opened it, her hands trembling so hard I knew she wouldn't be able to read it. "Athena?" She looked my way. "Would you?"

"Is it written in Greek?" I asked. "I can speak the language, but you know I can't read it. Not well, anyway." If I attempted to translate that letter, no telling what I'd come up with.

"I can," Stephen said. "If it's not too personal, I'll be happy to translate it for you. My Greek is still pretty good."

Of course it is.

"I'm sorry, but who did you say you are again?" Mama asked.

He extended his hand. "Stephen Cosse. I work with Athena. I'm a writer."

My mother took his hand, gripping it firmly. "And you read Greek?"

He nodded, and I passed the note his way, knowing Mama wasn't in any shape to be reading it. If it turned out to be private information, she could forgive me later.

Stephen's voice remained steady as he read the words in the letter. "Thera, if you're reading this note, I have gone to be with Jesus."

My brother grunted and muttered something under his breath.

Stephen continued. "May the gift I give you today bring you as much joy as you brought me as a child."

"Aw, how sweet." Mama managed a half smile. "Well, maybe she—" A pause followed and her smile faded. "Wait a minute. I never brought her joy as a child, though it wasn't for lack of trying. She always acted like she hated me. So what do you think she's trying to say about the dog? Is she sending some sort of subliminal message, perhaps?"

Zeus jumped up and growled at my mother, baring his teeth. Ack.

Stephen snapped his fingers and the dog settled down. He gestured to the letter. "There's more. Want me to read it?"

"I guess." Mama sighed. "Good old Athena. Always has to get the last word."

I turned to Stephen to explain. "Just so we're clear about this, my mother is talking about my dead aunt, Athena. Not me."

"Ah." The edges of his lips curled up for a moment. "Thanks for clarifying. I wondered. I'll file that away for future reference."

Hmm. There were a few things I wanted to file away as well. My wandering thoughts, for instance. How could I focus on poor Aunt Athena and her mangy mutt with such a handsome man standing next to me?

Who was this guy, anyway? He'd come all the way from Vegas to our gyro shop to translate a letter from my dead aunt? Seriously? Had all of this been orchestrated as part of some great cosmic plan, or could the timing of his visit today be deemed a coincidence?

Stephen read the rest of the note—basically instructions on how to feed and care for the dog—then handed it back to my mother. She folded it and put it in her apron pocket, shaking her head all the while.

"Well, now. I will pray about this, and we will decide what to do with the dog." Mama turned her focus to our guests, clasping her hands at her chest. "In the meantime, are you hungry? Come. I'll fix you the best gyro you've ever eaten."

Talk about switching gears. Clearly she did not care to address this any further. But all of the questions I had about Mean-Athena rushed through my head. She had left a lasting impression on my mother, and obviously not a good one. Was this gift an attempt to make things right, or some sort of subliminal message?

Mama reiterated her offer to feed our guests.

"I'm happy to take you up on that," Milo said. "Smells like home in here."

"It is." Babbas smiled. "Home to us, and now home to you. Any friend from Greece is a true friend indeed."

I should embroider that on a sampler and hang it on the wall.

"I ate a Super-Gyro last Saturday," Stephen said. "Which

69

is why I talked Rex and Lenora into coming back today." A boyish smile lit his face. "Haven't had a sandwich like that in years. Not since I was a kid, back in Jersey. Not just everyone can build the perfect gyro."

"You do make the best gyro in town." Rex offered my mother a smile.

Mama grinned. "I'm glad you liked it."

"Liked it?" A look of pure bliss passed over Stephen's face. "I've dreamed about it all week. And I promised Brooke I'd pick up lunch while I was out. She's waiting back at our place, so I can't stay long."

"Brooke?" My mama's joy seemed to fade as she repeated the name. "Your . . . your girlfriend?"

Could you be any more obvious, Mama?

"No, my daughter." As soon as Stephen spoke the word *daughter*, his face lit up and his eyes misted over. "Brooke is eleven. She's lived with me since she was four. Her mom . . ." He shook his head. "Anyway, she's not part of Brooke's life. Haven't heard from her in years. So I'm dad and mom. It's been challenging at times, but I wouldn't trade it for anything."

"Wow."

"Yeah, you should've seen me trying to French braid her hair the first few times," he said. "I finally resorted to getting the instructions from the internet."

"The internet?"

"Yeah. God bless YouTube. You can't imagine how much I've learned from watching videos. And my daughter has been pretty good about it, all things considered. Only . . ." Stephen shook his head. "Never mind. Don't know why I brought any of this up, anyway."

"I'll tell you what," my mother said. "You bring her with you next time. She can spend the afternoon with us. Play with the kids." Mama gestured to my sister's children, who had taken to playing with the dog.

Playing with the dog? What in the world? He wasn't growling or baring his teeth. No, the crazy mutt had rolled over on his back on the floor and was allowing the three-year-old to rub his belly. What was up with that?

"I couldn't burden you with an eleven-year-old," Stephen said. "She's quite a handful. You know what girls are like as preteens. Pretty emotional."

For whatever reason, everyone looked my way. Mama even rolled her eyes. Okay, so I'd had a few rough years in junior high. What girl hadn't? My cheeks heated up as I looked at Stephen.

"Don't you want her to meet people?" I asked, hoping to change the direction of the conversation.

"Sure." He shrugged. "I asked her to come with us today, but she declined. This has been a difficult transition for her, that's all. Just warning you she can be a handful when she's in a mood, which is a lot." A sad look passed over him. "She was such a happy-go-lucky little girl. It's kind of sad to see this change in her."

"I'm sure it's just a stage," I said.

"How could we turn her away?" My father slapped Stephen on the back. "We're Greek. You're Greek. We're all Greek. Bring her over and she'll fit right in."

"I wouldn't be so sure about that." He rolled his eyes. "First of all, have you spent much time with preteen girls? They're complicated. They cry. A lot. And for no reason. Very nonsensical."

"Well, you've landed in the best possible place," Lenora said, her face beaming. "Here in the land of Oz, everyone is so friendly. You bring your little munchkin over and these fine people will take her by the hand and lead her down the yellow-brick road." She licked her lips. "In the meantime, can we get this show on the road? I'm starved."

"Of course." Mama flew into action, preparing sandwiches

for everyone. I watched as Stephen ordered our Super-Duper Deluxe Gyro, loaded with peppers and onions. Mmm. A man after my own heart.

Watch it, Athena. You don't even know if you can trust this guy yet.

To his right, Lenora rambled on about tornadoes, flying monkeys, and poppy fields. She hollered for the dog to join her, calling him Toto. Strangely, he came when called and nuzzled up against her. Perhaps she'd won him over with her costume. Or maybe it had something to do with the nibbles of meat she slipped him from the tray on the counter. Either way, the dog was smitten.

For that matter, so was I. Staring at Stephen, I had to admit the truth—this guy had charmed me with his goodness toward my mother, his ability to calm Zeus, and his heart for his daughter.

If I wasn't so busy hating him for stealing my job—well, potentially stealing my job, anyway—I might be tempted to follow him right on down the yellow-brick road.

6

Hee Haw

On Monday morning I arrived at the studio, determined to give Stephen the benefit of the doubt. Ironically, both of my other writing companions had gone missing. Paul had stayed home with a head cold—for which I was grateful—but Bob simply didn't show up. I tried calling him at nine, but he didn't answer. Strange. He usually beat me to the office, especially on the days when I showed up with leftovers from Super-Gyros.

By nine thirty, I'd passed the food items off to Stephen, who grabbed a fork—*Thank you, Lord*—to eat the salad. With such a huge appetite, he didn't need much in the way of conversation. Right now it would be better if we just worked. Well, tried to work, anyway. I still hadn't figured out his approach to the sitcom, or whether or not he could even write. Part of me hoped he could, of course, and part of me hoped he stunk at this. Not a very Christian attitude, but I struggled with it just the same.

I'd never seen a man enjoy food as much as he appeared to enjoy that salad. The look of contentment on his face reminded me of my father. Interesting.

"So, let's talk about next week's episode," Stephen said between bites. "I had some thoughts about it. Tell me what you think about this idea." He dove off into some crazy idea about Angie and Jack opening up their talent agency to elderly Hollywood stars. Totally threw me. Guess we were really over the whole "Angie announces her pregnancy" idea. Bummer.

On and on Stephen went, chattering about the opportunity for chaos, should we choose to include elderly cast members. I found the idea strange at best. And perplexing. Was he missing the point of the show? Stars Collide was a talent agency for children. Children. Not elderly people.

Just about the time I worked up the courage to state my case, he took the conversation in a different direction.

"I've been taking a class on plotting," he said. "And I'd like to implement some of the things I've learned."

"Okay." I shrugged.

"So, here's the premise of the class. Twelve steps in the plotline."

"Right." I nodded. "It's called the Hero's Journey."

"Ah." He gave me a funny look. "You've heard of it."

"Of course." Did he think I was an idiot? And what in the world did this have to do with adding elderly cast members?

"Well, I think we need to be aware at every step of the game where Angie and Jack are in the plotline. That's how we'll keep the show moving forward. Right now we're in a new season, so we're basically back near the beginning. I'd say we're on Step 2."

"Which one is Step 2?" I asked. "Refresh my memory."

From the look on his face, I could tell he would enjoy telling me all about it. "It's the 'Call to Adventure,'" he said.

"That's where the hero—or heroine—gets called out of his or her comfort zone."

Ironic. That's the step I happen to be at in my own personal plotline.

"So, Jack and Angie are about to be called to do something new with the agency. Is that what you're saying? Hence the suggestion about senior citizens."

"Exactly." He lit back into his idea of bringing elderly cast members into the show, focusing on the positive changes this could bring to the season.

"But it's an agency for kids," I argued. "Always has been. I can't even imagine this show being about anything other than that."

"Right. I've watched this show from the beginning, so I know all about it," Stephen said. "Angie had her talent agency. Jack had his talent agency. They were chief competitors. Then, with some prompting from the kids, they overcame their obstacles—laid down their jealousies of each other—and fell in love. Got all that. I'm just thinking it's time to jump outside the box. Do something the viewers won't expect. Stir things up a little."

Things are being stirred up, all right.

He kept talking, but my thoughts parked on what he'd just said. I found the whole thing about Jack and Angie starting out as competitors strangely ironic, in light of my current situation. Stephen might not be a competitor, but on some levels he felt like one.

"Anyway, Jack and Angie have always represented kids," Stephen said. "I know that, and it's made for plenty of great antics along the way. But I think it would be fun to bring in a host of aging Hollywood stars—folks considered to be past their expiration date in the industry. Our two talent scouts can help them jump-start their careers. Well, the next phase of their careers, anyway."

I had to admit, it was an interesting idea. And I could almost envision the kids interacting with the aging men and women of Hollywood. Might be funny to see who we could get. A host of elderly stars came to mind, and I couldn't help but smile.

"We've already got Lenora Worth, for Pete's sake." Stephen reached for his coffee cup. "She's an icon in this industry. But she's not in very many episodes. We need to take advantage of the fact that she's already on the payroll and use her more."

"You might not know this, but she's in the beginning stages of Alzheimer's," I explained. "Working with her is tricky. She thinks it's still 1957."

"Ah." He nodded. "Gotcha. I've noticed her interesting clothing choices. Guess that explains it."

"Right. The folks in the wardrobe department stock her closet at home, but she doesn't know that. Kat makes sure she's always got the gowns she needs to make her feel content. We all do what we can to ease her concerns when things get iffy. We had a close call last season. When Jack and Angie got engaged on the show, she thought Scott and Kat were engaged in real life too."

"I remember reading about that in the newspaper. They did end up getting married in real life, right?"

"Right." I grinned, remembering how they'd pulled one over on us. "Anyway, Lenora gets confused. That was my point."

"And I'm sure if we bring in other elderly stars, we're bound to have a few issues like that," he said. "But it will be worth it."

"I must say, the kids adore Lenora." I paused to think this through. Maybe I'd been too quick to nix his idea. "Merging old people and young people might work."

"I think so, and I really like the idea of bringing in people who are considered to be washed up." He shrugged, a sympathetic look on his face. "I don't know. It's always nice to give second chances. There are so few of them in life, and even fewer in Hollywood. People out here always want the latest, greatest thing. They forget the people from days gone by."

"Yeah. Viewers are fickle," I said.

"Not just viewers. Directors. Producers. Network executives. They forget the generations of people who've gone before us, paving the way." He shrugged. "I don't know. I just think we need to give honor where honor is due, and there are a lot of people—like Rex and Lenora—who've given their lives for this industry. I'd hate to think they would get to the end of their days and not be recognized for what they've done."

Man. "Well, when you put it like that, of course we should include senior citizens in the show!"

"See?" Stephen reached over and touched my hand, sending a little shiver through me. "I knew we'd get along. From the moment you stepped on my foot, I had the overwhelming sense that we were a match made in heaven."

My jaw locked up at that proclamation.

"A literary match, I mean." He winked, and my heart fluttered. Goodness. Did this guy have a way with words or what? So much for thinking he had no writing talent.

I'd just opened my mouth to respond—though what I would say was still a mystery—when the door swung open. Bob stuck his head inside and hollered, "Papa's home. Is dinner ready?"

A wave of relief swept over me. Things would be less awkward with a third party in the room . . . even if it happened to be wacky Bob.

"It's about time," I said. "Where have you been? We've been trying to work on this week's episode, but—"

"Are you sitting down?" Bob interrupted me with a suspicious twinkle in his eye.

Stephen and I looked at each other on the couch.

"Um, yeah, dude." Stephen gestured to the divan.

"What's up?" I asked.

Bob stepped into the room and closed the door behind him. He lowered his voice to a hoarse whisper. "Remember I told you how George Clooney's production company was looking at my Amish vampire story?"

Who could forget? "Yes," I said. "But why are we whispering?"

"They want it."

"W-what?" I rose and crossed the room to meet him, my heart plummeting to my toes. "Are you serious? They're buying your script?"

A pained expression crossed his face. "Why do you look so surprised? I've told you all along that it would sell."

"Well, yes, but . . ." I should be happy for the guy, right? So why did I suddenly feel like the world had tilted off its axis?

"My agent just called to give me the news, so I had to rush over to his office to finalize the details. Sign the contract and all that. Not only that, they're going to try to get Keira Knightley to play the lead. What do you think?"

I'm thinking that this is all some sort of joke. That an Amish vampire is going to jump out from behind the desk and holler, "I don't exist! How could you possibly write a movie about me?"

"Production begins in a couple of weeks," he said, clearly oblivious to my internal wrangling. "So I have to sign off of *Stars Collide* ASAP to get ready. I can hardly wait. It's going to be a blast." Off he went on a tangent, talking about his plans for the next few weeks.

"Wait." I shook my head. "Sign off. You mean . . . quit?"

"Yep." He nodded. "Looks that way."

"Just like that? But you're under contract."

"Yeah, I know." He sighed. "Hoping Rex will let me out of it. My second cousin twice removed is a lawyer. Criminal defense, but I guess that part doesn't matter. He says I can get out of it if I handle things carefully. That's what I plan to do, anyway. You know me, Athena. I can schmooze my way through anything. I'll get out of this. I'll have my cake and eat it too."

"Better idea," Stephen said. "Don't quit. Just take a leave of absence. Ask Rex to hold your job for you. This kind of thing happens in Hollywood all the time, you know."

"Brilliant!" Bob's face lit in a confident smile.

"Besides, how long could it take to film a movie?" Stephen asked. "A couple months? Three at most. Right?"

"Who knows?" Bob reached for the Super-Gyros bag, coming out with a container of cookies. "I've never filmed a movie before. Shoot, even the layout of the script was different from what we use in television. I'll admit, this is all pretty new to me, but I'm looking forward to it. I like a good challenge." He opened the cookies and popped one in his mouth. Whole. He talked around it, rambling on and on about his future as a film writer. "Don't know if I want to come back to television or not," he added, then grabbed another cookie.

I plopped back down onto the sofa, my thoughts a jumbled mess. Bob . . . leaving? Sure, he'd threatened dozens of times, but to actually do it? I couldn't imagine it. We'd always been a team. The Three Stooges. Larry, Moe, and Curly. Now that Curly was leaving, we'd be Larry, Moe, and Stephen. Just didn't have the same ring to it. And Stephen could never fill Bob's shoes. Not really. Oh, he might be pretty to look at, but did he have that same sarcastic edge— the one I counted on from episode to episode? Probably not. And I still didn't know if he could write. Only time would tell on that one.

Another thing bothered me a little too. Bob had actually sold that Amish vampire screenplay. His career was taking a turn, propelling him forward.

Looks like he's on Step 2 in his plotline too. Getting a real-life call to adventure. Ironic.

Strange how bleak my future looked in comparison.

Calm down, Athena. Be happy for your friend. Jealousy is a sin, remember?

In between cookies, Bob continued to share, his enthusiasm apparently growing. "This is going to be great. My agent says the 15 percent he earns off me will be enough to buy a house. Can you even imagine how much my cut is going to be? I'm going to have it made in the shade. I'll get that place in Malibu I've been dreaming of."

Stephen crossed his arms over his chest and leaned back on the divan. "Well, don't put all your eggs in one basket, as my mama used to say. Sorry to be so cliché, and I sure don't want to put a damper on your spirits, but I'm afraid you're going to wind up in a jam if you're not careful. I'm speaking from personal experience. Sometimes what looks like the deal of a lifetime turns out to be a lemon."

"Yeah, promise me you won't do anything rash, Bob," I threw in.

"Like what?" He nibbled the edge of another cookie.

"Like taking the money you earn and moving off to Tahiti or something."

A faraway look came over him. "Hey, a guy could write a lot of movies in Tahiti." Bob grinned. "But no worries. I won't spend the money till I have it. And even then, I don't know that I'll do anything crazy." He offered a weak shrug. "Maybe I'll think about that leave-of-absence angle. Come back to *Stars Collide* after we're done filming. Might work."

I wanted to say, "Pray about it," but thought he might find my words a little too religious. I would pray about it, of course. We needed Bob to return. As crazy as he made me, I would miss him. Terribly.

"Not sure how you guys are going to keep this show going

without me, frankly." He flashed a crooked grin and closed the cookie container. "I'm the brains of this operation, you know."

I couldn't help the snort that followed. Still, I had to agree that things would be tougher without him. We'd always worked like a well-oiled machine.

"Can you stay a while today and work?" I asked. "Stephen came up with an idea to incorporate some older cast members into the show this season."

"Older?" Bob plopped down in the chair next to the divan. "Like who?"

Stephen named several well-known stars in their seventies and eighties. "Most were icons back in their day," he said. "I think it would be fun to give them a second chance."

"Second chances are good." Bob nodded. "So, what are you thinking? How would we use them? And what happened to the pregnancy idea? Did we nix that?"

"Just postponed it," Stephen said. He went on to explain his idea, and Bob seemed receptive. The more I heard, the better it sounded to me too. I could almost see it now—the kids playing jokes on the older cast members and vice versa. Plenty of opportunity for antics. And the whole thing would add plenty of stress—conflict—to Jack and Angie's relationship. Perfect, since comedy was built on conflict.

The ideas started pouring out, and before long we'd written the first five pages of the next episode. Maybe working with this new guy wouldn't be so tough after all. And I really liked all of his ideas related to Jack and Angie's marriage.

"All of this craziness will challenge their skills as a new bride and groom," he said. "But that will be half the fun. We'll stretch them in every area." The oddest look came over him for a second.

"You okay, man?" Bob asked.

"Oh." He paused, and for a moment I thought I saw

something that looked like pain in his eyes. Just as quickly he shook it off. "Just thinking about that whole marriage thing. My parents . . ." He shook his head. "Well, they had a horrible marriage. It didn't last. And I already told you my story. My wife took off when Brooke was young. No one in my family has a very good track record when it comes to marital vows."

"Mine either," Bob said. "My parents split when I was three. Barely knew my dad."

"We'll have to lean on Paul, for sure," Stephen said. "Maybe he can advise us."

"Think again." Bob snorted. "He's been married three times and has sworn off women altogether since his last divorce. If you're wanting information on how to keep a marriage strong, he's the very last person you want to talk to."

Both of the guys turned and looked at me.

"Well, you're it, then," Stephen said. "I happen to know firsthand that your parents have a great marriage."

"You could tell that after hanging out with them just one afternoon?"

"I could tell that within five minutes of meeting them." He smiled. "They're crazy about each other. How long have they been married? Forever, right?"

I shrugged. "Thirty-seven years. And you're right—they're still crazy about each other." I couldn't help smiling. Though my parents bickered like every good Greek couple, their love for each other was unquestionable.

"Maybe we can interview them or something," Stephen said. "Get their take on how Jack and Angie's marriage will be affected by all of the changes they're facing. Your parents are the ideal choice, since they work together and all."

"Oh, wow. Never made that connection before." My parents did work together, just like Jack and Angie. Yes, surely they would know how to make it through the challenges of a family-run business. Who better to give us advice for our characters? Why hadn't I thought of this? Brilliant.

Minutes later, we dove into the script once more, laughter resonating across the room. As we hit on a particularly funny scene, the office phone rang. I answered it, still chuckling. "H-hello?"

"Athena?" I recognized my mother's voice right away. "What's so funny?"

"Oh, we're in the middle of writing a wacky scene. Ironically, one that might end up involving you and Babbas." I paused. "Wait. Why did you call on the office phone? You never do that."

"I tried your cell six times and you didn't answer. Do you have the ringer turned off or something?"

"Oh, maybe." I stuck my hand in my purse, fishing around the gum wrappers, receipts, and lipstick, until I finally pulled out the phone. Glancing at it, I sighed. "Yes. Sorry. What's up?"

"It's that dog of yours. Zeus."

"*My* dog?" Surely I'd heard wrong. Just because I carried Aunt Athena's name didn't mean she'd left the dog to me. No, Zeus belonged to my mother first, and then the rest of us. Whether we wanted him to or not.

"Yes." Mama's voice grew more strained. "You've got to come home and do something about him. Soon. Before my last nerve is shot."

"What has he done this time? Could you be specific? Or is he just annoying in every respect?"

She began to reel off something in Greek, but she was speaking so fast I couldn't make heads or tails of it. Finally she switched to English.

"Before I left for the shop this morning, he'd chewed up the wood posts on my bed. And then I caught him shredding one of the pillows from the living room sofa. I . . ." A catch in her throat caught me off guard. "I can't take it, Athena. Something has to be done or the whole house will be destroyed."

"But, Mama, I'm a half hour away and won't be home for hours. Can't you think of something to calm him down?"

"I've tried everything." She sighed. "I went to the store as usual. Closed him in the bathroom. When I came back to check on him . . ." She began to cry. "Remember that beautiful rug I bought at the import store when you were in junior high? The green one with the pretty edging?"

"Of course."

"He . . . he . . ." She choked out the words. "He ate it."

"He ate the rug? Seriously?"

From across the room, Bob and Stephen gave me curious looks.

"Well, just the corner section," Mama explained, "but what good is a six-hundred-dollar rug if it's missing a piece? It's worthless now. And all because of a stupid dog that your great-aunt Athena made us take."

"She was your aunt too, Mama," I reminded her. "And dogs will be dogs. Maybe we just need to admit we don't know the first thing about animals and find someone else to take him. I think it's the only solution."

"You don't think that would be dishonoring her memory?" Mama asked through her sniffles. "Really?"

"I don't. It's good to know when to admit defeat. And clearly we're not meant to have a dog. At least, not this dog."

Stephen waved his hand to get my attention and mouthed the words, "I'll take him."

I stared at him, dumbfounded, and mouthed back, "Are you sure?"

When he nodded, I turned back to the phone. "Mama, the solution to this problem might be closer than we think. Just let me go for a few minutes and I'll see if I can work something out, okay?"

"O-okay."

"In the meantime, don't panic. What else can a dog do in just a few hours? It will be fine."

"I'll try putting him in the backyard," she said. "I just hope he doesn't jump in the pool again."

"Let him jump in," I said. "Might cool him down."

"Last time he came into the house soaking wet and shook off all over my clean tile floor." She sighed. "My luck, he'll eat the hibiscus plants in my garden if I put him in the backyard. Anyway, if you say we have a solution, I'm happy to hear it. I'll leave things in your hands. See you tonight, baby."

"Love you, Mama. Stay calm."

"Too risky." Her voice changed, and I could tell she'd started scolding the dog. Seconds later, she clicked off.

"Everything okay on the home front?" Bob's eyes showed his concern.

"No." I groaned. "My dead aunt sent us a present, and he's wreaking havoc in our home."

"Wait. Let's back up a bit." He shook his head. "Would you mind telling me how your dead aunt sent you a gift?"

"Long story." I sighed. "Just trust me when I say that our lives have been turned upside down." I turned to Stephen, hopefulness setting in. "Were you serious about what you said? You want to take Zeus off our hands? If so, why? And how?"

He rose and took a few steps in my direction. "I think it's a great idea. Brooke has been really lonely this summer. She hasn't made any friends yet. And the rental house we're in allows pets, so why not? We've been talking about it for days now. She's dying for a pet."

"Pets?" Bob scratched his head. "Your dead aunt sent you a pet?"

"A dog," Stephen and I said in unison.

"Ah. I thought maybe she'd FedExed a painting of her

heavenly mansion or something. Maybe a nugget from the streets of gold." He paused. "Heaven's streets are supposed to be made of gold, right? I remember hearing that."

"Yes." I nodded. Though I couldn't imagine Mean-Athena walking along them, from all the stories I'd been told about her. More likely she was hurling chunks of gold at the angels, just to be spiteful. *Slow down. You never really knew her. And remember what Milo said. There were extenuating circumstances.*

I released a slow breath, ready to admit I should stop passing judgment on a woman I'd never even met, then turned back to Stephen. "I can't believe you're offering to do this for us. You do remember which dog we're talking about, right? The one who jumped me and ate half of the salami in my family's store?"

"He'll be fine. And Brooke could use a friend. She's been . . ." He shrugged. "Out of sorts."

"If you're sure." I paused, deep in thought. "So, how am I going to get the dog to you?"

"Bring him here tomorrow," Stephen said. "We'll crate him, and I'll take him home after work. That's the best solution, I think."

"Bring that demon-possessed dog to the studio? No way."

"Yes. Bring his crate too. I'll teach you a few tricks of the trade. I've had a few dogs over the years."

When Stephen winked, my heart went into overdrive. Ugh. How dare this guy—this handsome, funny, practically-perfect-in-every-way guy—wink at me? Did he really think he could win me over with his charm?

Maybe. But he'd have to throw in a great script for next week's show too.

"Just to clarify, you're saying I should bring a dog with ADD to a television studio loaded with expensive equipment?" I asked.

"Sure. He won't be a bother."

You're nuts. "Before or after he chews up the cables that are strung across the floor in the studio and eats holes in the costumes? And what if he bites one of the kids? I can't take that risk." I shuddered, just thinking about it. Would the SPCA intervene? "He could hurt someone."

"He won't. The Greek Domestic is a docile breed. They don't bite."

"Wanna bet?" I held out my arm to show him Evidence A. "See that spot right there?" I pointed to the inside of my arm. "There's the proof. Teeth marks. Ask me what I did to deserve it. Go on. Ask me."

"What did you do to deserve it?" Stephen asked.

"Nothing. I was sound asleep in my bed, and that mutt jumped up there and tore into me in the middle of the night like I'd somehow threatened him."

"Wait. Was that the night it stormed?" Stephen asked. "Maybe he was scared."

"Hmm. Could be." I shrugged. "Still, I don't think bringing him to the studio is the best idea. The risk is too great, especially with little ones around."

"Just give me your address and I'll come by your house tonight after work." He smiled. "I'll bring Brooke with me. That way she and the dog can get to know one another in the car on the ride back. Trust me, by tomorrow at this time, everything will be fine."

I had to admit, meeting his daughter did sound good. I'd been dying to know what this eleven-year-old looked and acted like. Was she really the challenge he'd made her out to be?

We made our plans and then dove back into our work. As the hours passed, I felt more settled about, well, pretty much everything. Hopefully that feeling would stick.

7

Perfect Strangers

That evening I arrived home to pure chaos. Zeus had somehow slipped out the front door and sprinted away. My father followed him, leash in hand, calling his name. I could only imagine what sort of trouble the dog could cause while on the run.

Babbas finally returned, looking winded and frazzled. The mutt squirmed and whimpered in his arms. He looked almost as exhausted.

"Babbas?" I looked at the wrinkles in his brow. "You okay?"

Zeus jumped down, and my father leaned against the stair railing, taking a few deep breaths. "Nothing," he huffed, "an . . . extra dose of"—he paused for a breath—"blood pressure meds . . . won't cure." The rosy color in his cheeks made me nervous. By now the dog was circling us like a buzzard. Hopefully he wouldn't swoop in for the kill. "He made it twelve blocks . . . and approximately forty houses . . . before I caught up with him."

"Man. He's fast on his feet."

"Must be all the demons driving him." My father gave a woeful smile.

"No doubt."

The doorbell rang and I headed to the door to greet Stephen and Brooke, more than a little curious. After the big buildup, I had to wonder about the infamous preteen. Was she really as moody as he'd let on? If so, I'd better prepare myself.

My mother reached the door first. I stepped behind her, noticing the beautiful young woman with the curly brunette hair standing behind Stephen. She was petite with gorgeous brown eyes—eyes that stood in direct contrast to the unhappy look on her face.

Other than the expression, nothing about her stood out or seemed unusual. I wasn't sure what I'd expected. Attila the Hun? A gothic-looking kid dressed in black? Instead, I found a typical-looking preteen, maybe a little small for her age, who seemed shy at best. And that beautiful dark hair. Wow! She could do shampoo commercials with hair like that.

"You must be Brooke." My mama swept the young woman into her arms and began to murmur her welcome in Greek. "Oh, you sweet, sweet girl!"

Brooke seemed to freeze up in my mother's embrace. Obviously her tongue was frozen too. She didn't say a word, though her wide eyes spoke volumes. So did the glare that followed when my mother squeezed her tighter.

Mama never seemed to notice, thankfully. She took Brooke by the arm and led her into the living room, babbling on and on, half in English, half in Greek.

I kept a watchful eye on Stephen, whose gaze shifted from my mother to me to the various paintings of Greece on the walls, then back to me.

"Feels like home here," he said at last. "Smells like it too." He closed his eyes and appeared to be breathing in the scent.

"My dad's in the kitchen, cooking," I said. "He's going to ask you to stay for dinner, so prepare yourself. He loves to cook for people. No one is a stranger in his kitchen."

"I would think he'd get his fill at the shop."

"Oh no. My dad's a whiz at the stove. I think he would've done really well as a chef. Full Greek cuisine, I mean. Not just sandwiches."

A satisfied look came over Stephen. "I get hungry just thinking about all the foods my grandmother used to make. I lived with her for a few years when I was in elementary school and got an education that no public school could top. She was the best cook I've ever known."

Interesting. I wanted to ask more about that but never got the chance. Off in the distance, Zeus began to bark. For the first time, a hint of a smile lit Brooke's face.

"Is that our dog?" she asked.

"It is." I turned to face the girl, dazzled by the genuine sweetness in her smile as Zeus came running into the room. "He's a Greek Domestic Dog."

"A Greek Domestic Dog?" She knelt on the floor and began to tickle the mongrel's tummy. "Never heard of that breed. I'll have to look it up on the internet." She rolled her eyes. "But it figures. With my dad, everything is better if it's Greek." Her attention shifted back to the dog.

Mama turned to Stephen and grinned. "A good Greek boy." Her gaze traveled back and forth between Stephen and me, and I could hear her unspoken words: *Perhaps my daughter won't be a spinster after all!*

Thankfully, Stephen couldn't read her thoughts like I could. His attention remained fixed on his daughter. They seemed to have an unspoken conversation going on too. Funny how that worked. Parents and children just had a knack for speaking without words.

"Hey now," he said. "Nothing wrong with appreciating your heritage."

Brooke rolled her eyes. "I just have to hear about it all the time. And besides, you've never even been to Greece, Dad."

"I'll get there someday," he said. "It's only a dream so far, but I know it's going to happen. Wait and see."

Me too.

I knelt on the floor next to Brooke and petted Zeus. "I'd never heard of this breed either," I admitted. "Had to look it up myself. I know your dad said he's supposed to be a calm breed, but I've witnessed just the opposite. He's a real challenge. Do you think you're up for the task?"

"Yeah." Her expression grew serious. "I'm good with animals. They like me. I helped my friend Mandy train her dog to do tricks. He learned how to sit and stay and roll over. And he used to bark all the time, but I taught him not to." She grinned. "I watch *The Dog Whisperer*."

"She records every episode," Stephen said. "I think she's memorized Cesar Millan's tricks of the trade."

"It's so easy." She shrugged. "You just have to show him who's the pack leader."

"And that would be . . . ?" I looked at her and shrugged.

She pointed to herself. "Me. And he's going to know it too."

Five minutes later, with Zeus snoozing in her lap, I had to admit she hadn't exaggerated. She was good with animals. Her father appeared to be good with them too. The one or two times Zeus tried to make a move in the wrong direction, Stephen made a shushing noise that stopped the dog in his tracks.

As we sat together in the living room, Brooke opened up and talked about all sorts of things related to the dog. She commented on his beautiful black and brown coat and the texture of his ears. She let me know that he needed to have his nails clipped and could stand to take off a couple of pounds. From there, she shifted into a story about how she hoped to be a vet when she grew up.

I could tell two things from the expression on Stephen's face as he listened to this conversation. One, she rarely talked this much. And two, he'd had no idea she wanted to be a vet. Still, he didn't interrupt her as she carried on about her hopes and dreams for the future. Instead, the sweetest fatherly smile lit his face.

I watched it all, the oddest sensation gripping my heart. His love for her was almost palpable. I could feel it. And suddenly I wondered what it would feel like to have a daughter this age. What would it be like to have a daughter at all? Sure, I'd walked my sister through the births of her little girls—and then her son—but to have a daughter I could call my own? What would that be like?

I looked back and forth between Stephen and Brooke, my focus narrowing. They had the same eyes and similar noses. Her hair was a couple of shades lighter, and a teensy bit of preteen chubbiness had set in, so I couldn't really tell if she had inherited his overall physique. Still, when she smiled— which turned out to be more than I'd imagined—she looked just like him. In other words, I found her to be quite a stunner.

Two more thoughts occurred to me. One, her mother— whoever and wherever she was—was missing out on the most beautiful daughter in the world. And two, Brooke and her daddy were lucky to have each other. Thinking about this got me a little misty. It also made me angry that her mother had walked away. What kind of woman would do something like that?

Mama looked my way. "You okay, Athena?"

"Yes." I drew in a deep breath, doing my best to look composed. "Getting hungry, though. That food smells delicious."

"I agree." Stephen looked for a moment like he might leap

from the couch in search of the kitchen. Thank goodness he didn't have to.

"Did I hear someone say they were hungry?" My father entered the room, still wearing his Super-Gyros apron. "I've prepared a feast fit for a king. Hope everyone likes lamb. Oh, and I have the most beautiful vegetable dish. Can't wait for you to taste it."

Brooke turned up her nose, but I could almost see Stephen salivating. "You don't mind if we stay for dinner?"

"Of course not. You are our guests. We'll have dinner and visit. And then you'll stay for dessert. Hope you like baklava. Athena's is the best."

Stephen turned to look at me with a narrowed gaze. "I think I remember someone saying we might end up holding a duel to see about that."

"You bake too?" my father asked.

"He's the baklava king," Brooke said with a confident smile. "Nobody makes it like my dad."

Wow. That was the first time I'd actually heard her say something nice about her father, and it had to do with cooking? Interesting.

"Really." My father looked back and forth between us. "Maybe we'll have the two of you duke it out at the restaurant someday. How does that sound to you, Stephen? Ready for a Greek Iron Chef challenge?"

"I'm always up for a challenge, trust me."

Ugh. He had to say that. Those words reminded me that his latest challenge could very well be to take over my job.

Deep breath, Athena. No point in worrying about that tonight.

After putting Zeus in the backyard, we sent Brooke to the restroom to wash her hands. I took advantage of the opportunity to share my thoughts.

"She's a beautiful girl, Stephen," I said once she was out

of earshot. "And a real sweetheart too. Not quite what I pictured, from your description."

A sad expression registered in his eyes. "I feel like a real heel for sharing all of her negative traits before telling you how precious she is to me. It's just that you never know what you're going to get with her, so I always like to warn people. I don't want anyone to take her sour attitude personally."

"Haven't really seen that side. I'd expected her to be moodier, based on your description."

"I know. It's so weird. One minute she's pouncing like a lion, the next she's as gentle as a lamb. So confusing." He scratched his head. "There's no place for me to go to get a degree in mothering. You know? I can only teach her what I can teach her, which ain't much."

I reached to pat his arm, once again caught off guard by those impressive biceps. "Don't be so hard on yourself. You've taught her a lot. It's clear she's her father's daughter."

"You think?" As he spoke the words, his eyes brimmed with tears.

"I do. And I see a lot of potential there. Maybe she really will grow up to be a vet. Or maybe she'll be a comic like her dad. Or maybe a combination of both—a vet with a sense of humor."

"Now, *that* I can't picture." He grinned. "But I'd love it." Another sad look passed over him as he whispered, "Honestly, I'd just like to see her smile more. She's been so . . . down."

"Bring her around here more," I said. "We're a laugh-a-minute bunch. I think we'll loosen her up."

"I might just take you up on that." The look that followed was so tender it pricked my heart. For a moment there, I could almost envision Stephen and Brooke coming over for dinner. Hanging out with the fam. Playing with my sister's kids. Spending time with the cousins. Eating baklava.

Brooke came out of the bathroom, took one look at the

two of us standing so close together, and gave us a knowing look. "Someone has a crush."

"Oh?" Right away, I realized I still had my hand on Stephen's arm. I pulled it back. "We were just talking."

"Mm-hmm."

"Come," my father hollered from the dining room. "The lamb is getting cold."

As I led the way to the dining room, I tried to push aside the embarrassment that had risen at Brooke's proclamation that I had a crush on her father.

Or did she mean that he had a crush on me?

Either way, the idea left me feeling discombobulated. Thankfully, my family didn't pick up on my embarrassment. They entered the dining room in their usual boisterous way, loading up the table with all sorts of yummy delights.

We sat, my parents on opposite ends, my brother and I on one side, Stephen and Brooke on the other. As my father bowed his head to say grace, Brooke stared, wide-eyed. Not that I was looking, of course. After the prayer ended, she shook her head.

"What is it, honey?" I asked.

"You're just . . ." She shook her head.

"Just what?"

"Like a TV family. Ya know?"

My father snorted. "Hardly."

"No, really." She gestured to the large oak table and the china cabinet that sat nearby. "Do you know how many people would kill to have a real dining room table in their house? And people sitting around the table talking about dumb stuff?"

"How do you know we're going to talk about dumb stuff?" my brother challenged her as he sliced the lamb. "Maybe I have something brilliant to say."

She rolled her eyes for the umpteenth time. "Because TV families always talk about dumb stuff. They sit around and talk about things that don't matter, but that's what makes it all so . . ." She sighed.

"So different?" my mother tried.

"So crazy?" my father chimed in.

"So perfect," she whispered.

We could've heard a pin drop at that one. The silence lingered beyond the point of comfort, and I eventually broke it by clearing my throat.

Mama, probably nervous, began to pass the food. Before long, every plate was full, and contented sighs filled the room as we began eating. Still, I couldn't let the opportunity to say something pass me by.

"We do talk about dumb things sometimes, honey. And just so you know, we're far from perfect. But I also want you to know that I'm really grateful to have my home and my family . . . and my heritage."

Okay, I could tell from the yawn that I'd lost her at the word *heritage*. Maybe I'd taken it one step too far. Still, I think she got my point. And I happened to agree with her father—she needed to understand and appreciate her heritage. One day it would mean a lot to her.

"When I grow up, I want a house like this," she said. "One with a dining room table and lots of people around it."

I caught the look of panic in Stephen's eyes. Clearly, the man didn't own a dining room table. I'd venture to guess they made do with a couple of barstools, or maybe a small dinette. I'd never claimed to be a psychiatrist—though I'd written lines for one on the TV show—but I'd have to say the kid longed for something more. She clearly wanted a family environment. The table was just a symbol of all that was missing in her life. In that moment, I prayed she would get the very thing she longed for. In God's perfect timing, of course.

My brother, who'd always been a little slow on the draw, shrugged. "You think the table's full now. You should be here when the rest of the family shows up. This room is so full—and so loud—you can hardly hear yourself think."

"There are more of you?" Brooke looked mesmerized by this news.

"Yes, we have a sister, Larisa," I explained. "And she's married to Angelo. They have three kids—Mia, Becca, and their baby boy, Thad."

"I met them at the shop," Stephen added.

"Wow." Brooke grinned. "I like kids."

"How do you feel about older people?" Niko asked. "Just wait till you meet Aunt Melina. Now *there's* a family member you won't soon forget."

"What's up with Aunt Melina?" Brooke asked. "Is she crazy or something?"

"Not really crazy," I was quick to say. "Just has her own personality. Different. But in a loving way."

"Did I meet her?" Stephen asked.

"She was at the shop the other day," my father explained. "Melina is my older sister. She's in her early seventies. She . . . well, she has a few struggles."

"You couldn't miss her," I added. "She's a little hunched over. Always carries around a coffee mug." *Filled with booze, but it's probably too soon to explain that part.*

"Ah. I do remember her." A look of recognition passed over him. "She seemed nice. Very old world."

"Yes, Melina's only been in the States for three years," my father said. "She's still acclimating. I think this transition from Greece to L.A. has been difficult. Harder than she anticipated, anyway. But I'm prayerful she'll adapt before long."

God bless you, Babbas. You're such a good man, and such a great brother to Melina.

"So you've never been to Greece, Stephen?" my father asked.

"Only in my imagination. My nona—my grandmother—

came to New Jersey when she was in her thirties. My mom was born here and never saw Greece. Neither did I, except in the stories Nona told. I feel like I've been there, though. They were some pretty vivid tales. I could almost see myself there." A wistful look followed. "Still can. Like I said, it's going to happen."

"I know what you mean," I said. "I've been dying to go all my life, but I'm almost afraid it'll be a letdown after the big buildup. From the stories my parents and other relatives have shared, it's a heaven-on-earth sort of place."

"And so many of the smartest people came from Greece," my father threw in. "Plato. He was a student of Socrates."

Brooke rolled her eyes.

"And Aristotle," my mother added. "A scientist and scholar."

"And what about Archimedes," my brother added. "He was a mathematician and an engineer."

"All Greek," Mama said with a smile. "The smart ones always are."

Brooke groaned. "Okay, enough already. I get it. All the smart people are Greek."

"Well, not all, but it certainly doesn't make you less intelligent to be Greek," I said, then gave her a wink.

My mother dabbed her mouth with her napkin. "I think it's kind of a shame that none of our kids have gone back to the place of their ancestors. One day, perhaps." She put her napkin back in her lap and offered a coy smile. "Right now my daughter needs to focus on getting married and having babies. There will be plenty of time to travel later."

I stopped just short of smacking myself in the head at that proclamation. *Thanks a lot, Mama. Glad to know you're laying down all of your plans on my behalf.*

Brooke looked my way. "Speaking of kids, I'm dying to meet your sister's. I love working with children."

"She's great with them," Stephen said. "And with animals too. Obviously."

Brooke's eyes lit up. "How old are the kids?"

"Mia is three, Becca is two, and Thad is a baby, as I said. He's just at that sitting-up stage. Do you like to babysit, Brooke?"

"Oh, she's not really old enough to do that alone," Stephen said, looking more than a little alarmed at the prospect.

"I am too." She scowled at her father, then crossed her arms over her chest and slunk down in the chair. "If someone would give me a chance. It's not like I'm a baby. I'm almost twelve."

"I have an idea." My mother clapped her hands together. "You could come over here and help me with the kids when I'm babysitting. You would be a big help to me, especially if they wanted to go swimming. It's always such a challenge to handle three of them when there's just one of me."

"You have a pool?" Brooke's eyes widened. "Really?"

"Of course," my father said. "Doesn't everyone in Southern California have a pool?"

"Not us." She gave her father another look. "The dumb house my dad picked doesn't have one."

"We'll have a house with a pool someday," he said. "One thing at a time. We were lucky to find a rental so quickly." He looked my way and shrugged. "It was a fast move. Once Rex made the offer, I got here as quick as I could. Figured we locate temporary housing, then eventually settle into something else for a long-term stay."

I was starting to feel bad for the poor guy. He couldn't catch a break, could he? No dining room table. No pool. What next? Would we find out he had no dishes in the cabinet? No food in the cupboard?

Nah. Nix that last one. Brooke had said he could cook. They probably had a traditional Greek kitchen. Just no table to sit at.

I didn't have long to ponder these questions because the phone rang. Mama rose to answer it. When she returned, I could see the puzzled look in her eyes.

"That was Milo."

"Mean-Athena's Milo?" my brother and I asked in unison.

"Does he want the dog back?" my father asked. "If so, he's more than welcome to come and get him."

"No!" Brooke's voice had a nervous ring to it. "We're taking him."

"Okay, okay." My father gave her a smile. "I can see you're in love with that measly mutt. I won't send him back to Greece just yet."

"Milo didn't want the dog back, anyway," Mama said. "Though he did ask about him. He gave me the most surprising news. Apparently he's applied for citizenship."

"Wow." I could hardly believe it.

"He wanted to know if we could spend some time together," Mama added. "He sounded a little lonely."

"What did you say?" I asked.

"I said yes, of course. He was in love with my aunt, after all. I could hardly turn him down. In some ways, we're almost like family." She paused to take her seat. "Well, we would have been, if she hadn't broken his heart. I'm still not sure I understand all of that, but I do feel we owe him a visit or two."

"Wait . . . your aunt?" Stephen asked. "The mean one? The one who gave you the dog?"

"Yes." Mama fussed with her napkin, placing it in her lap. "It's so strange. I always thought Milo broke Aunt Athena's heart, but he told me it was the other way around. Seems strange that a man would pine after a woman like that." She shrugged. "Maybe I didn't really know her after all. I guess appearances can be deceiving."

Across the table, Brooke rolled her eyes. Her gaze met mine

and she quickly shifted it to the baklava. "Can I have one? I need to see if it's as good as my dad's."

"Sure, honey." My mama passed her the tray. "But prepare yourself for the best."

Brooke nibbled the yummy goodness, then gave me a look of admiration. "Mmm."

"Traitor." Stephen scowled at her. "How could you?"

"Sorry, Dad, but she wins. This is amazing."

She quickly gobbled down the rest, then licked her fingers and reached for another piece. When she finished it, I gave her a high five, and the loveliest smile lit her face.

When Zeus started yapping again, the resulting sparkle in Brooke's eyes reminded me of a photograph I'd once seen. What was it again? Ah yes. A picture Mama had taken of me in sixth grade, just after winning my first writing award.

Girls always smiled when they were in their element.

And right now . . . well, right now I felt like smiling.

8

Jeopardy

A week after Zeus went to live with his new family, I received an email from Stephen with photos attached. I laughed at the one of Zeus in an apron in their kitchen, but the one that really got to me was one with Brooke and that crazy mongrel rolling around on the living room floor together. The joyous expression on her face left me speechless.

I thought about it all the way to the studio that morning. The same dog that had brought my family such angst had apparently been just the ticket to pull a somber preteen out of her funk. God certainly had an interesting way of turning things around. I had to wonder if Mean-Athena was looking down from heaven at that eleven-year-old girl, remembering my mother at that age. Perhaps this was all part of some great heavenly plan to make up for how my aunt had treated Mama.

I pulled my car into the studio parking lot, grabbed the usual Monday morning bag of leftovers, and made the usual walk to the back door of the *Stars Collide* set, still deep in thought about Zeus and Brooke. As I approached, a man with a camera in his hand hollered out something I couldn't quite make out.

I turned to face him, perplexed. "I'm sorry. What?"

He leaned against the side of the building and messed with the lens on his camera. "Looking for that comedian. Stephen Cosse. You know, the guy from Vegas?"

"Ah. Not sure if he's here yet."

"Dying to get an interview with him," the guy said. He paused to wipe the sweat from his brow with the back of his hand. When he did, I could see the armpit stains on his shirt. Nasty. "If he's here, would you send him outside? Might be a twenty in it for you if you do."

"Excuse me?" I paused and shook my head. "You're a reporter?"

"Well, I, um . . ." His gaze shifted to the bag in my hand. "That smells good. What've you got in there?"

I ignored his question. "How did you get on the lot? I don't see a press badge or anything. Did you check in at the front gate? Not just anyone can come back here, you know. You have to have a pass." I put on my police cap and went to work, giving him a lecture about how no one could come onto the property without authorization.

"Look, can we skip all of that? That's not really the point. I just see a story with that Cosse guy and want to write it before anyone else does. C'mon. Give me a break. I told you I'll make it worth your while."

Yeah, I'll go a long way on twenty dollars in a town like L.A.

"What kind of story?"

"You must not get out much." He chuckled. "Haven't you been watching the news? They did a piece on him last night on *Entertainment Tonight*. It was all about his HBO special

103

and his sudden rise to stardom. He's a hot ticket right now, and I want to be the first in line to snap some pictures."

Entertainment Tonight? How did I miss that? Why hadn't he mentioned it?

I finally managed a four-word response. "I had no idea."

"Well, tell him—"

"I'm not telling him anything. But I'm going to tell you something. If you're not off this lot in five minutes, I'm calling security. And they won't be as easy on you as I've been. In fact, I have a pretty good suspicion there will be police involved before all is said and done. So if you want to keep your dignity—and your career—intact, you might consider hightailing it out of here."

"I like an assertive woman." The reporter winked, and I felt my hand begin to twitch. I wanted to wipe that smirk right off his face. I'd do it too, if only this morning's Bible verse hadn't told me to turn the other cheek.

"You don't have to play along, sister," the guy said, putting his hands up in mock defeat. "But you're not going to stop this ball from rolling down the hill. Cosse's big news right now. You know that, right?"

Actually, I didn't.

The fellow scratched his head. "Doesn't make much sense to me. He could have any job he likes. What's he doing here, writing for a weekly sitcom? He could be making movies or writing for Comedy Central."

Good question. A thousand other questions rolled through my brain too. Like, what made him such big news right now, and how long would it be before we were swarmed with reporters hoping to get the scoop on Stephen?

I gave the guy my talk-to-the-hand gesture, then made my way inside, pausing at the studio door to fill Rex in on what I'd learned from the reporter. He seemed to take the news in stride.

"Did you know about this?" I asked.

He nodded. "I knew Stephen was being considered for a national comedy award when I hired him. That's one reason I snagged him when the opportunity arose. Figured once he won—and I'm sure he will—we wouldn't be able to afford him. I know a good thing when I see it, and I'm getting more savvy about the timing issues. In other words, I hate to brag, but I did a good job this time around. Snagged a really great writer at the perfect time."

I couldn't think of a proper response, so I just nodded. So, Rex had known all along. Was I the only one in the dark? I'd never even heard of Stephen Cosse before, and I certainly hadn't seen his HBO special. I made a mental note to track down a copy somewhere. Might be interesting to watch.

From a distance, Kat waved. "Hey, Athena," she called out. I thanked God for the distraction.

"Hey, yourself." I crossed the studio to meet her in the middle of the ever-growing *Stars Collide* set. She pointed at several new set pieces. "What do you think of the new construction? This is all for next week's episode. I love the direction of the show, by the way. Bringing in elderly stars is going to be just the ticket. And that bit at the retirement center is primo. The kids will love it."

"You know the goal of all this, right?" I asked her. "The purpose of expanding Jack and Angie's business is to put pressure on them as a couple. It's going to wreak havoc on your—er, their—marriage. You okay with that?"

"Well, sure." She leaned in and whispered, "Half the fun in keeping a relationship alive is learning to work together. Scott and I are figuring that out in real life too. I mean, c'mon. We're together 24-7. We work together, live together, play together . . ." She wiggled her eyebrows.

"Whoa!" I put my hands up. "TMI, girl. But seriously, I figure if my parents can stand working together . . . if you and Scott can stand it . . . then Jack and Angie can stand it too. Besides, you know we're all about adding conflict to the story. Conflict is . . ."

"Key." We spoke the word in unison.

"I've taught you well. And remember, it doesn't have to be external conflict."

"External?" She looked confused.

"You know—man against man, man against nature, and so on. That's external. A good story has to have a lot of internal conflict too, where the characters battle their own thoughts and fears."

"Gotcha. We need to create internal and external conflict. That's what great stories are made of."

"Exactly."

"Well, I'm okay with conflict, as long as the ultimate goal is to strengthen Jack and Angie's relationship." She quirked a brow. "Hey, speaking of falling for someone you work with, where's Dr. Hottie?"

"Dr. Hottie?"

"You know, Stephen. The Manuscript Doctor. That's what Rex has been calling him, you know."

"Rex has been calling him Dr. Hottie?"

"No, silly." She laughed. "Guess I'd better set the record straight. That's what Jana and Nora have been calling him when no one's listening. Rex has been calling him the Manuscript Doctor."

The Manuscript Doctor? What was up with that? Did our scripts need doctoring? Ugh.

Lenora entered the set from the hallway, wearing a blue and white striped dress with a broad white belt. Wow. This one had me stumped. The vintage dress had to be really old. Maybe turn of the century, even.

"Guess who I am," Lenora said. "C'mon, guess."

I made a couple of attempts and so did Kat, but apparently she wasn't Ginger Rogers or Betty Grable.

In a warbling voice, she began to sing an unfamiliar tune. When I still didn't get it, she sighed and then offered an explanation. "This is the dress Judy Garland wore in *Meet Me in St. Louis* during that wonderful scene. You know the one, right, KK?" Her eyes sparkled as she looked at her granddaughter.

"'The Trolley Song'?" Kat tried.

"No, try again."

"'Under the Bamboo Tree'?" I suggested.

"No, silly. It's the scene where she sang that great song about falling in love with the boy next door."

"Oh, right!" Kat began to sing, "How can I ignore the boy next door?" eventually drawing the attention of a few of the others nearby.

Lenora gave her a wink. "Yes, that's right." She turned to me. "Speaking of the boy next door, where is that handsome writer you share a sofa with, Athena?"

I groaned, not so much at her comment, but the fact that she'd said it loud enough for everyone in the studio to hear. Jason, our cameraman, turned my way, giving me an inquisitive look. Tia, who happened to be standing just a few feet away, also glanced at me, surprise registering in her eyes.

I wanted to say, "Hey, listen, everyone. It's not true. I don't have eyes for the boy next door." But I couldn't. And I certainly didn't refer to him as Dr. Hottie. In fact, that whole Manuscript Doctor thing really had me rankled. Maybe it would be better if I just kept moving.

I entered our office, noticing at once the furniture had been moved. So much for our *Dick Van Dyke Show* ambience. Someone had flipped my world up on its ear. Who did I have to blame for this? Must be some sort of prank. Maybe the kids were behind it. Sure. They were always up to tricks. Well, this one went a little too far. I'd call them in here to put everything back where it belonged.

From across the room, I heard a funny grunting sound.

My gaze fell on Paul, who lay on his back on the floor, legs propped up against the wall.

"Paul? What happened to the room? It's as upside down as you are."

"I have no idea. It was like this when I got here. I thought maybe you did it."

"No way. That's so weird." I took a few steps in his direction, still trying to figure out what he was up to. Or, rather, down to. "You okay down there?"

"Yeah, my back's been bothering me. The doctor said I should spend some time in this position. Hope you don't mind. It relieves the pain and takes the pressure off."

"I see." Still, it made having a conversation with him a little awkward.

"Not feeling great this morning," Paul said. "I stayed up all night last night."

"Oh? Couldn't sleep?"

"Nah. So I plugged in a DVD of old *Dick Van Dyke* episodes. Did you ever see the one where Rob's brother comes to stay with them, and he sleepwalks but doesn't remember?"

"Oh, I loved that one," I said.

"What if we did something like that? Maybe brought in an older client to stay in Jack and Angie's house, and he keeps them up all night."

"Might work."

"Of course, we'll have to run this idea by you-know-who." Paul rolled his eyes. "Looks like he's the decision maker these days."

"Speaking of Stephen, have you seen him? Maybe he knows what's going on with the furniture."

"Nope. I avoid the guy like the plague."

"Ah." I'd suspected as much, but we hadn't really shared our thoughts privately about the new writer on our team.

Paul swung his legs around, let out another groan, and

eased his way up off the floor. "If you know what's good for you, you'll steer clear of him too, Athena. Don't get too close to the fire or you might just get burned. I've got a bad feeling about this one."

"Well, I'm concerned, of course. Concerned for both of us, I mean. Especially with today's news. I don't know if you heard or not, but he was on TV last night. There's some sort of award thing stirring. It's apparently a big deal."

"Right. I saw the bit on *Entertainment Tonight*."

"Have you seen the HBO special everyone keeps talking about?"

"Yeah. A few months ago, when it aired."

"So you knew who Stephen was before they hired him?"

"Sort of. I knew he was a comedian." Paul paused. "That HBO special was pretty good. Okay, it was really good. Brilliant, even. Look, I'm not saying the guy isn't funny. Just saying I'm not keen on his role here. And if he wins that award, it's only going to get more awkward around here. We don't need that."

"Right." I sighed. "Well, Rex and the others are pretty worked up about it. With everyone else singing his praises, don't you think we should show him a little respect? Maybe win him over with our friendship? He's part of our team now, you know."

"I'm showing him as little respect as possible. And we didn't need another team member, if you ask me. You and Bob and I were a great team." He muttered something under his breath about Bob, but I couldn't make it out. "Just feels a little crowded around here these days."

"Stephen has had some good ideas," I reminded Paul. "And I'm sure our ratings are going to go up once we take the show in this new direction. I think it's going to be good."

"I hope so." Paul took a couple of steps, then flinched, grabbing his back. "That whole ratings thing is wholly unfair, by the way."

"What do you mean?"

"If a show doesn't do well, the actors don't get blamed. The producers don't get blamed. You know who gets blamed." He walked toward the Super-Gyros bag and stuck his hand inside, coming out with a tray of cookies.

"Yeah." I couldn't help but sigh.

"The writers," we said in unison.

"This is the most unstable business in the world," Paul said. "Should've followed my dad's advice and become a cop. I'd definitely have better job security if I worked in law enforcement. At least we know there are always going to be criminals."

"Well, that's comforting."

Thinking about criminals made me think of Mean-Athena, for whatever reason. Thinking of my aunt caused my thoughts to shift to Milo. Why had he come to the States, really? To carry out my aunt's wishes, sure, but there seemed to be something more. He seemed lonely. In need of friends.

Thinking of Milo reminded me of Zeus, and thinking of Zeus reminded me of the lovely smile on Brooke's face. Of course, thinking about Brooke reminded me of Stephen, and thinking of Stephen made me wonder where he was. When he saw the mess someone had made of this office, he would probably flip. It would take us all morning to get things back in place. Ooo, those kids! Just wait till I told Rex what they'd done this time!

I went to sit on the divan, almost forgetting it had been moved. "You really have no idea why the furniture is off-kilter?" I asked again.

"Nope."

I grabbed a pencil and began to roll it around in my hand. "It's just so strange."

A noise from outside the door interrupted us. Sounded like a herd of buffalo heading out to pasture. Paul made the mistake of opening the door. Sure enough, buffalo—er, children—sped by, followed by their teacher.

"Sorry about that," she called out. "We just finished our classes for the morning, and the kids are ready for recess."

Paul nodded and closed the door. "Can't imagine how they do recess in a television studio."

"I think you just witnessed it. They run laps in the halls. And I have a sneaking suspicion . . ."

"Oh?"

"Yeah, they're on the run from us because we're on to them about the furniture."

"Likely." He stretched and winced once more.

We sat in silence for a moment, and I thought about this week's episode. A couple of ideas flitted through my brain, but neither of them were keepers.

After a couple of minutes, Paul's voice rang out. "You're doing that thing again," he said.

"Thing?" I looked up. "What thing?"

"Where you tap your pencil on the edge of the sofa."

"Oh, I tap my pencil?" I glanced at it. "I had no idea."

He rolled his eyes.

Should I remind him that he had a few annoying habits too? For instance, he slurped his coffee. And that eating with no utensils thing was getting old. Oh, and then there was the falling asleep and snoring when he should be working thing. That one really took the cake.

Calm down, Athena. You're worked up about other things, not Paul.

Minutes later, one of the primary things I'd been worked up about walked into the room. Stephen. I wanted to ask him all sorts of questions about his award—and about that reporter—but all of my preconceived ideas faded as soon as I saw him in that beautiful blue shirt. Wowza. He looked like he'd come straight from a photo shoot. Maybe he had. Maybe he'd be on the cover of *People* next month. My imagination went into overdrive as I envisioned him standing in front of cameras, prepping for a photo shoot.

Goodness. Could I possibly be any more fickle? Up one minute and down the next. I might as well apply to be an elevator operator. Half the time I had my head in the clouds.

Focus, Athena. Focus. He's looking at you.

Stephen seemed frazzled. I'd never seen him like this, and it piqued my curiosity. "You okay?"

"Yeah. Sorry I'm late." He tossed his laptop bag on the chair and shook his head. "Some reporter in the parking lot stopped me and drilled me full of questions. I feel like the O.K. Corral after the shootout. I'm bled out." He offered a weak smile. "But at least I'm still standing. He didn't take me down."

"I can't believe that guy was still here. I told him to take a hike. How did he get onto the lot, anyway?"

"Oh, I'm sure he paid off someone at the gate. I used to get a lot of those guys in Vegas."

"So, I hear something is stirring. What's going on?"

"It's no big deal, really." Stephen paused, his shoulders sagging a bit. "I was just nominated for an award. I guess the reporters want to know about it, is all."

"Right. I heard something about that. But what kind of award? Fill us in."

"The Comedy Awards." He shrugged. "My agent called last night to tell me. I was pretty surprised."

"Whoa." The Academy Awards of the comedy crowd. Maybe I'd underestimated this guy.

Paul cleared his throat and said something I couldn't quite make out.

"Stephen, that's great," I managed. "Congratulations."

He reached into the Super-Gyros bag. "It's a good thing, for sure. I could use this boost in my career right now. Less than a year ago, I wasn't even sure I'd have a career in comedy anymore, so this is good." He grabbed a jar of olives and opened it. Popping one in his mouth, he pointed to the room. "What do you think of the new design? Spent three hours last night getting it done."

"What? *You* moved the furniture?" So much for blaming the kids.

"Yeah. Hope that's okay."

"But we had a *Dick Van Dyke* theme going on in here," I said. "Just got the furniture the week before you got here, so it's all pretty new to us. We set the office up just like the one on *The Alan Brady Show*. We thought it would be inspirational."

"Right." He nodded and took a seat, still holding the olive jar in a firm grip. "Just seemed too . . . perfect."

"Perfect?"

"Yeah." He shrugged. "Every time I get into a room where everything is in an exact place, I just feel like switching things up. I strive for imperfection."

"I see." Only, I didn't. Why would someone strive for imperfection? And what was wrong with keeping the office like it was?

"Let's keep it like this for a while," he said. "See if it stirs up our creativity." He pointed to a new picture on the wall, one he'd taken of Zeus. "Thought that might inspire us."

"It inspires me to call Animal Control," I offered.

"It inspires me to call my ex-wife and check on the dog she got custody of," Paul added. A wistful look passed over him. "Man, I miss that dog."

I got a chuckle out of that one. The laughter seemed to relieve the tension in the room, helping me breathe easier.

"You guys ready to get to work?" Stephen asked. "I came up with a great idea over the weekend. One that involves several of our new cast members. The older ones, I mean. I think you're going to love it."

Pressing back the sigh that threatened to erupt was the easy part. Holding my tongue was tougher. Seemed like this guy was buzzing with ideas. Oh, they were mostly good, but where did he get off thinking he could lead the way? Wasn't that the job of the head writer? And who'd given him permission to move the furniture? Talk about presumptuous.

Determined to get some work done, I settled deeper into the sofa. Nothing about its current position felt right. In fact, it threw off my equilibrium and my creativity. Paul took his place behind the desk, which had been moved to the far side of the room. I could tell from the look on his face that he wasn't having any of this, but he managed to keep his mouth shut just the same.

Ironically, he was the only one keeping his mouth shut. The next hour or so was filled with people stopping by the office to chat, starting with Jana. She stepped inside the room, her arms loaded with costumes.

"Hey, Athena, I just wanted to run this by you." She held up a frumpy-looking floral dress in a hideous shade of green. "We're thinking Kat should wear this in next week's episode."

"Oh?"

"Yeah. You know that one scene where Jack and Angie dress up like old people and visit the retirement center?"

"Oh, right, right." I gave the dress a closer look. "Looks okay to me." *And since when do you run costumes by me?*

Jana looked Stephen's way and shuffled the costumes from one arm to the other. "We're thinking about this shirt and bow tie for Jack. What do you think, Stephen?" Her eyelashes— were those fake?—fluttered wildly. Good grief.

He looked up from his work. "I guess so. Didn't really picture him in the bow tie, but what do I know? I'm no expert on costumes. I really don't know much about them."

"You don't?" She draped the costumes across the back of the chair and sidled up next to him. "Oh, you don't know what you're missing. Costuming is the very heart of the show. I mean, think about it. You writers come up with an *amazing* script, and then the actors take it and do their part. But the folks in the costume department play a role too. There wouldn't be a show without us."

"We're grateful for that," I threw in. "I know we couldn't do it without you."

"We have to be creative too." She spoke to me but looked at Stephen, inching her way a bit closer. "What if you wrote a great, funny scene—something lighthearted and fun—and we dressed the character in a stiff, complicated outfit that didn't suit the scene? It's important that we catch the vision and run with it."

I'm catching your vision, all right, girl.

She scooted closer still. "We're on the same team, you know. You guys are the peanut butter and we're the jelly." Her eyelashes took to fluttering once again. "What good would one be without the other? You know what I mean?"

Yes. I know exactly what you mean. And I'm feeling a little nauseous.

Stephen offered a weak smile. "Guess this wouldn't be a good time to tell you that I'm not crazy about PB and J."

She chuckled. "That's okay. I'll come up with another analogy. You just keep writing those brilliant scenes and I'll keep dressing the characters. Deal?"

"Deal." He nodded and shook her hand.

Me? I was too busy being upset at her line that he needed to keep writing brilliant scenes. Had Jana forgotten that there were other writers involved? Paul and I had feelings. We needed encouragement too.

No sooner had Jana left than Nora arrived with some sketches. Hopefully she could lift my spirits. She always managed to put a smile on my face.

"Just wanted to talk you through how we're going to age

Jack and Angie in next week's episode." She spoke to me, so I expected her to take a few steps in my direction. Instead, she placed her sketches down on the coffee table and turned to Stephen. "I think you're going to like this. It's going to be so much fun aging Kat and Scott. Can't wait to show you projected images of what they're going to look like as elderly people. And you'll love the wigs we're using. Actually, Scott's is sort of a hairless number. He's going to be nearly bald with tiny wisps of hair."

I tried to inch my way into the spot next to her on the sofa, but I couldn't get a close look because she and Stephen remained hunched over the sketches.

"It's going to be great, Nora," he said. "I think the audience is going to love this scene, and it's going to be even better because of you."

"Thanks." Her cheeks turned strawberry-sherbet pink. "Just doing my job. You make it so much fun, Stephen. You really do. I was hoping you would like this."

Good grief. Since when do you run the sketches by the writers?

I rose and walked over to the desk, where I took a seat and began to play solitaire on the computer. After a few more minutes, Nora finally left. I was tempted to lock the door but decided people would get the wrong idea. Still, how could we get anything done if co-workers kept interrupting?

Tia entered the room about three minutes later, just as we'd finally started to get into gear. I groaned inwardly. Surely our director—a consummate pro—wasn't smitten with Stephen too.

"Sorry to interrupt," she said. "But I want to run some ideas by you guys. In case I haven't mentioned it before, that retirement center scene is brilliant. Just the ticket. And I want to make the best of it, so I'm thinking about a couple of interesting camera angles. Let me talk you through what I have in mind."

She stood in the center of the room, looking much like a conductor leading an orchestra as she shared her enthusiastic plan for how the scene would be shot. I knew a little about cinematography, but she lost me somewhere between wide-angle shots, aspect ratio, and focal length. Stephen seemed to understand every word. At one point he rose and joined her, putting his hands up in some strange gesture to represent a camera angle.

"We used this approach with my HBO special," he said. "And I really believe it made all the difference. It's innovative, but innovative is good. I'm one for change."

No joke. Look at the furniture.

Of course, he'd changed more than the furniture, hadn't he? Already he'd shifted the entire strategy for the show. Without asking me. The head writer.

As he and Tia rambled on and on, I found myself thinking about Brooke. Wondering how she felt about all of the changes her dad went through. Chances were pretty good the preteen just wanted things to slow down, not keep whirling out of control. She'd been through enough shifts in her young life already.

I was so lost in my thoughts that I almost missed Tia's exit. Only when she hollered, "See you on the set," did I jar back to attention.

"Man, this place is more crowded than Grand Central Station today." I sighed, wondering if we'd ever get anything done.

"No kidding. But I like their ideas. All of them." He gave me a funny look. "Can't you sense it?"

"Sense what?"

"Things are stirring. Changing."

Paul grunted. "They're changing, all right." His gaze shifted to the pen in his hand.

"I love it when that feeling of excitement is so thick you

could almost cut it with a knife." Stephen's face creased in a boyish smile. "And if we feel that way, imagine how the viewers are going to feel when these new episodes begin to air. I'm telling you, things are on the move. In a good way."

He grew silent and began to pace the room. I found it a little unnerving in light of the fact that his lengthy talk had dried up so quickly. After pacing a while, he finally stopped and turned my way.

"Okay, here's what I'm thinking. We've brought in two stars in their golden years for this week's episode, right?"

"Right." Paul and I spoke in unison.

"This is sure to up our ratings," Stephen said. "Viewers always respond well to older people, especially when they're funny. I know we're going to see our numbers improve."

Paul offered a grunt. I chose not to respond. Should I tell this novice that it often took weeks to get a feel for the true ratings? That the up-and-down nature of the business meant we might soar with the viewers this week but sink the next? Nah. He'd figure it all out . . . in time.

Stephen kept rambling. "It's time to start upping the ante. Something has to happen next week to take a toll on Jack and Angie's relationship. We're at Step 3 in the plotline now."

"The dark moment?" Paul asked.

"Not quite," Stephen said. "According to the class I'm taking, this is the 'Refusing the Call' stage. It's where the hero or heroine has a major opportunity but is afraid to step out and do anything about it. Fear stops him. Or her."

"So what's the big opportunity?" I asked.

"The chance to save the agency from ruin. But something has to foil the plan." He ran his fingers through his hair. "What we need is something that will force Jack and Angie into a position where they have no choice but to act. That's Step 5, by the way."

If he mentioned that stupid plotline one more time, I might

just snap like a twig. What kind of a sitcom writer had to take writing classes? *Are you a pro, or aren't you?*

"Look," I said. "We've never really worked this way before. We've always just sort of flown by the seat of our pants. It's worked fine for us. I don't see any reason to fix something that's not broken."

"Well, yes," he said. "But there's nothing wrong with trying something new, right? Especially if it helps stir our creativity. Besides, I already talked to Rex about this idea and he likes it."

Of course you did. Which puts me at Step 5 on my own personal plotline, doesn't it? I have no choice but to move forward.

Another twisted irony.

"Maybe one of the elderly clients has a former agent bent on taking them down," Paul said. "Or something like that. What do you think?"

"Sounds good." Stephen nodded.

"I see him as a Snidely Whiplash sort," Paul added. "Maybe he's out to steal some of their older clients, once they start getting famous again. Can you imagine how much we could do with that?"

"Ooo, great idea," I said. "And I love that Snidely Whiplash angle. Angie can have a dream that he's tying her to the train tracks, then Jack can rush in and save her." I turned to Stephen, hands on my hips, ready to beat him at his own game. "That would put us at Step 6 on the plotline, would it not? Isn't that the stage where the hero and heroine are trying to figure out who they can trust and who they can't? They struggle to know their enemies from their allies?" I hoped the stare that followed would convey my real meaning.

"Well, yes, but . . ." Stephen shrugged. "I'm just not sure we want to take this so literally. I was thinking of something a little more symbolic. Let me think about this whole 'tying her to the tracks' thing, okay?"

I brushed aside my wounded feelings and listened as he continued to share his ideas for how the scene could go down. Not bad, but my original idea was much better. In my own humble opinion, anyway.

He continued on, oblivious to my thoughts. "I was thinking we'd include Lenora in this episode," he said. "She'd be great, don't you think?"

"Even better." My enthusiasm kicked into overdrive. "*She can be the lovely Nell Fenwick, the one he ties to the tracks.*" My enthusiasm grew with each passing moment. "She'll be great at that, don't you think? And Jack and Angie can be the ones to rescue her from the evil Snidely Whiplash." *What fun! Oh, I love episodes like this. The viewers will eat it up.*

Stephen shook his head and ate another olive. "I'm not so sure. It's a little too old-fashioned."

"That's the idea. We'll use old-fashioned costumes and makeup. And we'll ask that the whole thing be shot in sepia tone to give it that old-film effect. What do you think?"

"I like it," Paul said. "Takes me back to the old *Rocky and Bullwinkle* cartoons. I loved those Dudley Do-Right bits. No one does comedy like that anymore."

We both turned to face Stephen, who shrugged. I could read the concern in his eyes. "I don't know. I'll have to think about this."

"It's going to be great. Jack and Angie rescue Lenora—and maybe some of the other elderly cast members. Chaos reigns, the kids get involved, and Jack and Angie end up at each other's throats." My enthusiasm now ran full throttle. "Only at the end of the episode do they remember they're on the same team. They come out stronger in the end, and the other agent gets his comeuppance."

I could tell from the look on Stephen's face that he didn't agree with the direction I'd taken this conversation. Still, to his credit, he said nothing.

I plowed ahead, laying out a detailed plan for the Snidely Whiplash episode, one sure to please both the sponsors and the viewers. Paul played along, clearly loving every suggestion and chiming in with even more. Stephen didn't really comment much, but that was okay. Maybe he'd finally grabbed hold of the idea that I was the head writer on this show. I had the final say-so on anything that went out of this office.

Yes, it felt mighty good to be in charge again. So good that I might just move the furniture back to where it belonged once Dr. Hottie left for the day.

9

Let's Make a Deal

The writing of the Snidely Whiplash episode went even better than I'd hoped. It took some doing to talk Rex into it, however. He didn't seem as enthused as we writers had been. Well, Paul and me, anyway. Stephen still seemed a little—what's the word . . . aloof?—about the whole thing. I couldn't tell if his feelings were hurt, or if maybe he thought I'd plowed over him. Regardless, it felt good to know I'd put out a show I could be proud of, and it felt even better to know Kat, Scott, and Lenora would get to act out that classic scene at the railroad tracks. I could hardly wait for the roundtable reading on Monday.

As we closed up shop on Friday, I looked around the office, still puzzled by the furniture. Paul straightened up the mess on the desk and put his laptop away. As I pulled open the door to leave, I found all of the younger *Stars Collide* cast members standing in the hallway. It was clear from the expressions on their little faces that trouble was afoot.

"Well, hello." I smiled at Candy, a precocious little blonde. She crossed her arms over her chest. "Miss Athena, can we talk?"

"Oh, we need to talk, do we?" Paul chuckled.

"Yes." She nodded and gestured to the room. "Can we come in?"

"Of course," I said.

They filed in—Candy leading the way, with little Toby, five, behind her. Then came Marcus and finally Katie, holding a doll in her arms.

"Please, have a seat." I gestured to the divan.

They sat in a row, looking so darling I found myself tempted to snap a photo. But the impatient look on Candy's face told me that they'd come on a mission.

"What can we do for you kiddos?" Paul asked, his arms crossed.

"We want to play a trick on Mr. Stephen," Candy said. "He's brand-new, so we think it will be fun."

"A trick? What kind of a trick?"

She giggled and her cheeks turned pink. "Well, remember how we were always playing tricks on Mr. Scott and Miss Kat last season, and they finally fell in love?"

I chuckled. "Yes, I remember. You managed to talk us into writing a few of them into the script. That bit where Jack and Angie got locked in a closet together was hysterical, if I do say so myself."

"The other pranks were great too," Paul said.

"The pranks worked," Candy said. "They fell in love and got married."

"So, is that the goal?" Paul asked. "You want Stephen to fall in love with someone?"

I suddenly felt like someone had reached inside my chest and yanked my heart up to my throat. So that's what this was about. The little vixens wanted to play matchmaker again. Hopefully they wouldn't involve me in this.

"Yes," Candy said. "We want him to fall in love with Miss Tia."

No way.

Picking my jaw up off the floor was the first order of business. The second was to think of something brilliant to say to the kids in response to their ludicrous idea. Stephen and Tia? Did they really think our show's director had eyes for him—or vice versa?

"Well, I'm all for love," Paul said. "But I have to wonder who came up with this idea. Seems a little far-fetched."

"What's *far-fetched* mean?" Toby asked, scratching his nose.

"It means it's probably not going to happen," Candy said. "But it is. Just wait. You'll see."

Toby looked around the room. "Where's the candy jar?"

I glanced his way. "Candy jar?"

"Mr. Bob always gave us candy." Toby released an exaggerated sigh. "And I loved his jokes. He was so funny. I really miss him."

"We miss him too, kiddo." Paul tousled the kid's hair.

"He knew every single knock-knock joke," Toby said. "Every one."

"Why did he have to go away?" Marcus asked.

"He's working on a movie," I said. "But maybe he'll come back in a few weeks."

Toby's face lit up like a child on Christmas morning. "Oh, good. Tell him to bring lots of candy with him."

"I'll do that. Now, can we finish the conversation about Tia and Stephen, please?" I asked. "Because it's getting late and we have to go."

"Miss Tia is sad and lonely." Candy's smile faded to a frown.

"She is?"

"Yeah." Candy sighed. "I heard her in the ladies' dressing room talking to Kat."

I gave her a scolding look. "You were listening in on their private conversation?"

"Not on purpose." Candy pouted. "Can I help it if I have really good ears? It's not my fault I could hear them whispering."

"I see. So, you decided Miss Tia needs a love interest."

"It would be so romantical." Candy giggled, but Toby slapped himself in the head. "Then they could get married like Miss Kat and Mr. Scott did, and everyone could live happily ever after."

"Happily ever after, huh?" For whatever reason, the idea of Stephen living happily ever after with Tia left me more than a little bothered, though I couldn't figure out the reason. Why should it matter whom he fell in love with? It was none of my business.

Still . . . Tia? She was the least likely person to fall for a guy like Stephen. She was all business, and he was all . . . I paused, deep in thought.

Paul looked my way. "I take it this idea doesn't suit you?"

"Oh." I shook off my ponderings. "Just wondering how that would work. Talk about opposites. He's the funny guy. She's serious."

"My ex and I were too much alike," he said. "I guess that was part of the problem. Might've been better if we'd been opposites."

I had to wonder which ex he was referring to. But no time for that right now, not with a group of small children watching my every move.

I turned back to Candy, who seemed to be the leader of this little band. "Why are you telling us this?"

"We want your help. We want you and Mr. Paul to write

some funny lines that will make Miss Tia and Mr. Stephen fall in love."

"I see. Well, we've got a busy weekend ahead of us, but if I come up with anything, I'll let you know." *In the meantime, do something childlike. Stop playing matchmaker!*

"Thank you, Miss Athena!" A smile lit Candy's face. She jumped off the sofa and led the procession of kiddos out the door and down the hall.

Paul followed on their heels, waving at me. "This should be fun. Maybe we'll come up with something."

"Yeah. Fun." I forced a wave, then walked back into the office and leaned against the wall. A few seconds later, Kat entered. She took one look at me and rushed my way.

"You okay? Feeling sick or something?"

"Or something." I paused. "Did you know the kids are trying to pair up Tia and Stephen? We just heard all about it."

Kat laughed. "No they're not."

"Yes they are. They just came into the office and laid out an elaborate plan."

"Athena, sit for a minute. We need to talk."

I plopped down on the sofa, still ranting about my visit with the kids. "I can't believe they would think Tia and Stephen would make a good couple. Then again, what do they know about romance? They're just kids."

"They know more than you think. Those kids are the reason Scott and I fell in love. It was their antics that pushed us together." She grinned. "Okay, it was really your doing. You writers scripted most of it. And all for the purpose of driving Jack and Angie together. But the real couple fell in love too, partly because of the trouble the kids went to. They saw something in Scott and me that we couldn't even see ourselves." She paused and then smiled. "Athena, you're a smart girl."

"Thank you. Mama says that all smart people are Greek."

Kat rolled her eyes. "You're a smart girl, but you've overlooked something rather obvious."

"What's that?"

"The kids have set you up."

"They what?" *No way.*

"They set you up. You don't find it a little coincidental that they come to your office now to talk about Stephen and some other woman? They were just in the dressing room earlier, telling Tia and me that they were going to play tricks on you and Stephen."

"But Candy said . . ." I paused to think about what she'd said. "Oh, that little monster."

"Exactly."

"So, you're telling me that they're not really trying to push Stephen and Tia together? They're trying to light some sort of flame between Stephen and me?"

"Exactly. And they're banking on the fact that you're not going to figure it out, so play along with them, okay?"

"I see." The most delicious feeling erupted. For a moment—just a moment—I could see their scheme working out. Just as quickly, reality hit. "You know that Stephen and I don't really get along, right?"

"Oh?"

"Yeah, and did you see what he did to the furniture?" I pointed to the office. "He mixed it all up. It's supposed to go a different way."

She glanced around the room. "Looks okay to me." She chuckled. "I still think it's funny that you go to such lengths to get inspired."

"You wouldn't believe how tough it is to be funny on demand. Comedy writing is serious stuff."

"So I've heard. Stephen and Brooke came over for dinner the other night, and he and Scott talked for hours about the writing craft. Scott's always wanted to write as well as act. Did you know that?"

I shook my head. "No way. I had no idea."

"Yeah. He's hoping Rex will let him help with an episode or two in the future. So Stephen's taken him under his wings and is teaching him the ropes."

"But Stephen's brand-new at this," I argued. If Scott wanted to learn to write comedy, why didn't he come to me? Or to Paul?

Ugh. Don't get worked up, Athena. Maybe Scott's just being nice to Stephen because he's new.

"I'm pretty sure it's just a guy thing. Scott really seems to connect with Stephen. And you have to admit he's a likable guy." Kat went off on a tangent about the budding friendship between the two men, then shifted gears. "So, tell me the plans for this weekend again. I told Scott that you wanted us to come for a few hours. Are we still on?"

"Yes." I relayed the message about spending the weekend studying my parents' marriage, and Kat smiled.

"I think that's a great idea. Your mom and dad have the best marriage of . . ." She paused. "Well, of anyone I know. To be honest, I don't know anyone who's still married after—what's it been? Thirty years? Well, other than Scott's parents, but they're in Arkansas. They're a little too far away to interview."

"My parents have been married thirty-seven years," I said. "And it's funny. Until the guys brought it up, I never thought about the fact that they're the only people I actually know personally who've stayed married this long. Strange."

"It is strange." She sighed. "I'm a child of divorce. But Scott knows what it's like to grow up in a family where the parents stayed together, so maybe he can help too. In fact . . ." She snapped her fingers. "This might be just the ticket. Talk about the perfect episode to get his feet wet. Would you mind if he helped you guys come up with some of the ideas?"

I shrugged. "No. Might be fun."

"Gotta love that man of mine," she said. "He was worth the wait." She reached over and put her hand on my arm. "Trust me when I say this, Athena. Sometimes the real-life romance can be even better than what you writers come up with." She paused, her nose wrinkling. "Not that your version isn't great, mind you. But I'll still take reality over fiction any day."

I would too, if I could ever experience a real romance firsthand. One that didn't end in heartbreak, anyway.

"Oh, and just so you know . . . the kids are aware that you and Stephen are going to be spending the weekend together. They've given me specific instructions to make sure you fall in love over the next forty-eight hours."

I rolled my eyes. "Well, I hope you're a magician then."

She laughed. "Hardly. But we might need to come up with a story to feed the kids once this weekend is over. They're going to ask what happened, you know."

"Tell them we fell in love and lived happily ever after."

"I'll do that." She winked. "Who knows. Maybe you will."

"Yeah, right." I rose and walked to the door, giving the furniture one last look. The room still looked topsy-turvy to me. And until we got it straightened out, I wasn't sure I'd ever write a decent page of comedy again.

10

Married with Children

I thought about Kat's words all evening, in between thoughts of Snidely Whiplash and the furniture chaos in the office. I found myself daydreaming about our upcoming episode as I made the drive home, imagining myself as sweet Nell tied to the railroad tracks. Would my hero sweep in and rescue me? My luck, he'd take one look at the cellulite on my thighs and change his mind. Rescue someone else.

Just as quickly I pushed aside those thoughts. *You're doing okay on your own, aren't you? Not every female needs rescuing.* In fact, the more I thought about it, the more I wondered what sort of message we might be sending twenty-first-century women with this episode. Hmm. Maybe we needed to rethink this whole thing, or at least add a clear takeaway at the end so that an "I am woman, hear me roar" message rang out.

Nah. That wasn't the right message either. Maybe we'd better just forget the whole thing. Start from scratch.

That night was spent wrestling with the sheets. I tossed and turned in between flashes of full-Technicolor dreams. On Saturday I awoke feeling more conflicted than ever about the episode we'd just written. Since when did I second-guess everything? Still, I tried not to fret over it. After all, we had all weekend to shift gears, should we decide to do so. Not that I wanted to shift gears. No, I just needed to lay down my anxieties and go with my gut. It had rarely failed me in the past.

As I showered and dressed for the day, I thought about the conversation I'd had with Kat. Maybe it wouldn't be a bad idea to ask Scott to help us with the script. Surely he would run interference with Stephen. Yes, the more I thought about this, the better the idea sounded. By the time I headed downstairs to breakfast, I'd decided to sweep Scott into the writing fold. Might be fun. Maybe he could fill in the void Bob had left.

Mama sat alone at the breakfast table, still dressed in her nightgown. She looked up from the newspaper as I entered the room.

"Good morning, Athena-bean."

"Morning. Anything exciting happening in the world?" I asked as I gestured to the paper. My words were followed by a yawn.

"Trouble in the Middle East. Seems like there's always so much happening near our homeland." She sighed and glanced at the paper. "There's another hurricane in the Gulf of Mexico, and there's talk of a volcano erupting on some Pacific island. Other than that, nothing big is stirring."

"Wow." I paused to think about what she'd just said. "Sometimes I forget there's a life outside of the script I'm writing. My whole world revolves around Jack, Angie, and a bunch of children."

"I'd imagine it's tough to separate fiction from reality in your line of work."

"Right." I reached inside the refrigerator and came out with the orange juice. "Sometimes I need a wake-up call that there's a life outside of the studio. I forget that my characters aren't the only ones with problems to be solved. Real people and real problems exist too." I sighed. "Wish I could write those resolutions as easily as I do in the script."

"No kidding." She closed the newspaper and laid it on the table. "But that's why we lean on God, I guess."

In theory. The next sigh that erupted took me by surprise. As much as I claimed to lean on God, more often than not I found myself leaning on my own ideas. My own creativity. My own want-to. Tough to admit but oh so true.

I shook off my fretting and focused on the weekend ahead. I would go with my mother to Super-Gyros, where Paul, Stephen, and Brooke would meet us and spend the day. The plan? To watch my parents. To see how they interacted in good times and bad. No doubt Stephen would tell me just where they fell on the plotline of life. I was pretty sure they'd reached the happily-ever-after stage. The resolution.

Maybe one day I'd get there too.

We arrived at the shop at 9:30, and I helped Mama and Aunt Melina prepare the phyllo dough for the day. Larisa arrived with her kids as well as two of my teenaged cousins, Mary and Trina, who had come to babysit. Hopefully they would sweep Brooke under their wings and make her part of the family.

As we settled into our work routine, Mama looked my way. "I hope you don't mind, Athena-bean, but I've asked Milo to stop by today as well."

"Oh? You did?" Interesting.

"Yes. I thought it would do him some good to share a good Greek conversation with someone. He seems so lonely, and he's really such a nice old man. Aunt Melina loves to talk. I think she'll remind him of home."

If his home happens to be a distillery.

Stop it, Athena. Pray for your aunt. Don't judge her.

I shook off my ponderings and agreed to do just that—pray. Not just about Aunt Melina but about the weekend ahead. Along with the day's activities, the guys also planned to come back to the house with us tonight and spend the night in our guest room. That should be interesting. According to Stephen, they needed to see my parents in both environments—work and home. I wondered if they would be interested in going to church with us in the morning as well. Time would tell. Sure would be satisfying to see Paul in church.

At 9:58 Paul arrived with his usual declaration: "I'm starved! What's for breakfast?"

Mama ushered him to a nearby table and served up a beautiful croissant and hot coffee, along with a tray of fruit.

A couple minutes later, Stephen entered the shop with Brooke at his side. For whatever reason, my heart fluttered as soon as I saw him in those jeans and that fitted T-shirt. *Be still my heart.* For a second there, I almost forgot we'd come here to work.

I quickly introduced Brooke to Mary and Trina. The preteen seemed shy around her peers at first, but before long I could hear the gaggle of girls laughing and talking from the back room. I also heard the squeals from Larisa's toddlers, who seemed to be enjoying the company of the older ones.

"Sounds like they're having fun back there," my sister said as she entered the room with a tray of sliced meats and cheeses. "Just what my babies needed today." As she set the tray down, she gave an exaggerated sigh. "It's hard having a houseful of kids when you work. And with my hubby in the Middle East . . ." She shook her head and dabbed her eyes. "Anyway, it's not the life I signed up for, but I'm doing the best I can with it."

"Balancing work and family is always tough," Stephen

said. "That's one reason we're here today, to see how that plays out in the real world."

"You've come to the right place." Babbas looked up from his work at the stove. "Welcome to the Pappas family."

"Thanks for letting Brooke come with me," Stephen said. "I don't think it would have worked out for me to come this weekend if she hadn't. I get tired of leaving her alone, and I know she gets really lonely."

"It's the perfect solution," I said. "We're happy to have her. And I think the girls will sweep her into the fold."

"Thanks. I thought about bringing Zeus too, but decided he could use a day at the doggy day care."

"Doggy day care?"

"Yes. He's being groomed. I even paid extra for the doggy massage and whirlpool."

"Whirlpool?"

"Yeah." He groaned. "I know. It was Brooke's idea. She felt like he needed the royal spa treatment. I opted to do it so we wouldn't have to be back till six to pick him up. Didn't want to miss a minute with you." The smile that Stephen flashed my way almost took my breath away. As I gazed into those gorgeous brown eyes and saw the twinkle there, I found myself captivated. Suddenly I didn't want to miss a minute with him either.

See how gullible you are? One minute you're questioning his ideas, the next you're attracted to him. What's wrong with you?

I couldn't help but notice the twinkle in my mother's eye. Likely she'd read too much into Stephen's words. To my great relief, she did not comment.

"How are things going with Zeus, by the way?" I asked, trying to keep my voice steady. "Ready to send him back yet?"

"Nah. He's definitely a member of the family now. I spent a fortune at the pet store the other day. I could have furnished a room with the money I spent."

"Oh?"

"Yeah. Dog bed. Food. Treats. Toys. Went all out. And you don't even want to know how much it cost to have his nails done and get him groomed."

"You're taking this very seriously."

"No, Brooke's taking this very seriously. I'm taking her seriously." He paused and appeared to be deep in thought. "I love her. And if caring for the dog gives her something to do—someone to care for—then so be it. I'll work overtime to pay for it."

Wow. His desire to show love to his daughter through the dog was admirable. I had to give it to him.

Mama's words interrupted my thoughts. "Tell me again why you're here," she said. "Not that I mind, of course. You're all wonderful people—so creative and fun. I'm just trying to understand what Athena was saying about the purpose of this visit."

"We're going to study you," Stephen said with a sly smile.

"Yeah. See what makes you tick," Paul added.

"Study us?" My mother gave me a funny look. "That's a little unnerving. What do you mean?"

"None of us have a clue what makes a marriage work," Stephen said. "We're all children of divorce or have been through divorces ourselves."

Paul held up three fingers, and my mama's eyes widened. She pulled him into her arms. "You poor, dear boy. May you come to know the greatest love of all."

He grinned—likely thinking she was talking about the love of a good woman. I knew otherwise. Paul could search for the rest of his life, but until he recognized the void in his heart that only God could fill, there would never be lasting love. Not the happily-ever-after kind, anyway.

"We want to see what makes a good marriage work," Stephen said. "If we can figure this out, then we'll know how to develop Jack's and Angie's characters so they can withstand even the most difficult challenges in their marriage. We still have to take them through Step 7 in the plotline."

"Step 7?" Mama looked confused.

"The 'Belly of the Whale' scene," he explained. "They have to hit a low point in their relationship where they feel trapped. We know, of course, that they won't stay there, but it's got to come. It's inevitable."

"Well, that's true," Mama said. "There are low points in every relationship whether we expect them or not. I love my husband, of course, but I'm ready to kill the man about every third day. Oh, I don't, of course. I suppose that's what makes our marriage work."

Not killing him is what makes your marriage work?

"I've often thought that if I murder him, I'll end up in prison," Mama said in her sweetest voice. "And what sort of life would that be?"

"Mama!" My mouth dropped open. In all my years I'd never heard her talk like this. So all of those years of thinking she and Babbas had a near-perfect relationship were nothing but a sham? And she had to reveal all of this with Stephen and Paul present?

Paul scribbled down notes as fast as she shared her thoughts.

"Wow. I'm so glad to hear this. I thought I was the only one who ever had a rough marriage."

Babbas stepped beside Mama and laughed. "Oh no. Marriage is hard work."

"I like to say marriage is *heart* work," Mama added. "And thank goodness, the high points in a marriage outnumber the low ones." She smiled. "Otherwise we'd be in big trouble."

"Exactly," Stephen said. "That's the work of great plotting."

"Great plotting, eh?" Babbas laughed. "Well, the only one plotting my life is the Lord. And frankly, I don't care to know what step I'm at on his plotline, thank you very much. I'd rather just be surprised by what tomorrow holds. For today I know one thing—you kids have come to the right place to learn about the love between a husband and wife. We might have our lows, but they make the highs even higher." He swept Mama into his arms and gave her a passionate kiss on the lips. Embarrassment flooded over me until I saw the smile on Stephen's face. It put me at ease.

I thought about my mother's words all morning long. Surely she'd been joking. Right?

By 10:45 the breakfast crowd had thinned, but by 11:30 half of Los Angeles had entered the premises. My parents continued to work, visiting with the customers and stopping on occasion for a peck on the cheek, or even a quick kiss on the lips. I had to wonder if they were going a little overboard with the affection because they knew they were being watched. Likely. Still, it did my heart good to see them so tender toward one another. Why not? So many people grew apart over the years. It felt great to know they still cared so much about each other. In between thoughts of murdering one another, anyway.

Stephen noticed it too. I observed him jotting down notes in his notepad. I would have added a few myself, but I ended up working on the sweets and baking breads. Aunt Melina fussed over the details of the baking process, pausing only when Milo entered the shop at noon. From that point on, she seemed distracted by him. Their back-and-forth chatter in Greek made me smile and feel a little homesick. Not that I'd ever actually been to Greece. Still, I pined for the homeland I'd heard so much about.

Paul's eyes seemed to glaze over as he watched the steady flow of traffic during the lunchtime rush. "Is it always like this?" he hollered out above the crowd.

"Yep. Saturdays are a nightmare." I watched Mama and

Babbas work together on sandwiches. Hmm. Better offer them some assistance. I tossed Paul an apron. "Here, put this on."

"W-what?" He shook his head. "Oh no."

I nodded, unwilling to take no for an answer. "They need our help."

Stephen fell into line beside us. "Good idea, Athena. If we're going to see what it's like to work together, this is just the ticket." He gave me a little nudge. "Maybe we could pretend to be husband and wife working together. What do you think?" The laughter in his eyes caught me off guard. For a moment—a teensy-tiny moment—I thought about playing along. However, a customer with a bad attitude brought me back to reality.

"Hello?" The platinum blonde glared at me. "Did you hear me? I need a refill on this coffee." She shoved the cup my way. I forced a smile, then turned to my pretend husband and passed it to him. "Coffee for one, dear. And step on it."

"Coming right up." He took her empty cup to the coffee-maker and returned with a full cup. "Here you go, snookums." He passed it my way and I took it, almost enjoying our little game.

Paul seemed to get a kick out of it and decided to play along too. "I'll be Athena's ex-husband," he suggested, "stopping by the shop to pick up some sandwiches for my buddies for the big game tonight."

"What big game?"

"Hmm." Paul shrugged. "Okay, skip the game. It's poker night at my place and I need gyros for seven guys."

"Hey, speaking of guys, whatever happened to Scott?" Stephen asked. "I thought he was coming today to help write the next episode."

"Oh, that's right." I'd almost forgotten. "He and Kat should be here soon. I think they'll be a great help with this scene. If anyone knows about working together as a married couple, they do."

Stephen nudged me. "Look at your parents," he whispered.

I glanced up in time to see Babbas pat my mother on the backside. She gave a little giggle in response, then went right back to work.

"I guess that's what makes it work," Stephen said. "They have fun together. It's enjoyable."

"Yeah. Guess you're right. Never really thought about it." My parents were the playful sort. Always had been. Maybe I'd picked up my comedic streak from them. Well, from Babbas, at least. He could get pretty silly at times. Not that I minded. Might be fun to be married to a silly guy—someone who could make me laugh and keep a smile on my face, even during the hard times.

After the crowd thinned, Stephen leaned against the counter, looking exhausted. "Do you want to sneak away for a few minutes to write?"

"What about Paul?"

"Looks like your aunt Melina and Milo are teaching him how to make baklava." Stephen winked, causing my heart to race. "Maybe you'll end up dueling Paul too."

I glanced at Paul just in time to see him drop the phyllo dough on the floor.

"Doesn't look like I have much to worry about there."

"No, you're right. I'm your only real competition."

Ugh. The way he worded things! Hopefully he referred only to the baklava and not my job.

"Paul's having a great time," I said. "I like to see him like this. I worry sometimes that he's too depressed."

"I've picked up on that too. Seems like an odd personality for a comedy writer."

"He makes it work. It's that sarcastic, dry sense of humor."

"I try to stay away from sarcasm as much as I can," Stephen said. "Sometimes it comes across as biting. Spiteful."

"Yeah." I sighed. "I've felt that way at times. The type of

comedy that makes people laugh at the expense of someone's flaws can be a little hurtful."

"Are you ready to get started?" he said. "I feel like we'll come up with something great with all the notes I've taken."

"Sure." I led the way to the storeroom. Pushing aside a couple of boxes, I took a seat at the little table near the back door. "This okay?"

"Perfect. Nice and quiet." A resounding "opa!" rang out from the front of the shop, and he laughed. "Well, maybe not quiet, but it's our own private space."

The words "our own private space" hovered over me, and I found myself feeling a little shy. This was our first time alone outside of the office. And with those amazing brown eyes riveted on mine, an increased pulse rate was to be expected. Right?

"Before we get started, I want to tell you how much I love your family. They're great. All of them. And I'm glad you came up with this idea to spend the weekend with them."

"Was it my idea?" Suddenly I couldn't remember. "I know my parents are glad to have you, and you can see them in action, both at work and at play." I paused. "Oh, that reminds me, we're going to church tomorrow morning, as always. Want to go with?"

"Sure." Stephen nodded. "I'd like that a lot. Brooke and I have been looking for a church ever since we moved here."

"What flavor do you like?" I asked.

"Flavor? You mean like orange, lemon, or lime?"

"No." I laughed at the image that presented. "I mean like traditional, contemporary, charismatic, etcetera."

"Oh, I prefer the etcetera flavor."

I laughed again. "Then you're in luck. We happen to go to an etcetera church. You'll fit right in."

"Awesome. Nothing like fitting right in." His laughter put me at ease. When the chuckling died down, his gaze lingered on my hair. For a second there, I wished I could read his thoughts. Then he seemed to startle back to attention. "I guess we should get to work." A hint of a smile lit his face.

I shifted my gaze to the notebook in his hand after I realized I'd been staring into those gorgeous eyes once again. "Y-yes. We should." *As soon as I can convince my heart to settle down.*

Suddenly he was all business. "Let's talk about Jack and Angie. You go first. I want to hear your take on the two of them."

"What do you want to know?"

"What makes them tick? When you think of their relationship, what makes it work? Where are their struggles?"

"Well . . ." I paused, thinking back to my first week as a writer on the show. "From the very beginning, we knew they had to be different from each other in every conceivable way. They started out as opponents, you know."

"Right. I remember that first season." A boyish smile lit his face. "They couldn't stand each other."

"Right."

"But then something happened." Stephen gave me a knowing look.

"Chemistry. When it's there, it's undeniable."

"Sure is." He looked up from the notebook, catching my gaze for a moment.

Focus, Athena. "And when there's chemistry—think 'science lab' here—there's potential for disaster." I pointed to the notebook. "Write that down."

He nodded and scribbled a few words. "That's what makes comedy work. Conflict is—"

"Key." We spoke the word in unison.

"Okay, so conflict. They've been through a ton of it over the years. And most recently they've survived the influx of elderly clients and the chaos that goes with that. This coming week we're putting them through the Snidely Whiplash thing." He paused to gaze into my eyes. "And by the way, you were right about that."

"Oh?"

"I didn't want to admit it, but that script is one of the funniest things I've read in years. I went over it again last night, just for kicks. It's perfect for where Jack and Angie are at in their relationship. And I need to give credit where credit is due. You were the driving force behind it."

"Why didn't you want to admit that you liked it?"

His gaze darted to the table. Then the wall. Then to the back door. Finally he got around to looking back at me. I could feel his discomfort.

"I don't know. Call it insecurity. Call it pride. I just struggle with . . ." His words faded away.

"Working with a woman?"

"No." He shook his head. "It's not that. It's just . . ." Stephen closed the notebook. "Look, here's the deal. I've only ever worked in live comedy clubs. That sort of thing. I'm my own boss. I write my own jokes. It's me, myself, and I." He shook his head. "See how self-centered that is? Sounds ridiculous when I say it out loud like that, but that's how it's always been. I'm used to working alone."

I wasn't sure how to respond, so I kept quiet.

"I've never had to be part of a team before. And I came in like a . . ." He raked his fingers through his hair. "A bulldozer." His rough edges seemed to fade away as he stared at me with those beautiful brown eyes.

"Ah." Not much of an answer, but what else could I say?

"See. You agree."

"Well, you had ideas. No sin in that. All creative people have ideas. Besides, that's why they hired you, to add your voice to ours."

"I just didn't know how to express my feelings without

hurting yours, and I didn't want you to think that I was trying to usurp your authority." As he reached out and took hold of my hand, an unexpected jolt of electricity shot through me. "I think you're a brilliant writer, Athena."

"O-oh?"

"You . . . well, you intimidate me a little."

"Huh?" Where in the world did that come from? Pulling my hand away, I repeated his words. "I intimidate you? Am I hearing right?"

"Well, sure. Rex thinks the world of you, and so do Kat and Scott."

"Wait. Rex thinks the world of me?" I wanted to linger on those words. "Because he doesn't really come out and say that, so I thought . . ." What did I think? That he saw me as dried up?

"He thinks you hung the moon. They all love you, Athena. I wish you could have heard Rex singing your praises when he hired me. He went on and on about how fortunate I was to be working with someone of your caliber."

"R-really?" Wow.

"Yes. In fact, he intimidated me with your résumé. That Amazon scene you wrote was brilliant. I'm surprised you weren't nominated for an Emmy for it, to be honest."

"You think so?" I felt my confidence surge. "Because I really loved it too." Joy settled into my heart. "That's one thing I love about writing. It really does transport you. Takes you to a different place. If you're having a crummy day, you can just write a funny scene and set it in a hut in the rain forest. Surround the characters with all sorts of animals and other distractions and then let them squirm."

"Internal and external conflict. It's the crux of every good story." He grinned. "Guess if someone wrote a novel about my life, it would be a bestseller."

"Mine too," I threw in. "Especially if they factored in my

family members. Then we'd have conflict all over the place. Especially if Mama ended up in prison for killing my father." I couldn't help the groan that followed.

"That's why I was so keen on adding more ongoing cast members. The more people you have, the more potential for conflict you have." Stephen shook his head. "I just hope the conflict stays on the page and not in my relationship with Rex. To be honest, the only reason he hired me at all was because he felt sorry for me."

"Okay, stop this train. I need to get off."

Stephen sat back in his chair. "What do you mean?"

"I mean this is the polar opposite of what I've been thinking. Why in the world would Rex feel sorry for you? You've had a brilliant career as a stand-up comedian. And that HBO special was really great." *Or so I've heard.*

"Thanks, but doing stand-up is not where my heart is. I have a daughter who needs a stable life. And our time in Las Vegas—even though it was great for my career—nearly did her in. When I contacted Rex and asked him for work—"

"Wait." I put my hand up. "You came to him for a job, not the other way around?"

"Well, yeah. I needed to get out of Vegas. And my agent was one of Rex's best friends back in the seventies. They'd worked on a couple of shows together, so he put me in touch with him. I took a chance and called him. Didn't have a clue if he'd be interested or not. And like I said, I knew he was already working with an award-winning team of writers, so I figured the chances were pretty slim. Just decided it was worth a shot, for Brooke's sake."

Relief washed over me, followed by shame. I'd misjudged just about everything. I stared at him, so overcome I could hardly speak. "You're actually an award-winning comic. And I thought you came because . . ."

Ack. I couldn't say it. The words wouldn't come.

"You were worried about your job? What?"

"Well, yeah. I thought maybe Rex wanted to prove some kind of point. Our ratings this past season haven't been as high as in seasons past. I know he's been worried about that. The sponsors have too. And he said it himself—bringing you in gave the show a fresh face."

"Some fresh face. Why do you think I'm taking that course on plotting? This is the first time I've had to write actual scenes with a beginning, middle, and end. And something with a strong takeaway value too."

"No way."

"Sure. Think about it. Most of my jokes are pretty short. Under three minutes. Until I started taking this class, I didn't know a thing about plotlines or 'Belly of the Whale' scenes. I'm on such a learning curve." He shook his head. "Honestly, I just hope Rex doesn't boot me too quickly. Brooke has already started school, and I want her to settle in for a change. Have some stability in her life."

I still couldn't get past his comment about the plotting class. The boy didn't know anything about scriptwriting? Nothing at all? And I'd been worried he would steal my job?

Okay. Time to offer a little encouragement.

"Stephen, I'm glad you're here. Rex is right. We needed to make some changes this season. Mix things up a little. The viewers have been really fickle."

"Well, that's always how it is when you finally bring a couple together after keeping them apart for so long. The sense of anticipation is gone." He stared into my eyes, and I suddenly understood that sense of anticipation he was referring to. *Be still my heart.* Thankfully, he kept talking. "As for adding a fresh voice, I guess there's some truth to that. Whether or not my ideas—my voice—will up the ratings is another thing. We'll see, I guess."

"I'm sure it will be fine."

"Probably. I just thought it was about time I let you know how grateful I am to get the chance to work with you. You and Bob and Paul have laid a foundation for the show, and I'm glad to be aboard. So if my enthusiasm ever comes across as anything other than that—enthusiasm—please just . . ." He shrugged. "Step on my foot or something."

I couldn't help but laugh at that. "Okay. I promise." A pause followed. "But if you ever catch me really stepping on your toes—hurting your feelings or leaving you out—let me know, okay? I . . . I want you to feel like you're part of the team." Suddenly I really did want that.

He paused and gazed at me so intently I could almost read his thoughts. In that moment, our words, our emotions, hung suspended in space. Then, from the shop, another "opa!" rang out, followed by a round of laughter.

He quirked a brow. "Better get back to work."

"R-right." I pulled a piece of paper from the notebook, folded it, and started fanning myself. Had someone adjusted the thermostat? The temperature in this room had suddenly gone up several degrees.

Time to get to work.

"Okay, so Angie and Jack are in love. They're going to live happily ever after."

"Right. But we have to throw a few kinks in that plan."

"Yep." I paused, pen in hand. "What can we do to up the conflict, beyond what we've already done? We've added the element of the older stars. We've created a potential takeover of their business."

He grinned. "I think we need another week or two of antics from the kids, and then maybe it's time for that 'Angie's Having a Baby' episode you've been waiting for."

I almost dropped my makeshift fan. "Really? You're okay with that?"

"I've always been okay with it, Athena. Just questioned

the timing. I thought it would be best to give them more conflict before adding a child to the mix." His voice rose to cover the noise coming from the restaurant. "That way, once the baby comes, there's chaos all around, especially if we have a full cast of children and senior citizens. Can you imagine?"

Suddenly I could, and what I saw delighted me. "It's going to be a blast. Pure chaos . . . but a blast."

"Exactly. That's what we're going for—chaos." He paused and his nose wrinkled. "Is someone baking fresh bread?"

"Always." I laughed. "Breads are my sister's specialty, and Saturday is her biggest baking day. That's why she gets the cousins to watch her kids on Saturday."

My mother entered the storeroom with a broom in hand. She took one look at us and grinned. "Sorry to interrupt. We had a little accident with the flour. Larisa's baking the bread, but Paul knocked over the flour bin."

"Need me to help clean up?" I took a step toward her, but she put her hand up.

"No, no. You stay here, Athena. You two need to . . ." She paused, and I could tell she bit back a few words. "Work. You need to work."

"Will you let us know when the bread is done?" Stephen asked. "It smells great."

"Of course," Mama said. "It's almost lunchtime anyway. We'll feed you, I promise. The Pappas family never lets a guest go away hungry . . . for food or for love."

Mama!

She winked and said, "We'll eat soon. In the meantime, make yourself at home. Our shop is your shop. Anything you want, it's yours." At the words "anything you want," her gaze darted to me. Lovely. But Stephen didn't seem to notice. If he did, he kept right on talking about how good the bread smelled and how he could hardly wait to eat.

"You know what we used to say in the old country, about bread?" my mother said.

"No." Stephen shook his head and closed his notebook.

"In the village where I grew up, bread was considered a gift of God. The old women would bless the bread and make the sign of the cross with a knife before slicing it. We never took it for granted. Every gift in our lives comes from God. The little gifts . . ." She looked back and forth between us. "And the big things."

I felt my heart begin to race as the meaning of her words set in.

"There's something wholesome about bread making. You start with something so small and end up with something so large." She paused, and the edges of her lips curled up. "It's kind of like a relationship between a man and a woman."

"Oh?" Stephen looked a little confused by this statement.

"Starts out small—maybe a thought, a glimmer of hope— and ends up growing over time." Mama clasped her hands at her chest. "In the end, both parties are in love. It's as beautiful as a fresh-baked loaf of bread."

I heard a sound at the door and looked up to see my father enter the storeroom.

"I've never heard you carry on like this about bread, Thera." He swept her into his arms. "But I love it. And I love you." He gave her such a passionate kiss that I had to look away. Unfortunately—or fortunately—I found myself staring directly at Stephen, who stared back. And smiled. And winked.

Either one of us could have looked away at any moment, but we chose not to. We didn't say anything. Didn't have to. Funny how the eyes could speak so much.

One thing was abundantly clear . . . the yeast had just been added to our relationship. And I had the strangest feeling it was about to start growing.

11

This Is Your Life

I couldn't shake my grin as I led the way out of the storeroom. Mama and Babbas didn't seem to notice. They were too busy holding hands and gabbing about how their love was like a loaf of bread—a gift from God above.

All this talk about bread was making me hungry. My stomach hadn't stopped growling for the last couple of hours. Hopefully we'd get to eat sooner rather than later.

From across the store, I caught a glimpse of Paul sitting at one of the tables with my brother, playing cards. "Glad to see you're hard at work," I teased.

"Hey, I was ready to start writing, but you two disappeared on me." He looked back and forth between Stephen and me. "Thought maybe you ran away from home. Left me with the kids." He gestured to the children, who played off in the distance.

"I would never do that to you." After a chuckle, I added,

"But I can see Angie doing that to Jack. Can't you? Maybe she leaves him alone for the day with all of the kids from the talent agency. He has to run a daddy day care for a day. Wouldn't that be fun?"

"Yeah, fun." Paul yawned and put his cards down on the table. "But can we talk about this after lunch? I'm starving."

"We had planned to wait on Kat and Scott," I said. "They should have been here by now." I reached for my cell phone, noticing I'd missed a call from Kat. She'd left a message, which I listened to right away. "Ah. They had to stop off at Rex and Lenora's house to drop something off, but they're on their way now. She said to save some food for them." My stomach grumbled again. "I think we'd better go ahead and eat without them."

"Perfect timing," Babbas said. "In a couple of hours this place will be full again."

A voice rang out from behind me. "In that case, I'll have the Super-Gyro with peppers and extra onions. Scratch the sauce. I've never been a fan."

I turned to see Bob walking my way.

"No way. Well, howdy, stranger."

"Howdy, yourself."

Paul took one look at Bob and let out a whoop. "Welcome back, my friend. The prodigal son returns to the fold."

"Well, only for a few days. We're on a break from filming." Bob handed me a gift bag. "I come bearing gifts."

"That's my line," I said. "And what in the world are you doing here? Aren't you supposed to be in Tahiti or something?"

"Nah." He handed me the bag. "We were in the Amish country shooting the scene where the buggy repairman reveals that he's a vampire in disguise."

"An Amish vampire story?" My mother did not look convinced.

Bob nodded. "Anyway, we ran into some problems. The director had to have his appendix out, so they've shut down production for the next week or so."

"I had my appendix out in '68," my father said. "Want to see my scar?"

He reached for the top of his pants, and I threw my hands up with a resounding, "No! Enough with the scars."

Bob laughed. "When I called Rex to tell him I was coming back to town, he told me you guys were powwowing, so I thought I'd crash your party. Is that okay?"

"Is it okay?" I threw my arms around his neck, nearly dropping the little gift bag. "It's more than okay. We've missed you. We need your spark."

"My spark, eh?" He brushed his fingers against his shoulder. "Guess I should have brought some matches. In the meantime, open your present."

I reached inside the little bag, pulling out a doll-sized quilt.

"Whoa. This is beautiful. Did you quilt this yourself?"

He laughed. "Hardly. Just decided I'd better bring you something from the Amish country." He pointed across the counter to the food. "Anybody gonna offer this poor traveler some food?"

Within minutes, we'd set up an assembly line with Babbas at the head of the line, Larisa in the middle, and me at the end. I'd sent Mama and Aunt Melina to a table to rest. Both had been on their feet all day, and I knew they still had hours of work ahead of them.

"Larisa and I will make the sandwiches," I said. "You guys just tell us what you want."

"Can I help?" Brooke's voice rang out, and I looked her way with a smile.

"Of course! We could use all the help we can get."

"Will you show me how? I've never made one of these before."

"Sure. I'd be glad to."

The guys got in line, and I showed Brooke how to make a gyro as we went along. She really seemed to get into it, especially the condiments part. Bob—never the patient sort—ordered first. He chose the Super-Gyro minus the sauce.

Stephen opted for the souvlaki sandwich—our top sirloin shish kebab on a pita with tomato, bell pepper, onion, and tzatziki sauce. Paul wanted the Super-Gyro. On and on the orders went. Just about the time we'd made enough sandwiches to feed everyone in the place, Kat and Scott arrived.

She approached the counter and grinned. "Hey, you."

"Hey, yourself." I glanced her way, noticing how happy she looked. "Good day?"

"Yep. How about you? How's it going on this end?"

If only you knew.

"Getting some good ideas for Jack and Angie's marriage?" she continued.

"A few." I was dying to tell her about my one-on-one conversation with Stephen but decided it had better wait. "Are you hungry?"

"Starving. I think I want the spinach chicken pita, and Scott wants the Super-Gyro."

I grilled the chicken for Kat's sandwich with Brooke standing at my side, gabbing all the while. When the chicken was done, I stuffed it into an open pita, and the preteen loaded it with sautéed spinach, onions, tomatoes, and dill, then topped it off with feta and mozzarella. All at my instruction, of course.

"You're really good at this," I said as I watched her work. "You could almost do this for a living."

"You think so?" Brooke's smile lit up the room. "When I'm old enough to get a job, maybe I'll work here. That would be a lot of fun." She nibbled a piece of cheese, and a contented look settled over her. "And the food's good."

"Oh? Greek food is growing on you?" I asked.

"I've always liked it," she whispered. "Just didn't want my dad to know. I love making him think I don't like Greek stuff. It's sort of a game I like to play."

"Quite a game." I grinned. "Well, if you work here, you can eat to your heart's content." I paused, trying to remember what still needed to be done. "Oh yes. Now for Scott's Super-Gyro. You watched me make all of the others. Think you can do this one yourself?"

She nodded. "I think so. It's lamb and beef, right?"

"Yep."

"And just about everything else in the restaurant piled on top?"

"Yep."

"All topped off with that—" Her brow wrinkled. "What did you call that sauce again?"

"Tzatziki."

She tried to pronounce the word but butchered it. Oh well. At least she gave it an effort.

When she finished, the sandwich looked a little sloppy, but—according to Scott, who ate every bite—it tasted great. Brooke beamed with delight at that proclamation.

I reached over to give her a hug. "Thanks for your help, Brooke. Couldn't have done it without you."

"You're welcome. But I'm starving."

"What do you want to eat? I can fix you anything on the menu."

She glanced up at the menu board. "There are a lot of things I've never had before."

"Have you tried falafel?"

"No. What is it?"

"Chickpea patties served in a pita with lettuce, tomato, and onion. You can have the tahini, tzatziki, or hot sauce on the side."

"Gross." Her nose wrinkled. "I feel sick just thinking about it."

"Okay, what about the cheesesteak?"

"Like Philly cheesesteak?" Her eyes widened. "I love that."

"Great. Cheesesteak it is. Coming right up."

"Can I help you?" The imploring look in her eyes touched my heart.

"Of course. C'mon back here, girl."

I spent the next few minutes teaching her how to put together the best cheesesteak in town. I made it extra-large so that we could share it. And man, the smell! As that beef sizzled, the heavenly aroma filled the room.

Kat joined us behind the counter as we nibbled on bites of the gooey goodness.

"You two look like you're having fun back here. You must be talking about boys."

"Boys?" Brooke laughed. "No. We're talking about sandwiches."

"Nothing very romantic about sandwich making," I said.

"Oh, I don't know about that. They say the way to a man's heart is through his stomach." Kat gestured to Scott, who took a big bite of his sandwich. "So I guess you could say that sandwich making is a tool of the trade."

"Never thought about it." I took another bite. "But I guess you're right." I nodded in Brooke's direction. "I was giving Brooke a lesson in gyro making."

"A lesson in *hero* making, eh?" Kat grinned as she stressed the word. "Sorry I missed that."

"What are we building over here?" Larisa asked as she joined us. "Heroes?"

Kat nodded. "Yes. Sounds like it."

"How does one go about building a hero, pray tell?" Larisa asked.

"You're asking a writer how to build a hero?" I giggled.

"Oh, honey. I could build you the best hero in town. You have no idea."

"You might not need to build one, Athena," Kat said. "Maybe he's already here." She glanced at Stephen, then back at me with a playful wink.

"W-what?" I felt the color drain from my cheeks.

"You have a crush on my dad?" Brooke's eyes widened. "I *knew* it."

Now what, Athena?

My silence apparently went on a bit too long. Kat gave me a knowing look. "Let me ask you a question, Athena."

"Uh-oh."

"If you *were* building a hero, what would you add?"

"What do you mean?"

"Just approach this like you would approach making a sandwich. We're going to list the ingredients you're looking for in a man."

"Huh?"

"C'mon now. Just play along." I picked up on the sparkle in her eyes. "What's your idea of the perfect sandwich?"

"Depends on the day." I stared down at the selections in front of me. "Lamb. Or beef. Kind of depends on what I'm feeling like. Has to have peppers, of course. And onions. Tomatoes. Oregano. Garlic. Yogurt."

"And if any one ingredient is missing?"

"It's just not the same."

"That's how the search for a mate is too."

"What?"

"It's true. Let's say you find a guy you think is just right. Maybe he's lamb and cumin with peppers and tomatoes. But no onions."

"I'm looking for a guy with no onion?" I laughed. "I'm not sure I get it."

"Athena, I'm trying to get at something here. What are you looking for in a husband? Have you made a list?"

"Yeah, how will you know Mr. Right if he comes along?" Larisa asked. "Maybe he'll walk in the door and you'll miss him because you didn't realize that's who—or what—you were looking for." She turned her gaze to Stephen, then jabbed me in the ribs with her elbow.

"Ouch." I rubbed my side.

Brooke started giggling. "This is fun. I like building heroes."

Easy for her to say. She was only eleven. She still had plenty of time.

"I don't know," I finally managed. "I mean, I'm obviously looking for the most basic things. He's got to love me and love my family. He's got to be a strong Christian. No wiggle room on that one."

"My dad's a Christian," Brooke said. "And he's a family guy." She pointed to herself. "I'm proof of that. What more do you need?" She glanced at her father. "And he's definitely handsome. Right?"

"Well, yes, he's handsome, but who ever said I needed a handsome guy? When it comes to the physical, I'm probably not as picky as you might think." *Hypocrite. Weren't you originally attracted to Stephen because you thought he looked like Adonis?* "Okay, maybe I am. But I'm no beauty, so I can't really expect a cover-model guy to be drawn to me. Ya know?"

Kat shook her head. "Don't let me ever hear you say that again."

"I'm not like you, Kat. I'm not a TV star. I'm just an average-looking girl from a loud, crazy family who wonders if there's a guy out there who might look twice at her without flinching."

Larisa slugged me in the arm.

"Ow!" I rubbed my arm and glared at her.

"You are an amazing woman, and any guy would be lucky to have you," she said.

"That's why I keep you on the payroll," I said. "Because you say things like that."

"Some payroll. You pay me in sandwiches." She giggled. "Not that I'm complaining. Anyway, let's go back to what you're looking for. Tall, dark, and handsome, I'm sure."

"Doesn't have to be. At my age, I'll take short, chubby, and moderately good-looking."

Brooke rolled her eyes, muttered something about adults under her breath, and then went off to join Mary and Trina on the other side of the store.

"Does anybody ever really get all of the things on their list?" I asked when she was out of earshot. "I mean, c'mon. What if you had something totally random listed, sort of as a test. You know? Like, what if you had 'must love fishing' or something strange like that."

"Must love fishing?" Kat looked at me, clearly confused. "Since when are you into fishing?"

I shrugged. "I'm not. But the man I fall in love with has to love it. It's a test. An out clause, basically. Either he's into fishing or he's not the guy for me."

"You're nuts." Kat shook her head.

"Must love fishing?" Larisa mumbled. "Crazy." Her gaze narrowed. "Do you even eat fish?"

"Sometimes. I had salmon last month." I squared my shoulders. "Anyway, 'must love fishing' is on my list and I'm leaving it there. That's how I'll know Mr. Right for sure if he comes along. Unless, perhaps, he has all of the qualities except that one."

"If he's missing one, then he's not Mr. Right," Larisa said. "That's my theory."

"I'm not sure I agree." I shook my head. "Because, honestly, preferences change. Today I might want outgoing and fun—just like today I wanted lamb on my sandwich. But tomorrow, quiet and reserved might sound more appealing. You know?"

"If you're still torn between lamb and beef, then you clearly haven't found Mr. Right," Kat said. "Because if you'd found him, you would know exactly what you wanted when you saw it. There wouldn't be any doubt in your mind."

"Wouldn't be any doubt in your mind about what?"

I turned as I heard Stephen's voice. In that second, that nanosecond, I had absolutely no doubt in my mind about what I wanted. I wanted the beef. Tall, dark, and handsome beef. My gaze lingered on him—perhaps a bit too long. Long enough for Kat to clear her throat.

"Hey, Stephen," she said. "How's your day going?"

"It's been great." His gaze darted my way and then shifted down to the display of meats and veggies. "Just wanted to come over and thank you ladies for letting Brooke join your assembly line. I can't believe she wanted to do it."

"She's a great girl, Stephen," Larisa said. "And she's been wonderful with my kids. I can tell you've taught her well."

"Thanks." He sighed. "I've done my best."

"I think she's lonely for family," Larisa added. "So bring her by any time. She seems to be getting along great with Trina and Mary."

"Yes, she's so excited about the sleepover tonight." Stephen shrugged. "I guess girls get worked up about that sort of thing."

"Yes, they do." Larisa looked my way. "Oh, I have an idea. While you writerly people are doing your thing tonight back at the house, I'll hang out with the girls upstairs in my old bedroom. We'll do pedicures and watch romance movies and talk about boys."

"But you're married," I said. "Do you still talk about boys when you're married?"

"We'll talk about the boy *you* will one day marry," Larisa said with a grin. "It'll be lots of fun."

Great. Now they were talking about my love life behind my back. At least she had the courtesy to warn me in advance.

"You're getting married?" Stephen asked, giving me a curious smile. "I must've missed that memo."

"Well, someday. Maybe. I guess. I mean, I don't know." A sigh followed.

"We were just discussing the qualities Mr. Right would have to have," Kat said. "He would have to be—"

When I kicked her, Kat stopped talking. Okay, she glared at me, but she would get over it. I hoped.

"Anyway, enough about all that," I said. "Are you and Paul still keen on spending the night at my parents' place tonight, or have we already scared you off?"

"Oh, we're spending the night. Bob's coming too. But I need to slip away for a few minutes to fetch Zeus on my way."

Fetch Zeus. Ha!

"Poor little guy's probably dying to get away from the doggy day care. Can I bring him to your place? I'll keep him crated, I promise."

"Sure. Bring him over. Surely with all of us watching he'll be okay."

My brother approached with an empty trash bag in hand. "What's this I hear? That mangy dog is coming back? Can't we shake him?"

This drew the attention of my parents, who joined us. "What? The dog's coming back?" Mama asked.

"Can't we send him out on some sort of a hunt and hope he gets lost?" my father said.

"Hey now. My daughter happens to love that dog," Stephen said. "And you never know . . . Zeus could turn out to be some sort of saving grace in all of our lives."

"If that mutt is a saving grace, then kill me now." My

father chuckled. "You comedy writers are nuts. You know that, right?"

Stephen and I nodded.

"But you're growing on me," my father said. "And you certainly keep things interesting."

Niko looked at me and sighed. "According to Stephen, I'm only on Step 2 in the plotline of my life. This wrestling thing is part of my 'Call to Adventure.' But I have a long way to go before I reach my final goals. What do you think of that?"

Good grief. Again with the plotline? Would we ever hear the end of that thing?

"You'll meet a wonderful girl someday and get married," Mama said. "Then you'll skip all of the other steps and go straight to the happily-ever-after part."

"Trust me, any girl I find will *never* pass Babbas's test." Niko sighed.

"Your test?" Stephen looked at my father. "People who marry into your family have to pass some sort of test?"

Why this intrigued him, I couldn't be sure. Maybe he was just taking notes for a future episode.

"That's right." My father squared his shoulders. "Anyone who wants to marry one of my children has to memorize all of the verses to the Greek national anthem."

Stephen didn't look terribly shaken by this news. "How hard could that be?" he asked. "Anyone can learn a song."

"The Greek national anthem has 158 verses," I explained. "I've never met a living soul who knew all the verses."

His expression shifted to one of disbelief. "Wait a minute." Stephen shook his head. "What about Larisa's husband? He must've learned all of the verses, right? Otherwise, how did he end up marrying her?"

Babbas grunted. "Crazy kids. They ran off and eloped. But don't you worry about that. I've got him up to verse thirty-seven. Before he dies, he'll pass the test. You can bet your life on it."

"Sounds like you're taking this very seriously," Stephen said.

"You betcha." My father gave him a pensive look. "Children are a heritage from the Lord. They're God's gift to me. I wouldn't give them to just anyone. They must find mates who are worthy. No one marries one of my children without passing the test."

"I'm never getting married," I muttered.

Stephen turned my way. "Oh, I'm sure there are a few guys out there who might be able to pull off the verses of that song. If they cared enough."

For a moment time stood still. I had the eerie sense that, for the first time, someone might actually care enough to give it a try.

From across the room, something—or, rather, someone— caught my eye. I watched Milo make his way from the counter to the tables. He passed Aunt Melina, who looked his way with a girlish smile. Melina—never one to speak much—lifted her glass as if to offer a toast. He gave her a little wink and just kept walking.

Looked like we'd had a lot of bread baking at Super-Gyros today. Someone had better cue the band. Before day's end, we just might sing a verse or two of the Greek national anthem.

In the meantime, I needed to spend a little time figuring out why I'd added "must love fishing" to my list. Chances were pretty good Stephen Cosse didn't even own a fishing pole.

12

Laugh-In

We spent the rest of the afternoon pounding out ideas based on our observations of my parents. Turned out Scott was loaded with ideas and fit right into our little writing circle. Even Kat chimed in with her thoughts. Around five o'clock Lenora began to look winded, so they all headed back to Beverly Hills. I promised to call Kat later. From the look in her eyes, I could tell she suspected my feelings for Stephen were growing.

My parents closed up shop earlier than usual that night so we could reconvene at home. I couldn't remember ever having such a great day. As I drove Brooke, Mary, and Trina back to my house, I listened in on their girlish chatter. Glancing at Brooke in the rearview mirror, I realized a light had come on. Her eyes shone with a new joy. Being part of a family would do that to a person.

When we reached the house, the girls changed into their swimsuits and headed for the pool.

"You joining us, Athena?" Mary asked.

Ugh. Me in a swimsuit . . . in front of the guys? At least the sun was going down. Maybe they wouldn't notice the cellulite on the backs of my thighs. And maybe—if I hurried—I could be in the water before Stephen got back with Zeus. That would be my only saving grace.

I scurried into my olive-green bathing suit—the one I'd paid a fortune for because it supposedly covered up many of my imperfections—and slipped on a cover-up. By the time I reached the pool, Paul and Bob were already in the water. They hovered in the shallow end, as far from the girls as possible. No doubt all the squealing was painful to their ears.

I'd no sooner gotten in the water than Stephen arrived with Zeus in tow. I'd made it just in time.

"Oh, Zeus!" Brooke scrambled from the pool and grabbed the pooch by the neck to give him a hug. "You look so beautiful. They put a bow on you!"

"They put a bow on him, all right." Stephen chuckled. "And for the price I just paid, they should have dressed him in a ball gown and given him a tiara."

"Oh, it was worth it, Dad. He's gorgeous. Thank you, thank you!" Brooke reached up and threw her arms around her dad.

I half-expected him to complain because she was wet, but Stephen just pulled her close and planted a kiss on top of her head. Sweet.

Then he looked my way.

I'd never in my life been more grateful to already be in the water. Getting to know a guy was one thing. Getting to know him while wearing a bathing suit was another. Then again, Mama had turned on the light in the pool. Maybe I wasn't as well hidden as I'd hoped.

Brooke jumped back in the water, hollering, "Come and get in the pool, Dad!"

Unfortunately, Zeus must have thought she was talking to him. The mongrel raced to the edge of the pool and did a swan dive over the edge.

All of the girls began to scream, myself included.

"So much for the grooming job." Stephen knelt at the pool's edge, calling out to Zeus.

I helped Brooke get the half-crazed animal under control and out of the pool. By now my thighs were in full view of everyone in attendance, rippling under the glow of the setting sun. Not that Stephen seemed to notice. No, once the dog shook off the excess water, Stephen was soaked head to toe.

"You have no choice, Dad," Brooke said. "You have to get in now."

"No kidding. Just let me get him into his crate and I'll join you."

He disappeared around the corner of the house, and I felt my heart go with him. Okay, when had that happened? During our conversation earlier today, perhaps? All of his glowing comments about my writing skills had gone to my head, maybe. They'd somehow linked my heart to Stephen's. Crazy.

I got back into the pool and chatted with the girls, but my thoughts—and my heart—were elsewhere. And when Stephen returned moments later in his swim trunks, I suddenly wished the sun hadn't gone down.

Could you turn up the lights just for a minute, Lord?

He got in the water, and the girls headed straight for him. Brooke jumped him and tried to shove him under, but he wasn't having it. Instead, he flipped her around and dunked her. She came up laughing. The wrestling match went on for a while, eventually involving everyone in the pool. I would have complained about being pulled into it, but as I felt Stephen's arms slip around my waist to propel me into the deep end, two things flashed through my mind. One, *Who has abs like that?* And two, *Dear Lord, please let this day last forever.*

The fun did go on for quite some time. Bob and Paul headed indoors when the smell of my father's cooking wafted through the air. And the girls decided they'd had enough when Larisa appeared with her toddlers, asking for assistance from the babysitters' club.

That left me alone in the pool with Stephen. Not that I was complaining. Oh no. By now, I'd pretty much decided that this had been the Lord's plan all along. Well, minus the whole bathing suit/cellulite part.

With the chattering girls gone, the backyard grew eerily quiet. Except for the crickets and tree frogs. Stephen flipped over on his back and began to float. I fought the temptation to dunk him. Only when his hand reached for mine did I realize he'd actually been waiting for the chance to be alone with me too.

I took his hand and began to float alongside him. For a moment neither of us said a word. From inside the house, I could hear the voices of the others raised in joyful chorus.

"Sounds heavenly, doesn't it?" I said at last.

"What's that?" he asked.

"All of it," I whispered.

He righted himself and pulled me close. "I could stay in here all night. You have no idea how much I'm enjoying this."

"Me too." My feet found the bottom of the pool, and I faced him, my heart going crazy. "Stephen, I may not get a chance to say this again tonight with so many people around, but Brooke is an amazing girl. You're so blessed to have her."

"I am." He brushed a damp hair out of my face and smiled.

"She's really in her element here."

"Oh, trust me, I've noticed. She's changing in so many ways when she's with you. All of you, I mean. So much of the time she's going through the motions. But here she seems to come alive."

"Well, of course she comes alive! She's eleven. Such a great age. What did you want when you were eleven?"

"Honestly?" He stared into my eyes so intently I could almost sense his emotions. "I wanted my parents back. And my grandmother. She died when I was ten. It almost killed me." He let go of my hands and took a couple of steps toward the side of the pool.

"You mentioned living with your grandmother before, but I don't know the story about your parents." I grabbed onto the side of the pool and stretched my legs out behind me.

"The state took me away from them when I was six and sent me to live with Nona, my mother's mother. She was the only saving grace in my life."

I wanted to ask why but didn't dare. Thankfully, he filled in the blanks for me.

"My parents were both drug users. They had me when they were young, but apparently they didn't take care of me. So when I started school, the teachers got wind of the fact that something was wrong, and CPS got involved. I remember the day they came and took me to my grandmother's place in upstate New Jersey. I was terrified, but at the same time, being with her gave me the only stability I'd ever known." He looked at me. "And that smell . . ."

"What smell?"

"The smell of lamb. And garlic. And cumin. And peppers. And bread baking." I could hear the catch in his voice. "Those are all smells I associate with Nona's house."

"I'm convinced God uses smells to minister to us."

"I agree. I think he uses the senses to touch us in ways that we can't otherwise be touched. Certain foods always remind me of my grandmother, and those memories are precious and few, so I love it when it happens." He paused, and for a moment I thought I'd lost him to his thoughts. When he spoke again, his words were laced with emotion. "I think that's why I like Super-Gyros so much. When I'm there, it's like she never died. Like she's with me all over again, standing in her kitchen, cooking for me and telling me stories about her parents growing up in Athens."

"Wow." I felt the sting of tears but didn't bother brushing them away.

"Like I said, my grandmother died when I was ten. And the years after that were hell on earth."

I opened my mouth to ask but never got the chance to. He plowed forward, his words coming faster now.

"I was put in the foster care system after she died. The only person I'd ever loved—the only one who'd truly loved me unconditionally—was gone. And I spent the next eight years being a nuisance to family after family after family."

No way. "What do you mean, being a nuisance?" I asked. "You were a bad kid?"

"No. In fact, I went out of my way to be the best I could be so I'd be accepted. But you have no idea how hard it is to fit in with someone else's family. And just about the time I'd get settled into one place, their 'situation' would change and I'd be booted someplace else."

"Man." The strangest feelings swept over me. I'd grown up in such a safe, happy environment. Oh, sure, I thought my family was a little kooky, especially after some of the comments my mama had made today. But even during the worst of times, I hadn't come close to experiencing what Stephen had. My heart went out to him.

"Now you see why I'm so determined to make a good life for Brooke. I don't want her to feel like she's a misfit. And maybe I'm overly concerned about her well-being, I don't know. But I can sense when she's unhappy. I see it in her eyes. And every time that look comes over her, I remember being that age, looking in the mirror, and wondering if anyone would ever just love me . . . for me."

"Oh, Stephen."

"She might be emotional. She might be a pain at times. But I love her more than life itself."

"That's all anyone could ask for," I said. "And you're such a great dad. I've seen you with her. She's so blessed to have you."

"No, I'm blessed to have her. And I want to give her the life I never had—the idyllic life, with the dining room table and lots of siblings seated around it. The life with the pool in the backyard and the mother teaching her how to . . . I don't know . . . be a lady."

He paused, and silence wrapped us in its embrace. "When her mom took off at such a young age, it was like revisiting my childhood all over again," he said at last. "Those feelings of abandonment are hard to erase. And I feel like I've spent a lot of my life trying to be the funny guy so that I don't have to deal with the harsh realities of single parenting. I don't want Brooke to spend the rest of her life in counseling, trying to get over the awful life she had as a kid. I just want her to be carefree. Have fun."

"She doesn't have a horrible life," I said. "And just for the record, all girls go through a bunch of emotions when they're preteens. I remember crying for absolutely no reason."

"Really?"

"Oh yeah. I was a mess. And I had the ideal family situation. Honestly, being eleven, almost twelve, is so hard. Your body is changing. Your emotions are changing. And I'm sure this move from Las Vegas to L.A. was pretty startling too."

"I thought she could have a better life here than in Vegas. That's such a strange place for a kid to grow up."

"She can have a better life here." I felt a smile wriggle its way up from deep inside me. "And now that she's landed on the Pappas doorstep, we'll do what we can to help. I promise."

"That's just it." His expression shifted. "You don't know how many times I came close to having an ideal situation as a kid. A couple of the homes I stayed in were really nice. But something always happened. The rug got yanked out from under me. What happens if I lose this writing gig at *Stars Collide* and have to look for work in another city? Then what? She loses your family and all of those relationships."

I hardly knew how to respond. First of all, it had never occurred to me that Stephen really thought his job might be in jeopardy. Second, I couldn't imagine my family leaving Brooke hanging like that. She'd become part of us. Even if she moved away—my chest began to ache at that thought—she would always know she was loved.

"Why do you think I'm trying so hard to come up with new and original ideas for the show?" he asked. "And why do you think I'm taking that plotting class?"

"To drive me crazy?"

"No." He laughed. "That's just an added benefit. I'm doing all of this to let Rex know he hasn't made a mistake in hiring me. I have to stick around. Being in L.A. means the world to my daughter. And now that she's met you . . ." He looked into my eyes and smiled. "Well, you and your family. Now that she's met all of you, it would rip her apart to pull her away."

"You won't have to. I have a feeling you're here to stay."

"I hope so," he whispered. His hand reached for mine, and he pulled me close. "That's what I want."

My heart began to race as I whispered, "Me too."

"Just for the record, I love working with you. And there's something to be said for being a sitcom writer. We have the most powerful job in the world. You know that, right?"

"Most powerful? What do you mean?" Most of the time I felt pretty powerless, actually.

"We get to push people around on paper all day. We write a scene and plop them down in it. The actors and actresses get all the glory, but in reality they're just doing what we tell them to do. They follow the script that we write."

I had to wonder what he was trying to get at.

"Following the script is easy when you trust the writer," he said. "That's kind of my philosophy about life too."

"Care to elaborate?"

"Sure. I believe that God is ultimately in control, but I know that he gives us free will."

"Right."

"It's what we do with our free will that matters. Do we bow to his plan for our lives—that is, stick to the script—or bolt? Write our own lines? Does that make sense?"

"Perfect sense," I said.

"Yeah." He drew me so close that I could feel his breath on my cheek. "Pushing characters around on paper is fun. But sometimes I find myself waiting around for the next real-life scene, thinking I can somehow control where things are going to go, like I do when I'm writing a script for the show."

"Really?" *Where are you headed with this?* I'd just started to ask him when the serious expression on his face shifted into a sly grin.

"Yes, really. For example, I'd be willing to bet you didn't pencil this into the next scene."

He wrapped his arms around my waist and leaned in to kiss me. My heart skipped into overdrive. What was happening here? For a moment I wasn't sure what to do. How would I have written this scene? Would the heroine fight off the advances—if, in fact, these were advances—or would she succumb?

I never had a chance to complete that thought. As Stephen's lips met mine, I melted like butter in the sun. Hmm. Too cliché. I melted like a chocolate bar on a s'more.

Enough with the food analogies. I melted. And as the kiss lingered, I melted some more. I found myself distracted, thinking about this moment in writers' terms. How would I describe this scene in a script? I'd have to say something about tingles running down my spine, right? Nah, that was probably overused. If this happened to be one of those cheesy romance novels, I'd throw in something about Stephen's rippling abs or his broad, manly shoulders. He did have great abs, and his shoulders were nothing to sneeze at, so I wouldn't have to exaggerate. Then again, if this happened to be one of those really sleazy, over-the-top romance novels, I'd have to add something about heaving bosoms. They always talked about heaving bosoms.

Nah. I was woefully underqualified to write about that. Now, if we were writing about cellulite in someone's thighs . . . *that* I could address with some degree of authority.

Focus, Athena.

Of course, if I decided to write about this, I'd have to use the word *fire*. Romance writers always equated kissing with fire, though for the life of me, I couldn't figure out why.

Stephen tightened his grip around my waist, and our kiss deepened. Now I understood why they used the word *fire*.

Okay, enough kissing.

By the time we came up for air, my eyes had filled with tears. I was a puddle. In a good way. Thankfully, we were already in a pool. I gazed into Stephen's eyes—eyes sparkling with merriment—and sighed.

Good grief. He was right—I'd never seen this one coming. Thank goodness. Being caught off guard was so much more fun.

From one of the upstairs bedroom windows, a couple of girls let out squeals. I heard Trina's voice as she hollered, "I *told* you they were going to kiss. You owe me a hundred dollars."

Brooke responded by calling out, "Dad, can I borrow a hundred dollars?"

"I see she has your sense of humor," I managed.

"Guess she does. I'll loan it to you at 17 percent interest," he hollered up at her. "Payable on a four-year loan. If you don't pay it all back by the time you're sixteen, you can't date. Ever."

"What? No fair!" She began to rant about his terms, and he chuckled.

"She's definitely my child."

Just when I thought things couldn't possibly get any more embarrassing, Mama came outside. "What's going on out here? I thought I heard shouting."

Stephen and I put a little space between us.

"They're kissing, Aunt Thera," Mary shouted down from the window. "We made a bet and Trina won. A hundred dollars."

"Kissing?" Mama looked my way and clasped her hands together at her chest. "There is a God and he loves me!"

I had a sudden, overwhelming desire to drown myself. Well, not technically drown myself, but to swim to some distant shore where no one knew I'd just been kissed. By a really handsome guy. In my family's swimming pool.

In the Pappas household, however, everyone knew everything about everyone. And right now, it looked like everyone included Bob and Paul. By the time Stephen and I had gotten out of the pool and wrapped ourselves in towels, our fellow writers had joined us.

"Something you want to tell us, kids?" Bob asked. "'Cause the girls upstairs are coming up with a whopper of a story about the two of you. Just verifying their tale to find out if it's fact or fiction."

I groaned. "Bob, do we have to do this? It's humiliating enough that the girls were spying on us."

"Oh, so it is true." He chuckled. "I knew it. Thought maybe I'd picked up on that vibe earlier in the day."

Aunt Melina joined the party next. "Athena, come inside and have some coffee and diples. A party isn't a party without you. We'll celebrate your new relationship."

Lovely. Next they'd offer to throw an engagement party.

"Diples?" Bob glanced at my aunt. "Do you mind if I ask what that is?"

"It's a Greek sopapilla that's topped with honey, walnuts, and cinnamon," she explained.

"Sounds great." He turned and disappeared into the house, chattering about how great it was to be back in California. Paul followed behind him, turning only for a moment to give me a curious glance. I'd have to explain later that Stephen wasn't really the threat we'd made him out to be. He was a great guy. A really great guy.

"I can't believe she made diples." Stephen looked my way and sighed. "Nona would have been proud. I've definitely landed in the right family."

"Oh you have, have you?" I shivered and pulled the towel a little tighter.

Stephen drew close, the moonlight reflected in his eyes. "I have," he whispered, then kissed the tip of my nose. "And just so you know, this has pretty much been the best day of my life."

"Following my parents around and finding out what makes them tick?" I asked.

"No." He brushed my hair off my face. "Following their daughter around and finding out what makes *her* tick."

"Great line, Dad," Brooke hollered from the window above.

"But I think you need to work on your delivery," Trina threw in. "You're a great writer, but not the best actor."

Stephen groaned, then glanced upward. "For your information, I'm not acting." He looked at me and shrugged. "Sorry. I forgot they were up there."

I glanced up, noticing that all three girls were going to topple out of the upstairs window if we didn't end this show by going inside. Still, there was one lingering thing I needed to take care of. "This was one of the best days of my life too," I whispered as I reached up and gave Adonis—er, Stephen—a kiss on the cheek.

"Hey, Dad," Brooke called down. "Just so you know, I'm pretty sure you two are at Step 9 on the plotline."

"What?" He looked up, squinting against the light coming from the window above.

"I've been reading your notes during the day when you're at work. You know, from that class you're taking. That kissing scene was a Step 9 if I ever saw one."

"Step 9, eh?" I grinned. "Wonder what that one is."

"A 'Moment of Triumph,'" he said. "It's a pretty good place to be at. Unfortunately, it's followed shortly thereafter by the 'Ultimate Test'—that point in the story where you have to prove you've got the goods."

"That's the point where the hero and heroine have to jump back into the action to see if they've learned their lesson," Brooke called out. "Have you?"

Good question. I really had learned a lot over the past few days. I'd learned to guard myself from judging people too quickly. I'd learned some things about myself too. Looked like the pain from my past relationship really was behind me now. I was free to move on. And who better to move on with than the man standing in front of me now?

From inside my house, I heard music playing. For a minute I thought the girls had put it on. Only when I heard the familiar Greek song did I realize the music was coming from the living room. Still wrapped in a towel, I took Stephen by the hand and led him into the house. Once inside, I rubbed the chlorine out of my eyes and found Aunt Melina and Milo dancing. Together. As a couple. They pulled Paul and Bob into their circle, followed by Mama and Babbas. Before long, Stephen and I had been ushered into the fold.

We formed a serpentine line, then wove around in circles, everyone laughing and singing. Well, Paul wasn't exactly singing. And I guess you couldn't really call it dancing either, but he gave it the old college try.

Brooke and the other girls showed up seconds later, their eyes wide.

"It's the Tsamiko," Trina said. She took Brooke by the hand and pulled her into the circle. I could tell the preteen wasn't keen on the idea, but she stuck with it just the same. I watched as she eventually ended up in her daddy's arms, the little princess twirling around the floor, safe in her father's embrace. In that moment, the most amazing feeling washed over me. How safe she must feel. How cherished.

Out of the corner of my eye, I watched Milo and Aunt Melina. He pulled her into his arms and spun her around the dance floor. She giggled as she lingered in his embrace.

Crazy. If I'd been writing this scene, I would have added . . . Actually, nothing. I would have added absolutely nothing.

Oh, we could have penciled all of this into a workable script, but it wouldn't have had the same punch. Some moments were simply divine. God-breathed. You couldn't plan or predict them. And, frankly, those moments suddenly held far more appeal than all of the scripted ones in the world.

Aunt Melina picked up the pace, leading us into another variation of the dance. Milo followed suit, a broad smile on his face. The two of them put on quite a show as they shouted "opa!" and lifted handkerchiefs in the air.

I wanted to shout too. For in that instant, with the people I loved dancing around me, I found myself in a near-perfect moment. A holy moment. And as Stephen glanced my way, his beautiful brown eyes locking firmly onto mine, I realized the yeast had done its work. Looked like our feelings were definitely on the rise.

13

The Facts of Life

The rest of the weekend was spent floating on a cloud. After years of being a happy single, I suddenly found myself caught up in a whirlwind of romantic bliss. Opa! Of course, I realized that my relationship with Stephen came with an extra surprise package—an eleven-year-old. How would Brooke feel about having a twenty-eight-year-old as a potential mother figure?

Am I a potential mother figure? Wow.

How quickly my feelings seemed to be growing. However, I realized in that moment what all of this must be like for Brooke. I didn't exactly fit the mold, did I? Sure, I played with the nieces and nephew. I'd spent a lot of time around kids. But what would Brooke think about me?

By the time Monday rolled around, I'd settled the issue in my mind. Instead of rushing ahead, I would take one day at a time. Wasn't that what the Bible said I should do? Sure. I'd ease my way into this relationship, and God would take care of the details. They were his to deal with anyway.

As I pulled into the studio parking lot on Monday morning, I did my best to push my personal life to the background and focus only on events related to *Stars Collide*. The Snidely Whiplash episode would be shot this week, and we were already hard at work on new material for next week's show. My parents had given us lots of fodder, especially that stuff about ending up in prison. No telling what would end up in our next script.

I'd no sooner parked my car than Rex and Lenora pulled into the spot next to me in her pink convertible.

"G'morning, princess!" Lenora called out. She gave me a queenly wave.

I watched as Rex got out of the car and went around to open her door for her. What would that feel like, to have a man care enough about you to open your door? Did I need that? Well, I might not need it, but as I watched the smile on Lenora's face, I realized suddenly that I wanted it.

Lenora pointed to her gown. "Can you guess who I am today, Athena? C'mon. Guess!"

"Hmm." I squinted against the morning sunlight, trying to figure it out. Only when she began to hum the melody to "Supercalifragilisticexpialidocious" did I get it. "Mary Poppins?"

"That's right!" She pointed to her dress. "This is the gown Julie Andrews wore when she flew into town on her umbrella." Lenora giggled and extended her hand in Rex's direction. "My parasol, young man."

He handed her a frilly umbrella, which she opened. Holding it above her head, she closed her eyes. Moments later, when nothing happened, she sighed. "Guess I've lost the magic."

"Oh no, sweet girl." Rex drew her close and kissed her cheek. "You'll never lose the magic. Not in my book, anyway."

Ah, love. How wonderful it made you feel. You really could rise above the circumstances when love swept in. Grab hold of the umbrella and fly away together—over the horizon.

These thoughts, of course, led right back to thoughts about Stephen. I scolded myself and tried to focus on my work, not my love life.

I followed Rex and Lenora into the studio, where we all stumbled upon Kat and Scott in a lip-lock. Wow. Was everyone feeling romantic this morning?

Obviously not. Tia and Jason stood off in the distance, arguing about something to do with camera angles. Nothing new there. They were always bickering about this or that. Still, there seemed to be a certain romantic spark in the air. I couldn't deny it, even when I listened to the bantering between director and cameraman. And when I made it to our office and saw Stephen for the first time—*Be still my heart! He looks amazing in those jeans!*—it was all I could do to keep my thoughts in line.

He whispered a playful, "Good morning," and I responded with a smile. I could feel Paul's eyes on us but did my best to ignore him. No doubt this had to be confusing to him. One minute I couldn't stand the new writer, the next I was dating him.

"Hey." Paul shook his head, a sour look on his face. "Where's the food?"

"Huh?"

"The leftovers from Super-Gyros. It's Monday. You always bring food on Monday. For as long as I can remember."

"Ah." I paused. "Well, we were together all weekend, so I figured . . ."

"You didn't bring food?" He shook his head. "Has the whole world gone crazy? Nothing is as it should be."

No, nothing is as it should be—and yet everything is as it should be. Only, I couldn't say that to Paul, now could I? He settled in at his desk, grumbling about his empty stomach. I looked around the room—that crazy, mixed-up room—and settled onto the spot on the divan next to Stephen. Talk about inspirational.

While the actors met for their roundtable reading of the Snidely Whiplash script, Paul, Stephen, and I pounded out our ideas for next week's show. I could tell Paul's heart wasn't really in it. Until Stephen mentioned something that got us all excited.

"Did you realize that Milo has done some acting?"

"No way." I looked up from my laptop. "He has?"

"In Greece. He was on a soap opera in the sixties."

"That's crazy. I had no idea."

"Yes, apparently he was quite a handsome fellow back in the day. I did a little research online, and he had a real following with the ladies."

"Wow. Who knew."

"It got me to thinking that we should use him in the next episode. And maybe . . ." Stephen grinned. "Maybe we could use your aunt Melina too."

"Aunt Melina?" *Yikes.* "I don't know about that, Stephen. Sounds a little risky. She's got a few . . . problems."

"I know, but they've got great chemistry. I think it would translate to the screen. Besides, it would be fun to add more seniors to the episode where Angie reveals her pregnancy, don't you think? The older women would have a lot to say about it."

"True." I thought about that. "So, is that where we are in the plotline? Are we ready for Angie to break the news about the baby?"

"Sure. Why not?"

"It's about time." Paul grinned. He reached into the toy box and came out with the soccer ball. "I've missed Little Ricky. Can't wait to add him back into the script."

The next several minutes were spent laughing and talking about the "Angie's Having a Baby" episode. Thankfully, Stephen went along with all of our earlier plans, which made for smooth sailing in the writing room.

"I love that Cuban bandleader idea," he said. "Hope we can get George Lopez on board. I think viewers will make the connection to the old *I Love Lucy* episode."

"Yeah, it's gonna be great," Paul said. He rose and began to pace the room. "Can't you see it now? Angie tries a hundred different ways to tell Jack, but he doesn't get it. In the end, he gets the news in a public setting. Crazy."

"That's the last place I'd want to share something that personal," I said.

"Which is what makes it so perfect." Stephen grinned. "Comedy is supposed to make you squirm. That's half the fun." He wiggled his eyebrows and I laughed, realizing just how much I'd squirmed in the swimming pool the other night, especially with Brooke and the other girls watching our every move.

On and on we went, talking about how perfect the upcoming scene would be. All the while, I kept thinking about how perfect the here-and-now scene in my own life was turning out to be. Brooke was right. Stephen and I were at Step 9 on the plotline. I was experiencing a long-overdue moment of triumph in my life and loving every minute of it.

We'd just pounded out the final line to the new episode when a knock sounded at the door. Kat stuck her head inside and smiled.

"Hey, you guys."

"Hey, yourself." I rose and joined her at the door, seeing Lenora standing next to her.

"Tia wants to know if you guys want to join us in the studio for our walk-through."

"Oh wow. You guys never do the walk-through till Tuesday. What's up with that?"

"You worked a lot of physical comedy into this episode," Kat said. "So Tia feels like we'll need to go ahead and map things out. That's why she wants you in there, so you can help with the blocking. She wants to get a feel for what you had in mind. What do you think?"

"Cool." Paul rose and joined us. "Sounds like fun."

I nodded. "Yeah. I'm okay with that. It's great to be included, and we've already gotten a lot done today anyway."

"Well, c'mon then," Paul said, leading the way. "Let's round up the usual suspects."

"Ooo." Lenora grinned. "*Casablanca*. 1942. Claude Rains." Stephen looked her way, clearly impressed.

"It's a gift," I whispered. "She can't remember what she had for lunch today, but she can remember almost any line from any movie."

"No joke?"

"No joke."

I tagged along on Lenora's heels to the studio, feeling Stephen's hand on my back as we made our way down the hallway. Funny how something as simple as a hand on the back could give you such confidence. I entered the studio feeling like a million bucks. And as I settled into a director's chair—at Tia's bidding—the world was my oyster.

Oh, what joy the next hour turned out to be. Every funny word we'd written danced across the lips of those delivering the lines. It all felt . . . magical. Like I'd waited my whole life for this moment.

I watched as Tia worked with the actors and cameramen. Seeing her in action intimidated me a little. And the few times she veered from the script, I did my best not to let it hurt my feelings. Who would cross her? Not me!

Sometimes I looked at Tia—beautiful, petite Tia—and wondered why some fellow hadn't snatched her up and married her. Other times I listened to her bark commands at people and knew exactly why some fellow hadn't snatched her up and married her. The woman—though tiny—was a force to be reckoned with. It would take some kind of man to stand up to all five-foot-two of her. I had to wonder if such a man existed.

Jason manned one of the cameras, focused as usual. At one point, though, I happened to catch a glimpse of him looking at Tia. I couldn't quite gauge his expression. In that moment, the strangest thought occurred to me. Perhaps his so-called angst toward her was just a ploy to get attention. Maybe what he wanted was something altogether different. Interesting.

"So what do you think about how things are going?" Kat asked. "Is it like you envisioned it?"

I startled to attention. "Oh, even better."

"Good." She grinned. "Because I think this is your funniest script ever, Athena. It's . . . amazing. Everyone agrees. I wish you could have heard us laughing at the roundtable reading this morning. I thought Grandma was going to bust her buttons."

"Or take off flying with that umbrella of hers?" I asked.

Kat grinned. "Something like that. It's really great when we've got amazing material to work with. Makes our job as actors so much easier. You have no idea."

"Aw, thanks."

"It's funny because you're funny."

"You think?"

"Of course. You're one of the funniest people I know. In a natural, God-given sort of way. Not contrived funny, if that makes sense."

"It makes sense."

"I really had a blast with you at the shop on Saturday," Kat said. "It was fun building heroes with you."

"Ha! I had fun too." I leaned in to whisper, "And I have *so* much to tell you."

"You do?"

"Yeah, after we got back to the house, things, well . . ." I felt my cheeks grow warm. "I'll tell you later."

"Yeah, I need to talk to you later too."

Tia called everyone back to attention, and before long the Snidely Whiplash scene was fully under way, physical gags and all. I managed to interject a few ideas along the way, adding more humor to the scenes. What a joy to listen to the laughter that rang out as the lines were delivered. Nothing could top that feeling for a writer.

Not that everything went according to schedule. In the middle of the rehearsal, a voice rang out. "Stop the presses, we've lost one of the kids!"

I turned, recognizing the children's teacher.

Tia brought the rehearsal to an immediate halt. "Who is it?"

"Toby." The teacher paled. "I can't find him anywhere."

"Toby?" I turned to Paul. "He's only five." A thousand awful thoughts went through my head. Had he been kidnapped? Maybe someone was holding him for ransom?

Seconds later, he popped up from behind the sofa on the set and hollered, "Boo!" Scared the daylights out of Tia and even distracted Jason, who jerked away from the camera.

The whole thing was a little scary, but somewhat typical of the kid. He was always up to tricks. Then again, they all were. That's what made the show work, after all. Having the kids aboard added all sorts of possibility for conflict—on and off the set.

Tia, ever the professional, got right back to work. Within minutes, everyone was laughing again. And when they finished, even the crew members cheered. I couldn't remember this kind of enthusiasm on the set of *Stars Collide* since Jack and Angie's wedding scene last season.

An undercurrent of energy laced Rex's words as he turned my way with hand extended. "Let's give our writers a hand."

I gave a little curtsy as the cast and crew applauded our efforts. Paul gave a deep, kingly bow, and Stephen . . . well, Stephen just blushed. He gestured to me, giving me the credit. Seriously? We'd done this together. And we'd write many, many more scenes together, if things went the way I hoped they would.

"Just wait till you see what we have next!" I said. Looking at Rex, I whispered, "Is it okay to tell them?" and he nodded.

"Jack and Angie are going to have a baby!"

A collective gasp went up from all in attendance, then everyone began to cheer.

When the applause died down, Kat looked my way, her brow wrinkled. "I just have one question," she said. "Pink or blue?"

"What do you mean?"

"Pink or blue? Girl or boy?"

"Oh, he's going to be a boy. We're already calling him Little Ricky. Funny, right?"

Several of the cast members chuckled at that one.

"We're using the *I Love Lucy* angle because we know viewers will connect with it. That's the goal, to help them connect. It's going to be really funny, especially if we can get George Lopez to play the Cuban bandleader."

"Wonderful idea," Scott said. He pulled Kat into his arms and gave her a kiss on the cheek. "My blushing bride . . . expecting! What a fun plot twist!"

"It's going to be hysterical," I said. "Just wait till you see all that we have planned. Hope you're up for a lot of fun."

"I am." Kat grinned. "I can't wait. But I'll bet I know something even funnier than anything you writers can cook up." She paused, her eyebrows elevating.

"Oh?"

"Yep. Let's just say that God has impeccable timing and an amazing sense of humor."

"Well, sure he does. I've always said that." I went off on a tangent, talking about the Scriptures on laughter. After a couple of moments, I couldn't help but notice that Kat was staring at me. She crossed her arms and sighed. Loudly.

"What?" I asked. "Did I lose you?"

"Athena, sometimes it's better just to come out and say something instead of beating around the bush." She looked directly into my eyes. "I'm having a baby."

"Well, yeah. I know that. What do you think I've been talking about? We just wrote the scene this morning—the one where you stand up in front of your friends and tell them that you're . . ." My words drifted off and my breath caught in my throat. "Kat, you do mean that your character Angie is pregnant, right?"

"Right." Kat nodded. "She's pregnant."

"Oh, good." I paused to giggle. "Because for a minute there—"

"And to make things even more ironic, so am I."

I continued to ramble until her words sank in. "You . . . you . . . you're . . ."

"Yep." She nodded, then began to cry. Happy tears, no doubt.

Scott pulled her close and began to sing in perfect pitch, "We're having a baby, my baby and me!"

Everyone swarmed them at once. I found myself surrounded on every side by well-wishers pouring out their love and affection on Kat and Scott. I wanted to hug Kat first but missed out when Rex grabbed her. Then Nora. Then Tia. Then everyone else on the planet. My heart swelled with joy as I watched the giddy expression on my best friend's face. Oh, the things I wanted to tell her! How had she kept this from me? We never had secrets. Never!

Then again, some things were meant to be between husband and wife. That was the point, wasn't it?

The crowd finally cleared, and I gave her a big hug. "I'm so happy for you, I could just scream."

"Join the crowd." She gestured to the cast and crew. "Looks like everyone loves the idea."

"What's not to love?" I paused a moment and whispered, "I'm assuming Lenora already knew?"

"Oh, heavens, yes. She's already hired a decorator for the nursery. She's sure it's going to be a girl."

"But the baby we're writing into the script is a boy, re-member?"

"I know." Kat grinned. "This is just all too funny. Can't wait to see what God does."

"Looks like he's already doing it."

"Yep. Looks like he is."

I lost her to several of the kids, who gathered around her, squealing and chattering about the new addition to the *Stars Collide* clan. Not that my feelings were hurt. She needed some time to share this news with everyone. We were one big happy family, after all.

Thinking of happy families reminded me of Stephen. I searched through the crowd until I found him standing beside Paul. He winked and gave me a little wave, which I returned. I was dying to ask him where this latest bit of news placed Kat and Scott on the plotline of their lives, but I didn't dare.

Only one thing I knew for sure as I observed the joy radi-ating from my best friend's face—if this was what a real-life happily ever after looked like, you could sign me up right now.

14

Bonanza

The three weeks following the filming of the Snidely Whip-lash episode were filled with great moments on every front. Stephen and I grew closer by the day. At some point I stopped asking where we were at on the plotline because I didn't want to know. As long as our days were filled with sunshine and rainbows, why should I care what potential catastrophes might lie around the bend? Wasn't this what the life of faith was all about, anyway? Mountains and valleys? Not knowing about tomorrow, but resting easy in today?

My relationship with Brooke turned out to be one of the sweetest gifts I could have imagined. She became a regular fixture at the Pappas household, helping Mama with the little ones on several occasions, and hanging out with Trina and Mary on a regular basis. A couple times she opted for an overnight stay with me just so we could be together. Getting to know and love her was the highlight of the autumn season. Next to falling for her dad, anyway. Nothing could top those sweet kisses he and I shared when no one else was around. Not that we had a lot of time to ourselves. Still, I treasured every precious moment.

The craziest thing that happened during those three weeks? We all—horror of horrors—fell in love with Zeus. That mangy mongrel weaseled his way into our hearts, winning us over with his slobbery kisses. How dare he worm his way into our family! I could hardly believe it. I almost found myself regretting the fact that we'd sent him to live with Stephen and Brooke. Almost. He was as much a part of our family as they were.

Other things stirred during those weeks too. I'd never seen my best friend so happy, or so fulfilled. Every day I watched as Kat bubbled with anticipation over her little bundle of joy. Already Tia, Jana, Nora, and I were planning a baby shower. Not for several months, of course, but when it happened, it would be the best ever.

Hmm. Better not tell Stephen. He'd probably try to script it.

All in all, life was pretty great. And in my current frame of mind, I could only guess that things would continue to get better and better, both in my personal life and in my professional life.

On the night the Snidely Whiplash episode aired, I joined my family—along with Stephen, Brooke, Mary, Trina, Milo, and Aunt Melina—in my living room. Mama made popcorn and we gathered around the TV. I hadn't really done a big buildup for the episode, so no one else knew this one was any different from the rest, but I knew it had special pizzazz. Time would tell if they agreed. Babbas usually had a pretty good eye for comedy. He would let me know if it worked.

My suspicions were confirmed as the show progressed. I'd never heard so much laughter in all my life. What a gift for a writer—to see people actually enjoying her work. Every time I looked at my father, he had tears in his eyes from laughing so hard. And at one point Aunt Melina had to excuse herself to go to the restroom because she'd laughed until her weak bladder gave out.

I had to conclude, everything about the episode worked. Every line. Every nuance. Every bit of slapstick. Everything. I had that rare sense that writers get, say, once in a lifetime when a miracle occurs. And I did not take it for granted. Indeed, as the show came to a conclusion, I found myself overwhelmed with sadness that it had ended. I rarely got that feeling anymore.

As the closing credits rolled, Mama looked my way, hands clasped together at her chest. "Oh, Athena, you've outdone yourself. It was brilliant."

"Thanks. I loved hearing you laugh. But remember, I didn't write it alone. Stephen and Paul and I worked together. We're the Three Musketeers."

"Well, the Musketeers need to keep on writing together," my father said, "because that was sheer brilliance. I can't remember laughing that much in years."

"We had fun," Stephen said. "I wasn't so sure it was going to work at first, but Athena's persistence paid off. She was right all along, and I'm man enough to admit it."

"Thank you." I kissed him on the cheek and released a sigh of satisfaction.

"A good man always knows when to let his woman take the credit," my father said. "You're a smart guy, Stephen."

"Thank you." He grinned.

"That was by far the funniest episode I've ever watched." Aunt Melina grabbed her sides. "I ache from laughing so hard. And I thought I was going to have to change my clothes a couple of times there." She giggled and Milo joined her, the two of them turning red in the face.

"It was great," Brooke said. "I loved that part where the bad guy tied her to the tracks and then Dudley Do-Right came and rescued her. So romantic."

"We based it on an old cartoon," I explained. "It's pretty cliché, but that's what makes it work. Sometimes cliché is okay."

"You made a rhyme." Brooke laughed. "'Cliché is okay.'"

"Yeah, I guess I did."

We continued laughing and talking about the episode, everyone chiming in about their favorite parts. In fact, we laughed so loud that I almost missed hearing my cell phone ring. I caught it right before it went to voice mail.

"Hello?"

"Athena, my phone is ringing off the wall." Rex's voice rang out in an overly cheerful tone.

"Oh?" *I hope that's a good thing.*

"Network executives want to call a meeting first thing in the morning. How early can you be at the studio? Seven thirty? I need to give them an answer."

"Oh no. Are they . . . unhappy?"

"Unhappy? No way. They said this was the best episode all season. And apparently a new sponsor is thinking about linking arms with us, which is always good. Executives just want to pat you guys on the back and talk about what's coming next."

"Awesome. Should I tell Stephen and Paul to come too?"

"No, that's not necessary. These guys know you're the head writer and they want to give you the respect you're due in a situation like this. So just you this time, okay? I think it's for the best."

"Okay, you've got it. See you in the morning."

I thought about his words as I climbed into bed that night, and even dreamed about them. I could hardly wait to hold my head up high as I met with network executives the next morning.

And that's just what I did. Dressed in my most professional attire, I entered Rex's office at 7:25. At 7:30 sharp, three network executives made their entrance, dressed in business suits. Well, the guys, anyway. The woman—a forty-something with pristine makeup and hair—wore the female version of a business suit in a rather bland shade of gray.

I had that usual tight feeling in my throat as we all took our seats. Kind of reminded me of that one time I'd been called into the principal's office as a child. In that case, I hadn't been in trouble at all. I'd been called in to receive an award for best student of the day. Hopefully today things would go just as well.

The next half hour was spent tossing compliments back and forth. Turned out Ms. Kearney, network exec, was a fan. A huge fan. I counted approximately twenty times she used the words, "I just loved it." And I'd never met anyone with a brighter smile.

By the end of our time together, we were all best friends. In fact, Ms. Kearney told me to call her Gail. So I did.

"I can't tell you how excited we are about the prospects for the rest of the season," Gail said. "I can hardly wait. After last night, I know the viewers are going to respond positively."

"Really?" I shook my head. "Who would have guessed something as simple as tying a woman to train tracks would resonate with viewers?"

"People love physical comedy. Slapstick is rarely done these days because people are afraid of it, but there's still a place for it in the twenty-first century. Clearly. That episode was all the proof we ever needed."

"Looks like it."

"There's nothing better than being innovative, and that's what that episode was. It was one of those rare ones that people will genuinely remember forever."

Oh boy, did I hope she was right. I could almost envision

people thirty years from now talking about the episode in the same way Bob and Paul and I always talked about the old *Dick Van Dyke* episodes. Did my words really have that kind of power?

The thought of it suddenly overwhelmed me. If my positive, funny words had power, I also had to believe that my not-so-great words had power too. Ouch.

At 8:15 Gail and I walked out of the room, laughing and talking all the way. Rex and the others lagged behind to chat. As I rounded the corner, I ran headlong into my mother. *My mother?*

My heart raced as I tried to imagine what had brought her here. "Mama? Is something wrong?"

"No, honey. Everything's fine. Brooke and I were headed out on a shopping spree and decided to stop by."

"Shopping spree? On a school day?" I asked.

"It's a teachers' in-service day," Brooke said. "Perfect day to shop. Nona Pappas said she would help me pick out some new jeans."

Nona Pappas?

"She needs my help with a few other things too." Mama gave me a wink. "Some things just need a woman's touch."

"I see."

At my feet, I heard the strangest sound. Was that . . . panting? I glanced down, horrified when my gaze fell on Zeus. "Mama, what in the world?"

She dismissed me with a wave of her hand. "Don't fret, honey. He's not staying. We were just on our way to drop him off at the doggy day care when Brooke remembered that she had her father's cell phone. We're only here for a minute, to drop it off."

I looked down at the dog crate. "You brought Zeus inside?"

"Brooke thought her dad would like to see him. Besides, he's such a sweet little dog," my mother said. "I couldn't bear it if something happened to him in the car."

Yep. Zeus had definitely weaseled his way into the family.

Thankfully, Ms. Kearney—Gail—didn't seem terribly shaken when she saw the panting canine. She glanced inside the crate. "Oh, what a cute dog. What breed?"

"A Greek Domestic Dog," I explained.

"Never heard of it."

"He traveled all the way from Athens to live with us," Mama explained. "His name is Zeus. It's quite a story, actually." She dove into the twisted tale, telling all about Mean-Athena.

Gail looked my way with a crooked smile. "Interesting story here, Athena. Maybe you could use some of that as fodder for an upcoming episode."

"Could be." I forced a smile, wondering how in the world I could work my dead aunt into an upcoming episode of *Stars Collide.*

From the crate, Zeus began to cry. "Oh, poor little guy." Gail knelt down beside him. "Are you lonely in there?" The dog's cries grew louder. He knew a sucker when he saw one, and Gail had s-u-c-k-e-r written all over her.

"Just ignore him," I said. "He's trying to get attention."

"Well, it's working." Gail reached over and unfastened the latch on the crate.

"No, no, no, no, no." Reaching toward the door, I did my best to slam it shut. "If he gets out—" I never had a chance to finish. Before I could complete the sentence, Zeus went barreling across the studio. He paused at the camera to lift his leg. "No!" I ran his way, but he took off just as I came closer, this time heading for the dressing rooms.

"I'm so sorry," Gail called out. "I didn't think he'd run away."

"Good news is, he can't get out," I said, still chasing after the dog. "Bad news is, if Rex hears about this, I'm out of a job."

"If Rex hears about what?"

I turned in slow motion, my heart gravitating to my throat. "Um, well, see . . ."

"If I find out there's a mangy mutt eating Tia's copy of this week's script?" He pointed to our director's chair. Zeus had made himself at home and was currently consuming several pages of script at once. *No way. Oh, you awful dog!*

"Give me that," I cried, yanking the script out of his mouth. "We worked long and hard on that."

"Athena?" Rex looked at me with panic in his eyes. "Would you mind explaining what in the world is happening here? Tell me I'm seeing things, that there's not really a dog in the studio."

"You're seeing things." I plastered on a tight smile. "There's no dog in the studio."

"Good attempt, but I still see him. He's eating the legs off the sofa."

"Ack!" I scrambled to snag the mutt, but he shot between my arms and ran onto the set, making himself at home on one of the wingback chairs. At this point, the network executives got involved. One of them—the older of the two men—reached out to grab Zeus, only to have the ornery mongrel snap at him. Yikes!

Zeus jumped from the chair and ran across the set, pausing to chew on a couple of wires. Heaven help me. Hopefully the building wouldn't go up in flames. As I chugged along behind him, I heard Rex's voice behind me.

"Keep him away from Lenora, whatever you do. She's got Fat Cat with her today."

I groaned. Lenora rarely brought her finicky feline to rehearsal anymore. Why today of all days?

Seconds later I was running down the hall, chasing Zeus. He made it as far as the hair and makeup room, where he turned and made a loud—and overly dramatic—entrance.

I'd almost caught him . . . almost . . . when he spied the cat in Lenora's arms.

Fat Cat took to hissing, then sprang through the air toward Zeus, his claws fully extended. What happened next left a lasting impression in my memory bank. The dog, never one to cower, tucked his tail between his legs and began to creep backward. Backward. I could hardly believe it.

"Well, there you go," I said. "The hairy beast is tamed by a lowly cat."

"There's nothing lowly about my cat." Lenora hunched over to scoop up the feline. Fat Cat continued to hiss until she offered him a bite of a cinnamon roll. "There you go, sweet baby. Don't let that mean old dog bother you."

The mean old dog—as it were—continued to creep backward, likely still scared by the mean old cat. I saw Stephen approaching from a distance. He took one look at Zeus, then looked at me, eyes growing wide. Putting his finger over his lips, he motioned for me not to say a word. I didn't. Instead, I watched in silence as he snuck up behind Zeus, grabbing him at just the right moment. Perfect. I breathed a sigh of relief.

Stephen's eyebrows elevated, and his voice went up an octave or two as he quoted one of my favorite movie lines: "I'll get you, my pretty, and your little dog too!"

Lenora looked over from her chair. "Oh, I know that one! *The Wizard of Oz.* Margaret Hamilton. 1939."

Stephen just shook his head and continued to clutch the dog, which squirmed in his arms. "You brought Zeus to the studio?" He looked at me with that "I don't quite believe it" expression on his face. "Seriously?"

"No. Mama and Brooke brought him. I just ended up with him somehow. Not my choosing, trust me."

"Brooke is here?" His face lit into a smile.

"Yes. You left your cell phone at home. She brought it to you."

"Ah. And we got a dog in the mix?"

"We did. One with lots of energy."

"It's all that expensive food I've been feeding him," Stephen said. "That stuff is loaded with vitamins and minerals."

"Of course it is."

I followed him into the studio, where he put the dog back in the crate and then swept his daughter into his arms to thank her for saving his neck by bringing the phone.

"I've been waiting on a couple of calls from my agent," he said. "Hope I didn't miss them."

He slipped Brooke some extra money for shopping, and she and my mama left with smiles on their faces. Thankfully, they took Zeus with them. And though I looked forward to my day at work, I envied them a little. What would it be like to spend the day helping Brooke shop for clothes?

Stephen and I made our way to the writing room, where we found Paul lying on the floor on his back, talking on his cell phone. The minute he saw us, he sat straight up, looking like a kid who'd been caught with his hand in the cookie jar. Odd. He ended the call, then reached for his laptop.

"Thought you guys would never get here."

"We're here," I said. "But it's been quite a morning." I filled him in, sharing the details of the dog story. By the end of it, Paul was laughing. "Crazy mutt. Hope he doesn't get you fired."

"Nah. Rex seemed to take it all in stride." I smiled. "Seems like everyone these days is on my side. Besides, he's a good dog. He really is."

Paul did not look convinced. "Are we talking about the same dog that stole my wallet the night we stayed at your parents' place?"

"That's the one."

"That dog makes me laugh," Stephen said. "Taking him in was one of the best decisions I've ever made. He's been a saving grace for Brooke. For me too, actually."

His words filled me with joy. And relief. "I'm so glad. I honestly think God brought that dog all the way from Greece to bring us together. Funny how a canine can do that."

"Oh, he still gets me riled up a lot too," Stephen said. "You should see what he did with the toilet paper he found in the bottom cabinet in my master bathroom. Covered my bedroom in four rolls of the stuff. Looked like it had been snowing in there." He paused. "But still, dogs will be dogs."

"And hey, he's Greek," I added. "You know that Greeks have a certain inborn temperament."

"True." He nodded. "Greeks *do* have a certain inborn temperament that's rather unique. And it's not just limited to dogs." He wiggled his eyebrows and we both laughed.

Strangely, Paul didn't join in. He didn't really seem like himself today. In fact, he spent the next several minutes checking messages on his cell phone and avoiding any and all probing questions.

Oh well. There would be plenty of time to quiz him later. Right now we had a new episode to write. Hopefully it would live up to the heightened expectations of our producer and network executives. If not . . . well, I didn't want to think about the "if nots." Just one more advantage to being at Step 9 on the plotline. I could simply relax and enjoy the ride.

15

Who Wants to Be a Millionaire?

The next several weeks sailed by. After the "Angie's Having a Baby" episode aired, the phones went crazy. Turned out the show's viewers were ecstatic at the news of the baby's impending arrival. And they particularly loved the whole *I Love Lucy* approach to sharing the news. George Lopez's performance as Ricky Ricardo had taken the cake. If things got any better, I might have to throw myself a party.

Turned out someone else took care of that for me.

On a Saturday morning in early December my mother's voice roused me from my slumber.

"Athena! Athena, come here!"

I rubbed the sleep from my eyes, tried to gather my thoughts, and ran into my parents' room, worried the house was on fire. Instead, I found my mother curled up in bed with her laptop.

"Mama? What's happened?"

"They've listed the Golden Globe nominees." She pointed to the computer. "It just posted to the site a few minutes ago."

"Oh?" My excitement grew. Kat must've been nominated again. Or Scott. Regardless, our ratings would go up the minute word got out that someone had received a nomination.

"Athena-bean, look." My father scrolled down, his finger landing on something that caught me totally by surprise. "*Stars Collide* has been nominated for Best Television Series for a Comedy or Musical."

"No way." My heart began thumping so hard I thought I might faint. "Seriously?"

"Yes, it's true. Look here." Mama pointed to the spot on the screen where the show was listed. What joy! I couldn't wait to tell Kat.

Oh, Kat. I scrolled the list until I saw her name listed under Best Performance by an Actress in a Television Series. *She did it! She's been nominated too!*

Grabbing my cell phone was the first order of business. Kat answered with a squeal. "I know, I know! Congratulations, Athena! I'm so happy for you!"

"And I'm so happy for you. This is the best season for *Stars Collide* ever."

"I knew it would be. The writing has been brilliant."

"Thank you. I feel like I'm dreaming this." After an exaggerated yawn, I laughed. "Maybe I am. Mama woke me from a dead sleep to share this news."

"You're not dreaming. The show has been nominated for a Golden Globe. And we're going to win too. I know it."

On and on she went, singing my praises as a writer and giving me full credit for the show's success. I'd never been one to have an overinflated ego, but her generous words in the next several minutes almost sent me over the top. *Guard your heart, Athena. Otherwise you might begin to believe your own press.*

I vowed to keep things in perspective.

Right after I called Stephen.

He didn't answer, so I left a "Call me as quick as you can!" message. Sadly, the phone didn't ring for the rest of the day. I had to wonder why. I tried to reach him that night before bed and got his voice mail again. I thought about sending a text to Brooke but decided it was too late. She was probably sleeping. Oh well. I could share my happy news with Stephen tomorrow. We had plenty of time to celebrate. We also needed to keep up the good work by further developing our writing skills. There were plenty more episodes to be written. Maybe I could stand to take a class or two. Brush up on a few things.

On Monday morning I arrived at the studio early to find everyone buzzing about the nominations. There were high-fives happening all over the place. Rex approached and opened his arms for an embrace.

"I'm so proud of you, Athena. All of you. I knew that episode was great, and I'm glad to hear that others agree."

"Thank you." I looked around. "Have you seen Stephen?"

"Not yet. I know he had some sort of meeting yesterday, though, because we were supposed to meet for dinner and he had to cancel. He's been pretty busy, I think."

"Ah." Well, that explained why he hadn't returned my call. Still, it was a little strange that he hadn't told me about his meeting. Not that we shared every intimate detail of our lives with each other, but it did feel odd. We were a couple, after all.

Kat stopped me for a hug. So did Tia. The three of us stood together, squealing like a trio of preteen girls. Off in the distance, Jason rolled his eyes at all the noise.

After celebrating with the ladies, I walked down the hallway toward our office, my heart so full I wanted to burst into a song-and-dance number. I arrived to find Paul inside, lying on the floor. Poor guy.

"Back hurting again?" I asked.

"Nah. Just thinking." He looked up at me with a woeful expression. "Turns out this is a good position for clearing my head."

"What are you thinking about?"

"My date tonight."

I stepped inside the room and pulled the door shut behind me. "You're going out on a date? I thought you'd sworn off women."

"It's not a woman. It's my ex-wife."

I fought the temptation to ask, "Which one?"

"Sylvia's back in town and wants to talk to me about something." He shrugged. "Could be something big. I dunno. I don't really want to go, but I feel like I should for some reason."

"Maybe she wants to give you back that dog she got custody of," I said.

"Nah, she can keep the dog. She got the house and the car. Might as well keep the dog too. I can't afford the vet bills. It's one of those goofy little toy poodles. Has all sorts of health issues. Some months we spent more on the vet bills than we did for our own medical stuff."

"Wow. Well, you'll have to keep me posted." *Or not. I guess it's not really my business.*

Paul swung his legs around and sat up, leaning against the wall. "So, did you happen to see the headlines in the entertainment section of today's paper?"

"No. What headlines?"

He tossed a copy of the newspaper my way. "Check it out. You might want to sit down first, though."

I opened the newspaper, thumbing through it until I came to the entertainment section. "Oh, cool. They did a piece about our show." I smiled as I skimmed the article, which talked about the Golden Globe nomination and the episode leading up to it. "Looks like everyone got a kick out of it. They're glad we've added the pregnancy this season, and they think the whole Snidely Whiplash shtick was clever. That's good."

"Remind me again whose idea that was?" Paul said, his expression tight.

"You and I came up with it." I shrugged. "Right?"

"Right." He gave me a pensive look. "Keep reading."

I did. When I got to the paragraph where the article credited Stephen Cosse with the writing of the now infamous episode—no mention of any other names—my heart hit the floor. Well, it felt like it did. I must've read it wrong.

"It's got to be some sort of misunderstanding. He would never take the credit for an idea he didn't come up with."

"How do you know?"

"Because I know him."

"Yeah, you know him all right." Paul rolled his eyes.

"I would think very carefully about what you're about to say," I suggested. "Because I have a strong suspicion your words are going to paint you into a corner, and it's going to be hard to get back out again."

He never flinched. "Let's just say that not everyone is who they present themselves to be."

Yep. Learned that with my former fiancé. And your point is . . . ?

"Read the rest, Athena. You'll see."

I glanced back down, picking up where I'd left off. Most of what I read seemed benign . . . until I got to a quote from Stephen. "Heading up the writing team is a blast. Can't remember when I've ever had so much fun at work."

My emotions almost got the better of me as I read and reread the lines. The Stephen I knew would never have put himself in the limelight, leaving the rest of us behind. This had to be some sort of mistake. I folded the paper and set it on the desk. Out of sight, out of mind.

"Now you see my problem," Paul said. "We've been work-ing with someone we thought we could trust. Turns out he's more like everyone else in Hollywood than he claimed to be. So much for that boy-next-door persona, right? He's been out to put a knife in our backs all along. Makes me sick to think he was just using us."

"I don't want to jump to conclusions, Paul."

"You don't have to. That article did it for you."

"There's got to be a reason. He was misquoted, maybe. Something."

"I just know it doesn't settle well with me. We were nomi-nated for a Golden Globe. A Golden Globe, Athena. We should be celebrating. Instead, we're talking about someone else taking the credit for our work. That's not right. You have to see that."

"I see what it looks like. But sometimes what we think we see isn't always what's there."

He rolled his eyes. "You're too naive. Always willing to trust, even when it's not reasonable."

At this point, I couldn't really tell what was reasonable and what wasn't. I only knew in my heart of hearts that Stephen couldn't possibly have taken the credit for something he didn't do. No way. Not that he hadn't played a role in writing that episode. Part of the credit was his, naturally. But not all. And he knew that.

I thought about all of this as Paul and I turned back to our work. When Stephen entered the room a few minutes later, I wanted to come right out and ask him, but I didn't dare, not with Paul present.

"Hey, Athena." A broad smile lit Stephen's face. "I've been trying to reach you." He pulled me into a warm embrace. "I'm so proud of you. And so happy about the Golden Globe nomination. Isn't it the best news ever?"

"Yeah. It's great news." I took a breath and contemplated

my next words. "I hear that your HBO special was nominated too. Congratulations."

Paul grunted. Well, maybe he grunted. Maybe he cleared his throat. I couldn't really tell for sure.

"Thanks." Stephen walked over to the divan and put his laptop down on the coffee table. "I was in a meeting last night with my agent. He wants me to play up the double nomination. We're trying to figure out how to take advantage of this opportunity."

"Looks like you already have," Paul said.

Stephen gave him a curious look. "What do you mean?"

I handed him the paper. "You did an interview with a reporter about the episode we wrote?"

"I did?" He looked stupefied. "Unless they interviewed me in my sleep, no. What did they say about me?"

"Just read it."

I looked on as his eyes skimmed the page. When he got to the halfway point in the article, Stephen looked up. "This is crazy. I never said this."

Paul coughed.

"No, really. I didn't say a word of this. Doesn't even sound like me. Can't you tell?"

"I don't know you well enough to tell," Paul said. "Are we supposed to believe some reporter just randomly came up with a quote from you?"

Stephen shook his head. "I have a feeling I know what happened. I'm sure my agent is behind this. But I can promise you, I had nothing to do with it. I would never do anything like this to you two."

"I need to get out of here before I say something I'm going to regret." Paul grabbed his coffee cup and swung the door open. He turned back for a moment. "Do you remember the 'Bupkis' episode from *The Dick Van Dyke Show*?"

"Wasn't that the one where Rob coauthored a song with a friend, then the song became a big hit?" I asked.

"Yes." Paul stared at Stephen. "Rob didn't get any credit for writing it, but his friend did."

Ouch. You had to go there.

"I've also been thinking about that episode where Laura wanted to write a children's story, then Rob rewrote it and made it his own. He took her heart and soul out of it." He shook his head, muttered, "I need to go clear my head," then disappeared down the hallway.

Stephen looked my way, his shoulders slumped forward. "Athena, you don't really think I would do something like that to you, do you? Take the credit, I mean."

"No. I know you better than that. It just stinks, that's all."

"Of course it does. And I'm going to make it right. I'll make sure they reprint the story. In the meantime, you've got to give me the benefit of the doubt."

I felt a lump in my throat but managed to speak above it. "Of course I will. This just takes a little bit of the joy out of our news."

"Don't let it. Please."

"It's hard enough being female in this industry, but to have a male writer get all of the credit when I'm the show's head writer . . . it just stinks." I trembled, in part because I felt tears coming on. "You'll never know how tough it is for me, and this just makes it tougher. I know you didn't cause this, but you have to see it's like a slap in the face."

"I'm so sorry, Athena. Of course I know how hard it is for you," he said. "Women have to work twice as hard to get half the acknowledgment in this industry. I know that. And I can only imagine how this must make you feel." He tried to draw me into his arms, but I wasn't having it. Not right now.

"This just reinforces the misperception that female writers aren't funny," I said with a shrug. "Otherwise why would a male writer be singled out over a female as the author of the funniest episode?"

"If that's the perception, then people don't know you. If they did, they'd know that you're a laugh a minute."

I bit back the tears to speak my heart. "I'm not laughing right now."

"Is it hot in here?" He tugged at his collar, then walked over to check the thermostat. "Feels like it's ninety degrees."

It was hot in here, all right, and getting hotter by the moment. "I get it that men have led the way in the industry. And I realize that most sitcom writers are males in their twenties and thirties."

"This is a male-dominated industry," he said. "You can't expect perceptions to change overnight. That's probably why that reporter assumed I wrote the funny episode, Athena. Because he's biased. He made an assumption."

"This whole conversation is ridiculous. This is the twenty-first century. Women have come a long way, baby."

"With a long way yet to go." He shrugged. "Look, I'm not saying I agree with the perceptions. I feel your pain. I knew a lot of comediennes back in Vegas who fought to get noticed. Always felt a little sorry for them because the guys seemed to have it so much easier. I'm not saying it's fair. I'm just saying that's how it is."

I found it hard to be angry with him when his beautiful brown eyes gazed at me with such tenderness. After a moment, he gestured for me to sit on the divan. I reluctantly took the place next to him.

"You want to pattern everything after *The Dick Van Dyke Show*, right?"

"Well, it was just an idea to arrange the office—"

"No, I get all that. And I was an idiot to change the room around. I've regretted it ever since."

Wow. Felt good to hear him acknowledge that.

"I just want you to think about that show for a minute, since it's apparently one of your favorites. Three comedy writers sitting in an office, cranking out jokes for *The Alan Brady Show*."

"Right."

"Rob, the brains, Buddy, the clown, and Sally, the one who typed the scripts and occasionally came up with an idea that they ended up tossing. Do you see now what I meant about perceptions between the sexes? It's been this way all along."

Ouch.

"Again, I'm not saying that's what I believe. I'm only saying that's how women have been perceived. Sally's role in that show was to act as a buffer between Rob and Buddy, and to bring an occasional bit of drama with her off-scene romance with nerdy Herman Glimscher. She was never meant to be the driving force of the team."

Okay, now I really wanted to punch him.

"You might as well relax," Stephen said. "I'm going to clarify what I mean in a second. And none of this is meant to be personal."

"Well, it feels personal."

"I'm on your team, Athena." He reached out and put his hand on my arm. I shrugged it off. "The only reason I'm telling you any of this is because I think you're better than all of us. You're better than Bob, you're better than Paul, and you're light-years above me. You're the best comedy writer I've ever met, and I'm not just saying that because my heart is involved."

Okay, well, those words softened me a little. So did the concern in his eyes. This time when he reached to touch me, I didn't pull away.

"Athena, it kills me to see you have to work so hard to get noticed. It also kills me that people make assumptions that leave you feeling wounded. I wish I could change that. I'm working to change that."

My heart—crusted over just seconds before—began to melt.

"These false perceptions about women in the industry are like a wall that needs to come down. You can speak to that mountain, and it's going to topple."

Only one problem—right now I didn't feel like speaking to any mountains. I just felt like going home and crawling under the covers.

"I think it's better if we change the subject," I said at last. "Honestly? I think I just need time to absorb everything that's happened."

Stephen moved to the chair behind the desk and leaned his head down. After a few seconds of silence, he looked up, his eyes locking with mine. "I can't believe all of this has happened right now, when we should be celebrating our nomination. You know what this means, don't you, Athena?"

"No, I have no idea."

He sighed. "We've just skipped Step 10 and have moved directly to Step 11 in the plotline of our relationship."

Ugh. Tell me you did not just say that.

"I'm afraid you're going to have to fill me in, Mr. Plotter. I'm a seat-of-the-pants kind of girl, remember?" Okay, my words sounded a little snippy. Still, I couldn't help myself. How dare he interrupt such a tense conversation to talk about writing? What was I, some sort of homework assignment?

"Step 11 is the 'Ultimate Test,'" Stephen explained. "This is where we see if we've got the goods."

"I see. So this step determines if we're going to make it?"

"According to the class I took." He raked his fingers through his hair. "It's a natural part of the progression of the relationship. The big gloom. The supreme ordeal. Whatever you want to call it. That point in every story where it looks like things can't possibly work out. That's where we are, isn't it?" He smiled. "Helps to see it in perspective, right? Besides, this is where we find out what we're made of."

"I can tell you what I'm made of. Jell-O."

"Jell-O?"

"Yes. That's what my insides feel like right now. Jell-O. So there's no point in thinking I'm going to have some terrific rebound and prove that I've got the goods—as a character in some script you're writing, or in real life. I'm just a girl. A girl with issues. I get jealous and I get angry. And right now I'm a little of both."

"There's no point in being jealous. I'm getting attention from the media, but it's undeserved."

"That's the part that has me a little angry." I sighed. "But being angry is unreasonable, so I'm also a little angry at myself for getting angry. Does that make sense? I should have a better handle on things. I need to get control of my emotions."

"There's another step on the plotline for that," he said. "Where the hero or heroine faces his or her inevitable flaws and challenges."

"Stephen." I put my hand up. "I appreciate the fact that you've studied this whole plotting thing. Seriously. It's good to know how to lay out a story. And maybe it's helpful for you to point out where I am in my journey. But some things can't be plotted. I have a feeling I'm off the plotline altogether, the way I'm feeling right now. So enough with that already. Give it a rest."

His expression shifted to one of regret. "Sorry. I'm on a learning curve here, so this whole thing about plotting is just for my sake. Maybe I'm taking it all too literally."

"I hate to be a plotting party pooper, but I'm getting a little tired of trying to figure out where I am and where I'm going. Can't we just say that we've hit a major bump in the road and leave it at that?"

"I'm going to smooth out this bump. I promise. My agent's going to own up to what he's done, and that story will be rewritten. We're going to get past this. The hero and heroine always get past the hurdles if they're meant to be together."

If they're meant to be together? How should I take those words?

I squared my shoulders, ready to put this behind me. "It's fine. Really. I'm probably just being overly sensitive. I am a woman, you know. And women are emotional beings. Right?"

"I never said that."

"No, your agent said it for you . . . not in so many words." I pulled the laptop onto my knees. "Anyway, we have a lot of work to do, so we'd better get to it. Should we wait for Paul or just dive right in?"

"I need to leave a little early today, so we'd better get to it."

"Leave early?"

"Yeah. I . . . well, I've got an appointment this afternoon."

I didn't ask what kind of appointment, though curiosity almost got the better of me. If I didn't watch myself, several things might get the better of me today.

All the more reason to take my hands off and just let God be God.

16

Get Smart

The next couple of days were tense at best. Paul came and went from the office, acting more than a little suspicious. I was dying to ask him about his date with his ex-wife but didn't dare. I knew he wouldn't want to share anything so personal with Stephen in the mix. Likely he wouldn't feel like sharing something so personal even with me in the room. The guy had always been private.

And speaking of private, Stephen's actions left me feeling unsettled. On Wednesday we faced another dispute, this one related to the show. It came in the middle of fine-tuning the following week's episode.

"I just feel we need to think outside the box," he said. "We've given Angie and Jack a lot of conflict, but nothing with any lasting consequences."

"Consequences?" Paul shook his head. "What are you thinking?"

"I'm thinking they need to be put to the ultimate test—something that would challenge both their marriage and their business."

"What sort of challenge?" I asked.

"Someone they love and trust—either the kids or the seniors they represent—could abandon them. Leave them in the lurch. Maybe they could actually lose the talent agency. Maybe they would have to start over."

"Lose the talent agency?" Paul groaned. "Are you kidding?"

His idea floored me, and not in a good way. "That talent agency is the foundation for the show. If we take it away—"

"I'm not talking about taking it away. Just saying we should spend an episode or two exploring the what-ifs. What if Jack and Angie lost everything they thought they needed to survive? Then what?" He paused. "That's life, you know. We put all of our energies into something, and sometimes that very something crumbles around us."

"This is a comedy," I reminded him. "We're going too deep. This isn't a nighttime drama. It's a *sitcom*. Situational comedy."

"It's all a matter of how we handle it." When Stephen turned to me, I saw tears in his eyes. "The lines between comedy and tragedy get blurred sometimes. Relationships get tested. And if we take them to the valley in their relationship, the only place to go is up. In other words, the resolution is on its way."

Funny. Right now it didn't feel like the resolution was on its way. It just felt like my loaf of bread was unbaking. If such a thing were possible.

I thought about a conversation I'd had with Kat about mountains and valleys. The deeper the valley, the higher the mountain. That was the theory, anyway. Maybe I needed to go through a few valleys to appreciate the mountaintops.

Or maybe I just needed to go crawl under the covers.

I shrugged off my thoughts and told Stephen we'd talk about it again tomorrow.

Ironically, he didn't show up for work on Thursday. Friday found him absent too. I'd missed a couple of calls from him, but there were no messages on my voice mail. Very odd. He was clearly avoiding me.

Okay, I'd been aloof too. How could I dive back into our relationship with so much hanging over us? Recovering from the article in the newspaper had been tough enough, but other media sources had picked up on it and were all sharing the tale that Stephen had been responsible for the famous episode. Seemed like every time I turned on the television or read a magazine, I heard the story again. By Friday the media sources were singing Stephen's praises as if he'd been the head writer of the show for years. Go figure.

As I struggled to know how to deal with all of this, I found myself reminded of that stupid twelve-step plotter. If we were really on Step 11, as Stephen said, there was only one step to go—the resolution. I knew from my years of writing comedy that the resolution was always the best part. Happily ever afters came during this final stage.

Only one problem with this theory—then what happened? Once we resolved our problems and forged ahead—if, indeed, that's what happened—then what? Did the whole crazy twelve-step thing start over again? If we got married, did we go back to Step 1? I wasn't sure I could take it, to be quite honest. Felt too much like a merry-go-round.

On Friday afternoon I ate my lunch alone in the office. The others were out in the studio, wrapping up the filming of this week's episode. I could hear the roar of the audience through the sound system. Obviously they were enjoying themselves. If only I could have said as much for myself. No, with the way I felt right now, spending the afternoon alone was for the best. I didn't want anyone to try to talk me out of my doldrums.

After the filming, Kat showed up. "You busy?" she asked.

"Not really." I gestured to the empty office. "Just going over a few notes."

"Missed you at the filming today. Everything okay?"

"Yeah." I shrugged. "Just needed some time to myself. Didn't want to be around people."

"I see." Her brow wrinkled. "Where are the guys?"

"Paul is acting strange, and Stephen . . ." I shrugged. "He's off, being famous."

"Being famous?" She took a seat on the divan. "Do I detect a hint of jealousy?"

"I'm not sure *jealousy* is the right word. I'm just confused. Or maybe *conflicted* would be a better way to say it. It's complicated."

"Care to elaborate?" She reached for one of my sweets and popped it into her mouth. "Mmm. This is great. I still say you're the best baker I've ever met, Athena."

"Keep that in mind when I open my bakery."

"You're opening a bakery?"

"It was just an idea I once had. I thought maybe it could be a backup plan if I ever lost my job here."

"Wait." She paused and stared at me with wide eyes. "Are you serious? You think they're going to let you go? We were just nominated for a Golden Globe."

I rolled my eyes. "Apparently you don't read the paper. According to Stephen's agent, I didn't play a role in writing that Snidely Whiplash episode. And maybe now that network executives think that, they won't want to keep me around."

"Of course you helped write it. You wrote most of it, from what Stephen told me. And I don't know why you're suddenly worried about your job. You're under contract. They can't just let you go. Right?"

"They can wiggle their way out of that if they want to."
I sighed. "Do you ever get the feeling you're just not wanted
or needed? Like you're . . . superfluous?"

Okay, that was a dumb question to ask the star of a weekly
sitcom. This whole show revolves around her. Of course she
feels wanted and needed.

When Kat's expression turned sad, I wished I hadn't asked
the question.

"I felt that way for years after my dad left," she said. "Rejec-
tion is a terrible thing to deal with. And it hurts even more if
you don't know why the person is rejecting you. Makes you
question yourself in a thousand different ways. So . . . yes, I
know what it feels like."

Ack. I felt like a heel for stirring up such a tough memory.
Still, she'd struck a nerve. "Lately I feel like I'm not needed
around here. I know why Rex hired Stephen, but I still have
to wonder if everyone thinks I'm . . . well . . . boring."

"You? Boring?" Kat's laughter shattered the near silence in
the room. "Is that some sort of joke? You're crazy and wild
and wacky and tons of fun. Where in the world did you get
the idea that you're boring? You're not boring. Far from it,
in fact."

"Thanks. I needed that."

"Honestly, Athena, I think you question yourself too
much." Kat reached for another pastry. When I gave her a
funny look, she giggled and said, "Hey, I'm eating for two
now, remember?"

"Oh, have as many as you like." I paused to reflect on her
words, then decided to share my heart. "There's this strange
misperception that humor writers are funny people."

"Are you saying you're not?"

"Well, I do think we have an exaggerated sense of humor,
but I guess what I'm trying to say is that we go through rough
patches in our own lives. It's not like we're just sitting around

making a joke out of everything. And we can't perform on demand. We're not court jesters."

"Though you would look great in the costume," she said with a wink.

"I'm just saying that comedy writing is tough work, especially when your personal life doesn't give you much to laugh at. Or about. Ya know?"

Kat gave me a sympathetic look. "I'm sorry, Athena. I always think of you as this happy-go-lucky girl. For as long as I've known you, you've been the one bringing a smile to everyone's face. So seeing you down and upset is throwing me off a little. I don't know what to do with this."

"I am happy-go-lucky most of the time. But coming up with comedy sketches week in and week out is tough. Being funny is hard work."

"I'm going to remember that." She grinned. "Being funny is hard work."

"You're not taking me seriously."

"I am. And honestly, I couldn't do what you do. The world is twisted enough without having to add a punch line." Her eyes narrowed as she stared at me. "But I think there's more to this than you're letting on."

"What do you mean?"

"Well, first of all, I have a theory about Stephen Cosse. Maybe it's one you're not going to like, but hear me out. Okay?"

"Okay."

"I think you're unnerved when you're around him."

"Well, of course I am. In walks this comedian, and my job is suddenly irrelevant."

"I'm not talking about your job here. That's not what I mean. I think you're unnerved for a completely different reason."

"O-oh?"

"I think things between the two of you are getting serious and you're scared."

"Why would I be scared?"

"I don't know, but that's a good question. Why are you scared? Don't you like the idea of your relationship growing and changing into something more?"

"Of course I do. I'm all about change."

"No you're not." She pointed to the room. "You freaked out when he changed the furniture. And your bedroom has been the same since you were seven."

"Hey now, that's not my fault. My mama—"

"Your mom told me that she offered to have the room redecorated years ago, but you turned her down."

Ack. *Mama, you traitor.* "Well, Strawberry Shortcake is coming back in."

"Sure she is." Kat shook her head. "And what about your food habits?"

"My food habits?" The girl had to go messing with my food?

"You're very limited in what you eat. I don't know if you realize it or not, but Greek and Italian . . . that's about it for you. Don't you find that odd? You never eat Mexican. Never eat Chinese. See what I mean?"

I sighed, realizing I'd been caught in her trap. "Okay, I admit it. My life has been the same . . . forever. For as long as I can remember, everything has been the same. I can tell you what every day of the week is going to look like. I bring leftovers on Monday, and we pound out a new idea for the following week's episode. On Tuesday we take our rough draft and fine-tune it. On Wednesday we present a cleaned-up version of the script to Rex and the rest of the crew."

On and on I went, talking about how my week was laid out. "On Saturday I work with Mama and Babbas at the shop and spend time with family. On Sunday we all go to church and have a fantastic meal after, then snooze the afternoon away so that I have the energy to wake up on Monday morning and start the whole process over again. See what I mean? My days are mapped out."

"Plotted." Kat pursed her lips.

"W-what?" Surely she did not just use *that* word.

"You're a creature of habit, Athena-bean. Stephen Cosse has interrupted your habit in more ways than one, and you don't know where things are going. And when you hit a few bumps in the road, you freak out, not because you haven't been through bumps before, but because there's someone else involved now. He's grabbed a piece of your heart."

"I might be a little predictable, but I'm not a creature of habit. Not really," I argued. "And as for him grabbing a piece of my heart . . ." My words drifted off.

She gazed directly into my eyes. "I think you see that things are moving quickly, and you're losing control. You're excited by the change but a little nervous because you're not calling the shots. Did I hit the nail on the head?"

"The only thing I'm concerned about right now is that people will think I'm not doing my job. There's a misperception out there that I'm not the driving force behind this show. Because of that misperception, I could lose my job, which would be totally unfair."

"I'm not sure why this keeps going back to your job. I'm not talking about your job. But what you just said is wrong, anyway. You're *not* the driving force behind this show." She gave me a pensive look.

"Oh." My shoulders slumped forward. I felt defeated. "I didn't mean that like it sounded. I really didn't. I guess I'm just worried people will think I'm slacking off."

"Why do you worry so much about what people think about you?" she asked.

"Don't you?" I shook my head. "C'mon, Kat. It's impossible not to worry about that. We live in Hollywood. We work in Hollywood. Everything is about perceptions."

"The only perception that matters is God's. And right now I have a feeling he's working out something inside of you that you're not even aware of. Of course, that's all mixed up with your growing feelings for Stephen and the fact that your life as a single woman could be coming to an end." She grinned. "Honestly? I think you're hearing wedding bells."

"Wedding bells?"

"Mm-hmm. And you didn't pencil them in, at least not while your career was in full bloom."

"How did we make the jump from my internal fears to weddings?"

"I can't remember," she said. "But just so you're aware, when you and Stephen get married, the Strawberry Shortcake sheets have to go."

If I'd had a script in my hand, I would have smacked her with it. Instead, I fought the heat that rose to my cheeks. The very thought of Stephen Cosse climbing into my bed if we got married . . . Hmm.

Didn't scare me as much as I thought it would.

Though the image of the Strawberry Shortcake sheets did throw me a little.

Okay, maybe I *was* hearing wedding bells. And maybe the idea that I could actually marry and have a life outside of *Stars Collide* scared me to death on a subconscious level. Maybe that's why I cared so much about what network executives thought about me right now, because every other area of my life was shifting. Changing.

Kat rambled on about my love life as if I were paying attention. "Since we're talking about weddings and all, don't forget that you promised I could be a bridesmaid. Not sure how that's going to work, now that I'm married and pregnant."

"Wait, now you're planning my wedding?"

"Someone has to." She rose. "Athena, listen. We're always joking around about you writing the script of my life. But sometimes I think we get so caught up in the play-acting that we forget there's a story going on that's much bigger than any sitcom. And it's not like God's in heaven pushing us around like chess pieces, giving us lines to read from a script. He gives us free will."

"True." I wondered where she was going with this.

"So don't discount the fact that there are multiple stories going on at once here. There's the sitcom stuff, and there's the real-life stuff. Keep them separated as much as you can. And give God room to move. He wants to, you know."

"Right." I rose and gave her a hug. "And I feel like a real heel right now, Kat."

"Why?"

"I haven't asked you how you're feeling. This whole conversation has been about me."

She shrugged. "I'm okay. The morning sickness has been a problem. It's a good thing you weren't on the set when we filmed last week's episode. It was so embarrassing."

"Embarrassing? Why?"

"I had to run off the set in the middle of the scene." She laughed. "It wasn't funny at the time, but I can laugh at it now." She rubbed her palm across her stomach. "This little one will be worth it. He or she will make all of the morning sickness in the world worthwhile. But right now, to be honest, I feel pretty drained, physically and emotionally. I think my hormones are out of whack. And with all of the stuff going on with my grandmother . . ." Kat sighed.

"She's not doing well?" I asked.

Kat shook her head. "Rex took her to the doctor last week. She didn't even realize what sort of doctor it was. Thought they were going to see a dermatologist. Rex didn't tell her any differently. But the doctor said . . ." Her words drifted off. "The disease seems to be progressing more rapidly now. It breaks my heart." Her voice broke, and tears rose to cover her lashes.

I gave her another hug. "I'm praying for her, Kat. And you too. I know she means the world to you."

"She's really been the only mother I've known. Well, since I was seven, anyway. If something happens to her, I don't know what I'll do."

I decided I'd better change the subject. Thank goodness someone else took care of that for me.

The door to the office swung open, startling us both. Paul stepped inside, eating an apple. He spoke around a full mouth. "Did you guys hear the news?"

"What news?"

"Stephen's been offered a job writing for *Saturday Night Live*."

"W-what?" My jaw dropped. "Are you sure?"

"Sure am. They flew him out to New York to meet with the producers. That's why he hasn't been here."

Suddenly my heart felt as heavy as a block of lead. "I don't believe it." So much for the conversation about weddings and happily ever afters. Looked like my Romeo was on his way to the Big Apple.

"You know how I feel about the guy," Paul said. "I've told you before. I do respect his talent, just don't know that we can trust him. Maybe it's going to be better that he's found a different job. Maybe we can get back to the way things were."

Get back to the way things were? I sighed, thinking about the way my life was before Stephen.

"Sure, it's going to be different around here without him, but we'll get used to it." Paul slapped me on the back. "We were a great team before he got here. And besides, Bob will be back soon. Talked to him last night, and they're wrapping up the filming of his movie in a couple of weeks."

Back to Stephen, please. "Are we sure Stephen's really leaving, or is this just some kind of rumor?" I asked.

Paul tossed his apple core in the trash. "Well, it's probably in the rumor stage right now, but Jason and several of the other guys know all about it. Rex told them. I just know that some sort of offer has been made. Stephen must be considering it. I know I would be."

"Not me."

"Oh, c'mon." Paul looked me in the eye. "If someone offered you the job of a lifetime, you'd take it. Right?"

"Even if it was across the country?" Kat shook her head. "You'd better believe she wouldn't. Athena is staying put."

I shrugged. "I don't know, I'm such a family girl. No running here. I like to stay put. Besides, I'm not so sure it is the job of a lifetime. I feel like I've already got that."

"I'd go in a heartbeat." Paul nodded and crossed his arms over his chest. "Wouldn't even stop to wave goodbye."

"Thanks a lot."

He grinned. "Nah. I'd wave goodbye. *Sayonara. C'est la vie.* So long, former life . . . hello, big, new world."

His words went in one ear and out the other. Frankly, I couldn't imagine Stephen writing comedy for *SNL*. No way. And Brooke . . .

For whatever reason, my heart broke as I thought of her having to go through yet another life shift. How would she take the news of moving to New York? Where would she go to school? How would she adjust to a new school? Who would befriend her?

My heart grew heavy just thinking about it. Or maybe it grew heavy at the idea of Stephen leaving me. How had this happened? I'd gone from being mad at him for taking credit for the episode to realizing just how much I loved and needed him.

I thought of his parting words to me a couple of days ago:

"You know what this means, don't you? Our relationship is at Step 11 in the plotline."

Ugh.

I picked up this week's script and twisted it in my hands, wishing I could toss it across the room. "I hate that stupid plotline," I mumbled.

Paul gave me a funny look as he took a seat. "What do you mean?"

"It just makes me so mad. Why does everything have to be so complicated?"

"Conflict, my dear." He wiggled his brows. "Good stories are built on conflict. Remember?"

Yeah, I remembered. Stories were built on conflict. And mine had plenty of it. But that certainly didn't mean I had to like it. In fact, the more of it I experienced, the more I wanted to crawl under my Strawberry Shortcake sheets and hide away. Maybe I'd just do that and forget this whole thing.

17

Full House

On Friday evening I arrived home to a chaotic scene. Mama was on the phone with someone and appeared to be crying. I could barely make out what she was saying through her tears, but I knew in my gut something terrible had happened.

I waited a few anxious seconds, then finally interrupted her call. "What is it?"

"Oh, Athena." She passed the phone off to me, whispering, "*Kyrie eleison*. Lord, have mercy."

At the sound of those familiar words, my heart did a back flip. Someone must really be in trouble.

I flinched when I heard Stephen's voice on the other end of the line. "Athena? Is that you?"

"Yes. It's me."

"It's about Brooke."

"Brooke?" My mind flooded with possibilities. Had she been in an accident? "What about her?"

"I can't find her."

"What do you mean? She's missing?"

"Yes. Less than an hour after we got back in town. She took off with the dog after we had a—well, a fight."

"Are you saying she ran away from home?" I paused and shrugged off my purse. "What did you fight about?"

He hesitated for a moment. When he spoke, I could hear the strain in his voice. "I wanted to tell you this another way, but I . . . I've had a job offer in New York."

"Right. The *SNL* thing."

"You knew about that?"

"It's all over the studio," I told him. "And trust me, I have a lot I could say about it, but I won't. Is that why she ran off?"

"Yes." Stephen groaned. "She went with me to New York, and I thought she had a great time. I took her shopping. We went to FAO Schwarz, rode the subway . . . everything."

"Wow. You've been busy over the past two days." And he'd kept me in the dark. Hadn't shared a word of it. That bothered me more than I could say, especially now. I'd love to give him a piece of my mind, tell him what I thought about the fact that he'd disappeared without talking to me, but this wasn't the time.

His words interrupted my thoughts. "I've been so busy. It's almost like a tornado touched down and picked me up. I was caught up in it for days and couldn't get back to the place where I started."

Should I start humming "Somewhere Over the Rainbow"?

"I was going to tell you all of this, but it happened so fast. And when I left, things were so weird between us. I wasn't sure you would want to know. Maybe I thought you'd be glad I was leaving."

My heart lurched at that proclamation. How could he say that? "Stephen, we can talk about all of that later."

"I know." He paused. "I . . . can't go," he said.

"You can't?"

"No. But she thinks we're moving, I guess. So she took off. And now I don't know where she is."

I pressed away the sting of tears as I imagined what this must be doing to him. "You tried Mary and Trina's place?"

"Of course. Called them first thing. No one has heard from her."

"You called Mama next?"

I turned to discover my mother still standing behind me. She mouthed the words, "I haven't seen her."

"Yes, your mother said she didn't come by the shop today, so I'm clueless. Will you . . . will you go with me to look for her? I can come by your place and get you. Maybe she's gone to that park by your house. The one with the high slide. She went there once before when she was upset."

"She did?"

"Yes. Ages ago. These past few weeks, she's been happier than I've ever seen her. I really thought things were turning around." He groaned. "I feel like we've taken ten steps backward now. That's the last thing I want to do to my little girl. I want her to have the stability I never . . ." His voice broke and I could hear him crying. "That I never had."

Suddenly every bit of angst I'd been carrying washed away like the evening tide. "Come and get me. I'll be waiting. She's out there, Stephen, and we'll find her."

"I'm leaving right now."

When I ended the call, my mother opened her arms to hug me. As I fell into her embrace, the tears came—tears for Brooke, and tears for myself too. This whole situation with Stephen had taken its toll on me.

As my mother held me, praying in that soft, soothing voice, I suddenly knew everything would be okay.

"I'm going to change into my jeans," I said after getting my emotions under control. "And wash my face. He'll be here soon."

I sprinted up the stairs and headed straight for my bed-room. When I got there, I found the door slightly ajar. I walked into the room, startled to find a big lump in the middle of the bed. It took me a minute, but when I saw movement under the comforter, I realized I had a stowaway hiding under my Strawberry Shortcake bedspread. Make that two. A wagging tail stuck out from under the corner of the sheets.

I'd never sensed relief like I did in that moment. Now I knew what the father of the prodigal son had felt like.

"Brooke?" I pulled the covers back, my heart flooding with joy as I looked at that beautiful, tearstained face. "You scared us to death. Your dad is looking everywhere for you."

She shook her head, the tears now pouring. "Don't tell him I'm here. Please! I don't want to talk to him." She pulled the covers over her head once again, and her sobs rang out, breaking my heart.

I gently eased the covers back and ran my hand along her back. "Honey, I know you're upset, but it's going to be okay. I promise."

At this point, Zeus got in on the act, using his nose to push back the covers. Then he began to lick the tears from her cheeks. At first she pushed him away, but after a few seconds, she wrapped her arms around his neck and let him minister to her in the way that only a dog can do.

Brooke eventually crawled out from under the sheets and pulled her knees up to her chest. Zeus settled at her side. "We're moving . . . again," she whispered. "And I don't want to."

I sat down on the bed next to her and drew her close, planting a kiss in her hair. "I don't think your daddy's going to move after all."

"He isn't?" She looked at me, disbelief registering on her face. "Are you sure?"

"Pretty sure. I just talked to him. But honey, even if he

had decided to move, it would be so that you could have a better life."

"I already have the best life in the world," she said, wrapping her arms around my neck. "Right here. With you."

Okay, if that didn't break my heart, nothing would. And I couldn't help but agree with her. The life she'd lived over the past couple months had been pretty ideal. A tiny apartment in New York could never compare. Here in L.A. she had friends, family . . . Family.

We really were her family now, weren't we? Why else would she have come here? I gave her a warm hug and my own tears fell. We sat in silence for a moment, wrapped in each other's arms, Zeus fighting to get between us so he could get his share of affection too.

Everything about holding Brooke felt completely natural and right. She was the closest thing to my own child, and I would give my life to protect her. To make her happy.

Right after one more round of scolding.

"Promise me you won't ever scare us like that again."

"I promise." She looked up at me, her beautiful brown eyes brimming over. "I didn't want to scare you. But I didn't know what else to do."

"How did you get here?" I asked.

Her gaze shifted downward. "Uncle Milo."

"Uncle Milo?" I sat up. "Milo knows you're here and didn't tell us? How could he do that?"

"He didn't know I was running away or anything," she said. "I just called him and acted like you had invited me over. He came and picked us up." She smiled through her tears. "He didn't want to let Zeus in the car, but I convinced him."

I tousled her hair. "You're a mess. You know that?"

"Yeah." She sighed. "But you love me anyway, right?"

"Of course. And I know your daddy does too."

Daddy!

As soon as I spoke the word, I realized I needed to tell Stephen. I picked up the cell phone to call him at the very moment our doorbell rang. My mother's voice sounded from downstairs. "Athena! Stephen's here."

I put my finger to my lips and motioned for Brooke to follow me to the hallway at the top of the stairs. Of course, Zeus tagged along behind her, tail moving in a frenzy. Brooke stepped beside me and looked down at her father, choking back a sob. The moment Stephen saw her, he gasped and ran—literally ran—up the stairs.

This, of course, made Zeus a little crazy. He went into full-out attack mode, thinking someone had come to harm his owner. I tugged at the mongrel's collar and shushed him while father and daughter melted into an embrace.

I backed up, knowing they needed their privacy. Still, a part of me wanted to be in on the action.

Stephen held Brooke close, lifting her feet off the floor. "Brooke, you scared me to death. Don't ever do that to me again. You hear me?" Tears streamed down his face. He kissed her multiple times on her hair and cheeks, then told her how much he loved her. She responded with a few "I'm sorry's" and an "I love you, Daddy."

Wow. I felt like I'd just witnessed a reenactment of the prodigal son story, played out between father and child.

My father's solution to all of this emotion, of course, was to feed everyone. We gathered in the kitchen, and he placed a mountain of food before us. We ate until our stomachs ached, and talked about everything under the sun . . . except what had just happened. From across the table, I watched as Stephen interacted with Brooke. She was all smiles again, and all the more when he told her they would be staying in Los Angeles. In fact, everyone smiled at that news.

I wanted to ask him a thousand questions but didn't know when—or if—we'd find the time. My parents eventually retreated to the living room after dinner to watch a movie, and Brooke joined them. Stephen motioned for me to follow him out to the back porch. I carried my cup of coffee out into the darkness.

"Hang on a second and let me turn on a light," I said.

"No." I could hear the emotion in his voice. "Leave it. I like it like this."

"You want to talk in the dark?" I fumbled around until I found the small glass patio table and set my cup on it. "Why?"

He cleared his throat. "Might be . . . easier. You know?"

"Easier to talk without seeing me?"

"Yeah." He groaned. "But don't take that the way it probably sounds." He paused for so long I got a little nervous. When he did speak, his words were shaky. "Athena, the last few days have been horrible. You have no idea how much I've missed you. Every time I thought about moving to New York, I felt sick inside. And obviously the idea tore up Brooke too. I never expected this kind of reaction from her."

Should I tell him that the idea of losing both of them made me feel sick inside as well?

"I guess she didn't really think I'd be interested in the job. Maybe she just thought it was a two-day vacation to the Big Apple. I don't know." He released a lingering sigh, one that got me plenty nervous.

"Are you?" I asked. "Interested in the job, I mean."

"The whole thing was flattering. Very flattering. But I can't do it—for Brooke's sake, and for my own. I can't possibly leave when . . ." His voice broke, and for a moment his words were left hanging. "It was the offer of a lifetime," he whispered at last. "I know that. But I already had the woman of a lifetime waiting for me right here. What they offered me in New York didn't even come close to what I already had."

I had to admit, it did sound pretty good hearing those words in the dark. Though I had to wonder about the expression on his face. Was it pain? Angst? Remorse? Joyous bliss? Who knew? Then again, maybe guessing was more fun.

"Are you going to say anything?" he asked.

"Oh." I startled back to attention. "I was just thinking."

"About what? What a schmuck I am for actually getting on that plane? Or about how I should fire my agent for setting up that article in the paper?"

"He set it up on purpose?" I asked.

"I think so. I never got a straight answer out of him. Every time I asked the question, he danced around it. I know he thought it was some sort of savvy career move, but he caused a lot of people a lot of pain."

"Stephen . . ." I reached for his hand, hitting the table instead. "Can you come here?"

I felt his presence, strong and comfortable, in front of me. I somehow managed to slip my arms around his waist, and he pulled me close. Our lips met—well, almost met—and we shared a kiss that made everything in the world right again. Funny how one passionate kiss could speak a thousand words. We managed two "I'm sorry's," one "I adore you," and even a couple of "I think I'm falling in love's" without ever speaking a word.

In that moment, as heaven and earth collided, I found all of my pain from the past few days slipping away. Suddenly I didn't even care if the furniture in the office stayed in its current topsy-turvy state. We could hang it from the ceiling for all I cared.

As the kiss intensified, I found myself distracted, wondering once again how I'd write a scene like this into a TV script. Would I mention the swell of emotions? The racing heart? The near swooning? Nah, swooning was highly overrated. Twenty-first-century women didn't swoon. Not when they were kissing, anyway.

Or did they?

For a second there, I thought my knees were going to buckle. Perfect! Unfortunately, I never lost my balance. Well, forget the buckling knees. I'd just have to come up with something else.

Or pay attention to what was really happening instead of daydreaming about a dumb scene. Especially when the kiss offered such forgiveness, such hope for new beginnings.

When the kiss ended, I rested my head against his and whispered the words, "Welcome home."

"This is home," he said. "Not the city. Not even this house. But being with you . . . is home. It's where I belong. And it's clearly where Brooke belongs." He began to get choked up again. "She . . . she knew where to come. She wanted you."

"Honestly, she wanted you," I said. "But I think she was scared that you would . . ." I shrugged.

"Disappoint her?"

"Maybe. I don't know."

"I really do want the best for her," he said. "If you had any idea how much I love her . . ." His voice cracked. "I . . . I would die for her."

"I know you would. And I know you want the best possible life for her. The good news is you've found it. It's been here all along."

He kissed me again, this time surprising me with the emotion behind it. Oh, sweet bliss. This was a spine-tingling, knee-buckling, swoon-worthy kiss if I'd ever experienced one.

As it ended, I finally decided to turn on the porch light. Then we sat on the porch swing and rocked back and forth like an old married couple. I half expected him to say something about the weather. Instead, Stephen kissed my hair and whispered, "Man, I've missed you."

"Same here."

"Did your dad tell you I came by the shop the day before I left to talk to him?"

"No. You did?"

"Yes, I wanted to ask him a question."

"O-oh?"

"It was related to the show. Since we're looking at adding tension to Jack and Angie's relationship, I wanted to know what would be the worst kind of attack on a couple working together. His answer was problems from within."

"Problems from within? Like, maybe someone having an affair or something?"

"No, not anything along that angle. We were talking about business-related problems. Big stuff."

"Losing the business would put a terrible strain on my parents' marriage," I said. "Their whole identity is wrapped up in that sandwich shop."

"Exactly. And Jack and Angie's whole identity is wrapped up in Stars Collide, the talent agency they've built together. And our whole identity is wrapped up in our work. Our writing. It shouldn't be that way, but it usually is."

"I know." A sigh threatened to erupt. "I'm working on that."

"Being attacked from the outside is awful, but according to your dad, there's something worse. Finding out that someone you loved and trusted is willing to turn on you."

I waited to hear the rest.

"Athena, I would never turn on you. I want the best for you and for the show. I wouldn't jeopardize you in any way. And if you think that my being on the team has somehow made people overlook you or think you're somehow less important than you really are, then I need to step aside. That's why I went to New York. I thought if things went back to where they were at in the sitcom, you could take the credit for that Golden Globe nomination like you deserve."

"No." I snuggled up against him. "No more of this *you* business or *me* business. From now on, it's *we* business. Got it?"

"Got it." He kissed me on the tip of the nose and then

whispered, "We're going to have an awesome future." A few quiet seconds ticked by before he came back with, "Want to guess where we are on the plotline now?"

I started to slug him but decided against it. If we'd just moved forward to Step 12 on his ridiculous plotter, who was I to mess it up again? Nah, I'd just stay right here, head cradled against his shoulder, and enjoy my happily ever after.

18

The Mod Squad

Bob came back to the *Stars Collide* set just two weeks after Stephen and I kissed and made up. His return, of course, had nothing to do with our unscripted kiss. It was pretty powerful, but not that powerful. No, his return to the fold just happened to follow on its heels. And boy, were we happy to have him.

Bob brought the perfect balance to our little writing room. Oh sure, his head was still in the clouds after the filming of his movie. And it turned out he'd left his heart behind in the Amish country. I could hardly believe it when he told me he'd fallen head over heels for a woman he'd met in a woodworking shop. Would wonders never cease! Hopefully she wouldn't convince him to move away and take up whittling.

Having Bob back at home on the *Stars Collide* set was the icing on the cake. The four of us—Bob, Paul, Stephen, and I—were pretty invincible. Sometimes we laughed so hard I

235

wondered how we'd get anything done. And as we inched closer to the Golden Globes, I found myself happier than ever with both my job and my personal life.

Monday, as always, was spent nibbling on leftovers from Super-Gyros and pounding out new ideas for the show. Thank goodness, these days they flowed like water. In fact, we hadn't experienced this much enthusiasm for our work since the very first season.

"Ooo! Tell me what you think about this idea." I paced the office late that morning, tickled pink by a brilliant-beyond-brilliant idea that had just flitted through my mind. I could hardly wait to share it.

"Oh?" Bob stopped eating a piece of baklava long enough to listen.

"What's that?" Stephen looked up from his laptop.

"What if the older cast members decide to throw a sock hop and invite the children?"

"What's the point?" Paul asked.

"Hmm." Oh yeah. There had to be some sort of point to it all. "Maybe . . ." I paced some more, then snapped my fingers. "Yes, maybe they're raising funds for local firefighters. It's the annual firefighters' extravaganza, and the Stars Collide team is there to lend a helping hand."

"Firefighters?" Bob did not look convinced. "With all of those children and elderly people in the room?"

"Sure, why not?" Stephen said. "Maybe something can catch on fire in the middle of the episode and the firefighters will save the day."

"Perfect." I clasped my hands together. "A fire is just the ticket. And I think this would be a great episode to use Milo and Melina. They can do a little Greek dance in the middle of the sock hop. Something like that. Anyway, the whole thing could have a Greek flare."

"Why Greek?" Paul asked.

"Why not?" Stephen and I both replied. We looked at each other and smiled.

"All this talk about Greek food is making me hungry," Bob said. "The leftovers you brought today were slim pickin's."

"I know. The customers ate us out of house and home on Saturday. Babbas is restocking today."

"I'm dying for a Super-Gyro," Paul said, rubbing his stomach. "And it's almost lunchtime. Do you think we could . . ." He quirked a brow. "Get out of here?"

"Oh, go out to lunch, you mean?" I nodded. "Great idea. Aunt Melina will be at the shop, and I'd be willing to bet Milo will be there too. We could talk to them about doing the episode."

"Those two have become quite an item, haven't they?" Stephen chuckled.

My eyes filled with tears as I thought about it. "Yes, and my aunt . . ." I could barely get the words out. "She's a changed woman. I haven't seen her take a drink in weeks. She's been . . . transformed."

"That's what love will do to you." All four of us spoke in unison.

Okay, I knew Stephen and I were in love. And Bob had fallen for his woodworking girl from the Amish country. But Paul? I gave him a curious look and he shrugged.

"So, maybe my ex and I weren't exactly over each other."

I let out a squeal that could have pierced ears, then rushed his way and threw my arms around him. "You should have told us!"

"Why? So you could add it to a script? No thank you. I think I'll keep my personal life personal."

"Why?" Bob, Stephen, and I asked.

"It's so much more fun to put it out there," I said. "So we want details."

"Nope." He shook his head. "No details. Let it go."

Bob shook his head. "How you ever got to be a comedy writer is beyond me."

We all laughed, but in my gut I knew Paul was right. He needed time to work out his relationship—not just with his ex, but with the Lord. Over the past few weeks I'd watched as Stephen gently nudged him in that direction. The whole thing had been handled with such grace, flowing naturally out of our conversations, that it caused me to marvel. Stephen had a real gift for evangelism, though he probably wouldn't have called it that. I could definitely tell Paul was on a journey in the right direction. Hopefully the relationship with his ex-wife was part of his life story. And how wonderful to think he'd gotten that silly little dog back.

Hmm. I wondered where that would place him on the plotline. Step 3? Step 4?

Stop it, Athena. Toss that plotter out the window and just enjoy life.

"So, what did you think about that lunch idea?" Paul asked, glancing at his watch. "I think my creative abilities would be greatly enhanced with the right food, and I know just where we can get it."

"And we would be researching, after all," Bob added. "If we're doing a Greek episode. We could write it off."

"Write it off? That's funny." I laughed. "Since when have my parents ever charged you for food?"

He grinned and shrugged. "We can write it off in theory."

"Exactly." I stretched, then reached for my purse. "So what are we waiting for? Let's shake this place."

We tiptoed out of the studio, inching our way past the roundtable reading room, where the cast read through the script we'd pounded out the week before. I could hear Kat's voice. Scott's too. What really got me tickled, though, were the voices of the kids. We'd given them plenty of antics for this week's show. Likely they were all happy campers.

We stole through the studio, doing our best not to be noticed by the camera guys. Jason happened to catch my eye as I slipped by and gave me a smile.

Paul, Bob, Stephen, and I made it outside, where we squinted against the sunlight. Or maybe it was just the glare of the sun shining against Lenora's pink Cadillac convertible. We all climbed into Stephen's SUV and made our way to Van Nuys. The drive was spent talking about the upcoming sock hop episode, which we'd now decided should feature songs that firefighters would love. Go figure. We'd keep the fire bit to up the conflict. After all, great stories were built on conflict.

As always, my heart came alive as we pulled into the Super-Gyros parking lot. This place had captured me on every conceivable level. As I looked up at that sign, the one with the superhero, I was reminded of the day Kat had helped me put together the list of all the things I wanted—needed—in a mate. I'd found them all in Stephen.

Well, all but one. There was that whole fishing issue. I'd never mentioned it to anyone except Kat and Larisa. And the Lord, of course. But he had remained silent on the issue, so I'd forged ahead with the relationship, pushing the issue to the background.

Why did I put that on the list? Ludicrous.

Oh well. Maybe I could just overlook that and assume the Lord had brought Mr. Right into my life, even if he didn't care about fishing.

Stephen opened the door of the sandwich shop and gestured for me to walk through. As I did, he leaned over and gave me a kiss.

"Remember the first time we met in this very spot?" I took hold of his hand.

"How could I forget? You left a lasting impression . . . on my big toe."

"Obviously my plan worked. I caught you, didn't I?"

"You did. You trapped me in your snare with that broken-foot tactic." He reached over and kissed me soundly, causing Bob to groan.

"You're holding up the line. I'm hungry."

"Sorry." I giggled and continued into the store, pausing only to drink in the wonderful aroma of meats and spices. Yum!

Babbas took one look at me and called out, "Athena-bean!"

I raced his way and gave him a hug. "Hope you're okay that we stopped by."

"Are you kidding? You've made my day!"

"We decided we couldn't live without some good Greek food. And we're researching for next week's episode, so that gave us two good reasons to come."

"You're just in time." My father's eyes twinkled. "I've come up with a new sandwich for the shop. Adding it to the board now. You're going to love it."

I couldn't believe it. The menu had stayed the same for years. "What is it?"

"I named it after Zeus. I'm calling it the Greek Dog. It's a hot dog made of lamb, with peppers and olives on top."

"Perfect. Sounds a lot like the gyro, though. Sure you don't want to build a different sort of hot dog that's more traditional?"

"You mean like a regular hot dog with chili on top?" He shrugged. "I'm naming it after Zeus, you know. He's Greek. The sandwich is Greek. It's all Greek!"

Indeed, everything in my world was truly Greek. I waved at Mama, who worked alone at the counter on the phyllo dough. "Is Aunt Melina here? I need to talk to her about something important."

My mother wiped her hands on her apron and took a few steps in my direction. "Yes, she's in the back room, doing inventory. It's taking her a long time. Guess she's got a lot of paperwork or something."

"She's a hard worker." I walked across the shop and into

the back room—the same room where Stephen and I had shared our first heart-to-heart talk. A tiny giggle alerted me to the fact that someone—or a couple of someones—stood behind the boxes at the back of the room.

Inventory, my eye.

As I tiptoed by, Melina's voice rang out. In Greek, of course, but I could make out the words.

"Ah, Milo. When you kiss me like that, I feel like I'm a young woman again, hiding behind the school building, kissing the boy I love."

Okay then.

I cleared my throat to warn them of my arrival. Melina gasped, and the next thing I knew, several boxes came tumbling my direction. She and Milo ran toward me, grabbing boxes right and left.

"Oh, Athena." My aunt's cheeks flamed red. "We were just . . ."

I put my hand up. "Never mind. None of my business." I grinned and gave her a playful wink.

She hugged me. "Thank you, sweet girl."

Milo pulled her close and planted several little kisses in her hairline. "I'm not embarrassed to be caught kissing you." He looked at Melina, love radiating from his eyes. "I've come all the way from Greece to find you."

"And here I am," she whispered, leaning into him.

He shook his head. "My life has been so full of sadness. But no more." He paused and whispered, "How can I not believe in God? He led me straight to you."

My heart came alive at his words.

Tears streamed down my aunt's cheeks, and she muttered something in Greek that I couldn't quite make out through the emotion in her voice. The next words were a little easier to understand. "I've been through so much sadness too. But my mourning is over now."

Well, her mourning might be over, but as I watched this scene unfold, I suddenly felt like crying. I could feel the sting of tears in my eyes.

"I've outlived two husbands," she said. "But I haven't been living. Not really. I've been drowning my pain. Only, it never died. Not till now." She pressed herself into his arms, tears now flowing. "You've brought joy and laughter back into my life, Milo. How can I ever thank you for that?"

Tears flowed down my cheeks at her impassioned speech.

Milo responded by kissing her on the cheek. "Your love is all the thanks I will ever need."

Okay, so I thought that last line was a little cheesy. Sounded like something I heard on a soap opera once. But Melina seemed to buy it, and that was all that really mattered. They melded into a passionate lip-lock, and I stood by watching, the whole thing now feeling a little awkward. I needed to sneak out of here, but there just didn't seem to be a good way. Or a good time.

The kiss continued for some time. I glanced at my watch, wondering if the others were missing me yet.

When the kiss ended, Melina looked my way. "I'm sorry, Athena. We got carried away."

"No, it's all good." I smiled. "But I've brought the writers from the sitcom with me, and they want to talk to you about something, so if you two are done now . . ."

Melina reached up to wipe the lipstick prints off Milo's cheeks and lips. "We're done now."

They tagged along on my heels into the shop, where I found Bob, Paul, and Stephen eating gyros and telling Babbas about the sock hop episode. He chuckled and dove into a story about what life was like as a youngster growing up in the fifties.

I finally got the train back on track, and we asked Milo and Melina if they would like to be in next week's episode.

I thought my aunt was going to faint. Milo puffed out his chest, said something about how he'd been waiting for this opportunity for years, and then kissed her. Again.

The room went a little crazy at that point. Everyone began to talk at once. A couple of customers entered the store, took one look at the chaos, and joined right in, adding their stories to ours.

When the noise in the room finally lowered to a dull roar, Milo gave me a hug. "Sweet girl, you've been so kind to this old man."

"You're easy to love, Milo. Truly."

"Well, you've made my day. And because you have, I think it's finally time to make yours."

"Make my day?" I gave him a quizzical look. "What do you mean?"

He clapped his hands to get the attention of everyone in the room. "Pappas family, I have an announcement. Something I've been hoping to share for a while. Just wanted to wait till the time was right. I know in my heart this is the day."

Melina's eyes sparkled. Had he popped the question? Did he plan to do so now, in front of her whole family? I didn't have a clue, but he'd hooked me with his line. Maybe Milo had missed his calling as a writer. He certainly had a penchant for grabbing the audience by the throat and holding them captive.

Shut up, Athena, and just let him make his announcement.

For once I actually took my own advice. I closed my mouth, leaned against the counter, and waited for Milo to speak his mind.

19

The Price Is Right

Milo paced the room, not saying anything for a moment. Finally he turned to us, a suspicious smile on his face. "Pappas family, there's something I need to tell you. Or, rather, something I need to give you." He reached into his coat pocket and came out with a small envelope, which he passed to my mother.

"Another letter?" she said. It trembled in her hand.

He nodded. "From your aunt Athena. It was written several days before she passed away. I've carried it for months, waiting for the right moment."

"You're just now giving it to me?"

"Yes. I was given specific instructions about how and when to share it with you. I'm sorry about that, but I had to follow those instructions. You will understand shortly."

Wow. Talk about getting my curiosity up. This was better than any suspense novel.

Mama gently opened the envelope, her hands still shaking. She pulled out the letter and unfolded it.

"It's in Greek," she whispered.

"Do you want me to translate?" Milo asked. "I'm happy to do it if you like."

Mama shook her head. "No. I think I'd better read this one myself. I can do it."

I looked on as she scanned the page, trying to guess what it might say. By the time she reached the bottom of the first page, her eyes had filled with tears. And by the time she finished the letter altogether, those tears ran in little rivers down her cheeks.

"*Kyrie eleison,*" Mama whispered.

We all echoed, "Lord, have mercy."

What he was having mercy *on*, I couldn't be sure. But it must be something big.

"Mama, what did she say?" I asked at last. "Tell us."

My mother's hands shook so violently as she attempted to fold the letter that it slipped through her fingers and drifted to the floor.

I reached down and picked it up. "Is it okay to let Stephen translate it?"

She nodded and stammered "yes," then dropped into a chair and began to cry.

We'll deal with this. Whatever it is, we'll deal with it.

I passed the letter to Stephen, who began to read aloud as I looked over his shoulder. By the time he finished the first paragraph, my heart began to thump so hard that I thought I might pass out. "Mama . . ."

"I know." Her eyes grew wide as she looked at Stephen. "Keep reading."

And so he did. The second paragraph shed light on the first, and by the time he got to the third one, I could barely contain my tears. "Oh, Mama, I don't believe it. I don't believe it."

"Me either." She covered her face with her hands and

sobbed. "Oh, sweet Athena. Everything I ever believed about you was wrong." Mama looked up at us through her tears. "She did love me. She did."

"Obviously." I paused to think about what Stephen had just read. It changed everything. Absolutely everything. "So, let me get this right. The whole thing about sending Zeus to us was really just a test?"

Milo nodded. "Yes, that's right." He paused. "Well, in part. She really did want to find a good home for him. But all of it was done with a purpose in mind."

Mama rose and put her hand on Milo's arm. "Please tell me I've read that letter correctly. I've inherited a million-dollar estate in Athens?"

"Two million, actually," he said. "Give or take. But yes, it's yours. She only had two conditions—that ninety days after receiving Zeus you would have adopted him as your own, and that you would learn to love me as part of the family. You've done both."

"Oh yes, you're definitely family." Melina gave him a kiss on the cheek. "But that dog . . ."

"Technically, we passed him off to Stephen," Mama said. "Does it really count?"

"Stephen is part of your family, yes?" Milo asked.

Stephen drew me close and planted a kiss on my forehead. "For all practical purposes, yes. And you'd be hard-pressed to tell my daughter she's not kin. She's pretty much adopted all of you."

"We've adopted her too," I said.

Stephen nodded. "And as long as Zeus stays with us, he stays in the Pappas family. You can take those words to the bank."

I would. As soon as I got my heart to slow down.

"There you go," I said at last. "It's all settled. We're one big happy family."

Even as I spoke the words, the greatest thrill filled my soul. Stephen, Brooke, and I really did feel like one big happy family. Okay, Stephen, Brooke, Zeus, and I. Not that I minded the little Greek dog. He'd forever linked me to the man of my dreams. And apparently he linked my mama to a story that stretched back nearly fifty years. Who knew?

"Obviously we passed Mean-Athena's test," Babbas said. "Interesting, since we didn't know we were being tested."

"Is this really true?" I looked at Milo, still not quite believing it. "You're going to have to give us more details. Help us understand."

He nodded. "It's all true. Every word. In spite of Athena's desire to keep her family's estate, I tried to persuade her to marry me . . . live with me in my home . . . but she refused."

"That's so sad," I said.

"Yes, she died a lonely old woman who never knew love, and all so that she could preserve the estate for future generations. But, as you can tell from her letter, she regretted her decision all of her life. All she ever wanted was love from family . . . and from a husband." His eyes filled with tears. "The husband she never had."

"And so she left the house to Mama so that it would stay in the family?" I asked.

"Well, that, and she wanted your mother to know the truth, that love comes before possessions. That's why she sent the dog. And me." He grinned. "She wanted that message to ring out loud and clear. And I'm so glad you passed the test."

"I just can't believe she left the house to me." Mama shook her head, a stunned expression on her face. I could tell she wasn't quite buying this story. "Milo, you're convinced this is legitimate? Do you have the legal documents?"

"Yes, I've had them all along. I only had to wait the ninety days stipulated in the letter to make sure you didn't give up on Zeus. He had to become part of the family."

"That crazy dog," Melina said. "Who would have known?"

"Hey, that's a two-million-dollar dog," my father said. "For that we'll put up with his antics. No problem. From now on he drinks out of a gold bowl."

"Well, he came from the lap of luxury," Milo said. "Athena gave him every good thing from the time he was a pup. He had the run of her estate."

Mama's tears began again. "Oh, you've triggered such memories. That home! That beautiful home. The two years I lived with Athena were lonely—she wasn't really one to play with me—but I spent hours exploring her incredible estate. You've never seen such luxury. It was a little intimidating for a child, but it left a lasting impression on my mind. I've never seen anything since to compare."

"She never really flaunted her money," Milo explained. "So it wasn't a prideful thing. But she did have an amazing home. We're talking about a house that's nearly two hundred years old."

"Wow." That was about all I could manage. I thought about Aunt Athena's dilemma—to keep the home or to marry the man she loved. She'd missed her opportunity because something got in the way. And now, all of these years later, I stood facing the man I loved, determined not to let my work, my writing, get in the way. I didn't want any "lost" years. I didn't want to get to the end of my life and face regrets for poor choices. No way.

"I want you to know something, as Athena's family members." Milo paced the room, then finally stopped and faced us. "I was young when I fell in love with Athena, but my feelings were very real. And I know now that it broke her heart to send me away. I believe that's why, in the end, she wanted to make sure the people she loved saw me as part of the family. I thank God that she still cared enough about me to include me in all of this, and I so clearly see the puzzle pieces coming together now."

"The people she loved . . ." Mama shook her head. "That's the strangest part of all. She rarely showed that love, if at all."

"Maybe that's why it was so important to her that you show love for her." Milo shook his head and drew Aunt Melina close. "I don't know. I only know that she sent me on this mission and I came, not knowing what awaited me in America. Now I know, and it has changed everything."

"Everything," Melina whispered as she leaned her head against his.

"I let my first love slip away from me," Milo said. "I will not let you slip away, Melina. I will die before I let you go." He eased himself down on one knee, and a collective gasp went up from the crowd, including the customers. "So, with that said, would you do me the great honor—"

He never had the chance to finish his sentence. Her resounding "Yes! Yes! Yes!" filled the room from top to bottom, side to side. Stephen extended a hand and helped Milo stand. The process took a few seconds, but he finally managed. Once standing, Milo swept my aunt into his arms and gave her a passionate kiss.

Looked like they'd better get married . . . and quick.

"Oh, look, honey," a customer said, pointing our way. "I think they must be acting out a scene from a movie. Do you think there are hidden cameras in the room?" She began to fuss with her hair. "Maybe we're on television right now."

"No, they're not acting," I told her. "It's the real deal, trust me. None of this was scripted."

Nope. None of it was scripted. And yet, it was some of the best writing I'd ever seen.

Only one person I knew of could write a scene like that. He didn't need a laptop, and he didn't need the help of fellow writers. All he looked for was willing hearts.

A cheerful "opa!" rang out, and Babbas turned up the sound system so that the Greek music played even louder.

Mama pulled several of the customers into our circle and taught them the dance. One poor woman looked like she'd rather bolt, but we eventually got a smile out of her.

Wasn't that what life was like? You went into the dance not knowing where it might take you. Not knowing the steps. Not having a feel for what was around the next bend. But once the music got going—once someone took you by the hand—the steps came so easily you felt as if you'd known them all your life.

My gaze shifted to Stephen. When I held his hand, when I listened to his voice, when I shared my heart with him, I realized I'd become comfortable with our dance.

The yeast had done its work. The loaf of bread had finished baking. Now we chose to break it together—to celebrate the goodness that only love from a gracious heavenly Father could bring.

20

Fast Forward

I'd heard of short engagements before, but never one that lasted less than a week. Melina and Milo got engaged on Monday and married the following Sunday after church. Our pastor was happy to perform the nuptials. I'd never seen a more radiant bride or a more eager groom. And why not? They had everything in the world to celebrate.

I thought about their whirlwind romance as I drove to the office the following Monday morning. I'd been so distracted that I'd actually forgotten to bring leftovers. Paul and Bob would be miffed, but there was nothing I could do about that. Surely they would understand. I hoped. They'd been in great moods lately, after all. Maybe I'd swing for Chinese takeout. Try something new for a change. Get off the script. Fly by the seat of my pants.

I arrived at the studio to see Lenora and Rex getting out of her pink Cadillac. She looked radiant in a cream-colored gown. In fact, I'd never seen her more beautiful.

"Oh, Lenora!" I gasped. "That's the prettiest one yet. Who are you?"

"Who am I?" She shook her head. "What do you mean?"

"I mean, which movie star are you today? Ginger Rogers? Doris Day?"

The strangest expression followed—almost blank. "Why, I'm Lenora Worth, star of stage and screen. Perhaps you've seen my movies."

A hush fell over our little trio. Rex looked at me with tears in his eyes and gave me a little shrug. "She is quite the star, is she not?"

"She is," I whispered.

He took her by the arm and led her across the parking lot as she rambled on about some movie she'd filmed in the fifties. My heart lurched—partly because I realized she was truly slipping away from us, and partly because of his tender love toward her. Talk about laying your life down for others.

Surely the Lord must be smiling on their relationship. I knew I was. And though Rex probably faced some tough times ahead, he seemed to be taking it in stride. Likely he wasn't spending his days asking where his journey fell on the plotline. Instead, he just lived life to the fullest, taking advantage of every moment.

I entered the studio, smiling as I walked through the re-decorated set. I thought about all of the changes to the cast and crew this year and how the actors, young and old, had played along. God bless them all. They'd made my job so much easier and much more fun.

"Your dress is beautiful today, Lenora," Jason called out.

"Why, thank you!" she said. "My mother thanks you. My father thanks you. My sister thanks you. And I thank you."

For a moment he said nothing. Then a smile lit his face. "Oh, I know this one. *Yankee Doodle Dandy*. James Cagney. 1946."

"1942," Lenora said with a wink. "But good try."

I marveled at her ability to remember lines from movies when everything else in her life seemed to be fading. Still, for whatever reason, it gave me hope that she would be with us for some time to come.

Pausing by the makeup room, I waved at Nora, who worked on Candy's hair. "Good morning."

"Same to you." She lifted the curling iron and waved it my way. "You look chipper this morning."

"I feel chipper this morning."

She turned back to Candy, who appeared to be giving Nora advice on her love life. The girl chattered on and on. Nora didn't appear to find this strange at all. Instead, she paused every few seconds to take notes. "Oh, that's a good one," she said. "I'll have to try that." They both laughed.

What a crazy world I lived in. Still, I wouldn't change a thing.

Next I passed Jana, offering a cheerful, "Welcome to a new week!"

"Can't wait to see what you writers come up with this week," she said with a wink.

"Me either." I chuckled. That was half the fun, after all. Coming up with something new and fresh. Giving the reins to God and seeing where his inspiration led.

As I made the trek down the hall, I thought about that verse in Genesis about how the Spirit of God hovered over the waters during creation. Goose bumps ran down my arms as I envisioned what that must have been like. When I gave my writing gift over to God—when I stepped back and allowed him to create—he truly took control. His Spirit hovered over the waters of that creation. What an awesome, powerful thought. I could hardly wait to tell Stephen.

I walked into the office, stunned to find the furniture back in place. Stephen sat at the desk, typing away on the old typewriter. Hanging my purse up on the coat rack, I looked at him.

"Stephen?"

"Yes?" He barely glanced up from the typewriter.

"Something you want to tell me?"

"Yes." Another quick glance and a smile. "You were right about the room. The whole *Dick Van Dyke* ambience is very inspirational. I've been writing all morning."

"Writing a scene for the show?"

"No. Writing something else. I think you're going to like it." He yanked the paper from the typewriter and teased me with it. I grabbed for it but he wouldn't let go. "Have a seat."

"Are you going to read it to me?"

"Maybe."

I took a seat on the divan and watched as Stephen headed my way. He tripped over the ottoman and did a crazy somersault.

I gasped, but he popped up and grinned. "Saw that on *The Dick Van Dyke Show*. Opening credits. Thought you might enjoy it."

Good grief. My heart rate slowed back down to normal. "Do you mind if I ask what in the world you're up to?"

"Oh, just wrote a little script. A story about the two of us."

"O-oh? You're writing our story now? I thought only God could do that."

"Well, I took a few liberties. Came up with a little somethin'-somethin'." He held out the piece of paper, and for the first time I noticed his hand was trembling. "Would you read your lines? I'll read mine."

"You've scripted our conversation?"

"Uh-huh." He nodded. "C'mon. Play along, okay?"

"Okay." I took the script in hand. "But if you say one more thing about where I am on the plotline of life, I'm going to smack you."

Stephen laughed. "No. Nothing about that plotline, I promise. Where we are in the grand scheme of things is God's business."

"And yet you're scripting our lines."

He wiggled his eyebrows in playful fashion. "Just for this scene. Read already."

"Okay, okay." I looked at the page and began to read, using my best acting voice. "Stephen, I'm so glad you came to Los Angeles. I don't know where I'd be right now if I hadn't found you. You're the handsomest, kindest, sweetest . . ." I shook my head. Looking up from the paper, I couldn't help but chuckle. "Now I see what you're up to."

He cleared his throat. "Keep reading."

"Okay." I read a few more glowing words about Stephen's character, then did a double take as I glanced at the next words. "It . . . it says Stephen gets down on one knee."

"Mmm-hmm." He did just that.

My heart went a little crazy at this point. Surely this was all some sort of play-acting. Right?

"It says . . ." I shook my head again. "Stephen pulls out ring box."

"Mmm-hmm." He reached into his pocket and came out with a tiny box.

At that moment, the door to the office flew open, and Bob and Paul walked inside with Rex and Lenora behind them. They were followed by Kat and Scott and then my parents. After them came Milo and Melina, and then Brooke, who'd obviously skipped school. Jana, Nora, and the rest of the crew slipped in next. Before long, our tiny office was maxed out.

"I, um . . . I don't see anything about all of them in the script." I pointed to the page. "Are we off the page?"

"They're in there." Stephen grinned. "Just read between the lines."

"I see." So he'd been planning this all along. How had it eluded me? He'd planned to propose on a Monday morning in our office? Only a writer would get the significance of that.

He wiggled his eyebrows again. "You know what a plotter I am. I think it's time to toss the script, though, and do the rest of this by the seat of my pants."

I tossed the paper in the air. It landed on the edge of the piano.

Lenora came rushing our way. "Are you proposing, young man?"

"Trying to," he said. "But not doing a very good job of it."

"Oh, I'm sure it's going to be wonderful." She leaned against the desk and sighed. "I wish I had some popcorn."

"Popcorn?" Rex asked as he took her by the arm and eased her back a couple of feet. "Why?"

"I love popcorn when I watch a really good show, and I have a feeling this one's going to be a doozy."

Oh, it was a doozy, all right. Our "Stephen and Athena Get Engaged" scene had pretty much taken on a mind of its own.

"Tell her that you love her, Stephen," Lenora suggested.

"That you can't live without her," Brooke added, her eyes filled with tears.

"That you want her to have a whole family of soccer ball babies," Bob threw in.

I slapped myself in the head at that one.

"And you plan to stick with her, no matter what life throws your way," Paul said.

We all turned to look at him.

"Hey, that's where I went wrong with my ex. We didn't go into it with a 'forever' way of thinking." He smiled. "We're working on that now, by the way. We've made a lot of progress."

We all began to cheer. For a moment I thought Stephen was going to stand up. Forget about his plan to propose.

Fortunately, Lenora put her hand on his shoulder and told him to keep going.

He did.

His next words were completely off the script. Not that it really mattered. I couldn't remember one thing he said once it was spoken. I was too distracted by the tears in his eyes and the pure joy radiating out of his smile. Well, that, and the fantastically large princess-cut diamond in the now-open ring box.

When he finished, I gave him a resounding "Yes!" and everyone began to shout. The ring went on my finger, and the women gathered around, Brooke leading the way, to examine the merchandise. My heart raced like never before, and all the more as I examined the ring.

I'm getting married? I'm getting married!

"Ooo, that was a great proposal," Lenora said, grabbing my hand and leaning down to see the shimmering diamond. She turned to Stephen. "But you need to kiss her now. Seal the deal."

"Thank you. Don't mind if I do." Stephen rose and pulled me into his arms. He whispered, "I'm so sorry, Athena. I'm not sure how you feel about this happening in front of a crowd, but they wouldn't take no for an answer."

I laughed. "Stephen, every major event of my life has happened in front of a big crowd. That's what happens in Greek families. You share it all together—the joys, the sorrows . . ."

He put his finger over my lips. "No sorrows today. We've been through enough of those. Only joys from now on."

"Oh? You've penciled in joy but not sorrow? What about conflict? What about having a plotline that moves up and down, in and out? Our story won't be much fun if it's all joy."

"You two are crazy," Kat said. "You do know that, right? Do you always interrupt your love scenes to analyze them?"

Stephen and I looked at each other for a moment and then laughed.

"Yep," I said.

"Sorry if that blows any romantic notions," Stephen said. "But we're just a couple of crazy writers who overanalyze everything. That's what makes us so perfect for each other."

"Crazy can be good," Bob said. "You wouldn't want the writer of the show to be normal, after all. How boring would that be?"

"Yes, how boring would that be?" I whispered in the ear of my husband-to-be.

"Back in the old days, a Greek man would propose to a Greek woman by tossing an apple to her," Milo said. "Anyone got a fruit basket lying around?"

"Skip the fruit," I said. "His proposal was perfect. Wouldn't change a thing."

My father drew near, a somber expression on his face. Uh-oh. I could feel something coming, and it wasn't going to be good.

"We're not quite done here yet," he said. "There's one more piece of business to attend to."

"O-oh?" Stephen paled. "I . . . I asked you for her hand, sir. You said yes."

"Yes. I agreed that you could ask for her hand," Babbas said, looking far too serious. "But have you forgotten my rule? Do you not remember what I once said about the Greek national anthem?"

Oh, help.

My father looked straight at Stephen. "Any man worthy of my daughter has to memorize all 158 verses."

I saw the look of panic in Stephen's eyes. Clearly he'd forgotten this little tidbit.

Or had he?

With voice shaking, he dove into the first verse. We all sang it with him. Well, those of us who were Greek, anyway. Jana and Nora looked a little lost, as did Bob and Paul.

As we sang, my heart swelled with pride. I thought of Mean-Athena and how her story had ended. She'd gone her whole life without love, only to share the greatest kind of love in the end. I wanted to know love firsthand. To taste it, feel it, experience it. As a married woman.

That's why I was particularly thrilled when Stephen made it through verse two. And three. And four.

He hit verse five and kept going, mesmerizing us all with his memorization skills. Things got a little iffy around verse eleven, and I knew we were in trouble when he got to the seventeenth verse. In fact, I was pretty sure he made up about half of it. Some of the words didn't even match, and he had that "I'm not sure what I'm doing here" look in his eye. Still, he plowed ahead. I had to give him credit for trying.

Verse eighteen was more than a little rocky, and verse nineteen was pretty much a wash. Still, by the time he reached that point, he'd won my father over. And my mother too, for that matter. And Aunt Melina. And Milo. And the rest of the Pappas clan.

"Son, welcome to the family." My father slapped him on the back so hard Stephen took a couple of steps forward. He caught himself with one hand against the piano keys.

"Thank you." Stephen offered a broad smile, then collapsed onto the piano bench, looking exhausted.

Everyone in the room began to talk at once. Fortunately, they were all talking *about* me, and not *to* me. That left me free to talk to the one person who mattered most. I sat next to Stephen and leaned against him.

He pulled me into his arms and kissed the tip of my nose. "I love you, Athena-bean."

"Ugh. You had to call me that?"

"Of course. It's a love name. I'm all about love names."

"Fine. Then I'll have to come up with one for you."

He smiled. "Don't you find all of this strangely ironic?"

"Ironic?"

"Yes. Jack and Angie started out as opponents and then became co-workers. They ended up in love in the end."

"I know." I giggled as I thought about it. "Crazy coincidence."

"I don't believe in coincidences." He brushed a light kiss on my right cheek, then my left. "I've been through a lot of pain where love is concerned," he said. "I didn't think God would open the door for me to find a wife, let alone a wife with such a delicious sense of humor."

"Oh, I have a delicious sense of humor?"

"You do. And we're going to need that humor to keep things fresh." He looked at me with such love that my heart felt like it might explode. "I can't wait to see how our lives play out. It's going to be a blast."

"No doubt."

A thousand questions were going through my mind. Where would we live? Would Brooke accept me as her mother? Would Stephen and I still go on working together after we got married? Would we really have a houseful of soccer ball babies? If so, would I keep working for *Stars Collide*, or would I give it all up to be a mom?

Calm down, Athena. You've been watching other married couples work together for months—your parents, Kat and Scott, Lenora and Rex. Everything will come together. Watch and see what God does.

Yes, married couples could certainly work together. They might have to jump a few hurdles, but it could be done . . . and done well.

"So, when's the big day?" Kat raised her voice to be heard above the roar of the crowd. "Have you given it any thought?"

"I don't have a clue." My mind reeled. I looked at Stephen and shrugged. "What do you think?"

"Greece is beautiful in the springtime," he said with a wink.

"G-Greece? Really?"

This seemed to get everyone's attention. Mama and Babbas turned my way. So did Milo and Melina.

"Oh, that's perfect!" Mama said. "Absolutely perfect."

"Of course. Is there anyplace else to go on our honeymoon?" Stephen asked. "I've wanted to go all my life."

Everyone went a little crazy at this news. Mama announced that the wedding should take place in Greece as well. I wasn't so sure about that part. Getting married in my own church sounded pretty ideal to me, but a honeymoon in Greece? I could hardly wait!

Within minutes everyone in the room was chattering once again. I took advantage of the chaos to pull Stephen to the side. "I can't believe I get to go to the place where my mama lived. And Mean-Athena." I stopped myself and said her name once more. "I mean, *Aunt* Athena."

"Funny how hindsight helps you see things in perspective, isn't it?" Stephen ran his fingers through my hair and smiled.

"No kidding. I'm guessing she was never mean at all. Maybe she lived her whole life brokenhearted, sacrificing the only chance she ever had for love so that her family could one day benefit from the gift she would leave behind."

"Reminds me of that verse about laying down your life for your friends," Stephen said. "She pretty much did that, didn't she?"

"She did. And you do too, Stephen. You've always been the kind of guy to put others first. Don't think I wasn't watching when you brought those aging Hollywood stars back into the limelight. You knew they needed another chance."

"Everyone needs another chance, Athena." Stephen lowered his voice, though I knew no one could hear us. "That's the truth. Mean-Athena needed one. Zeus needed one. Milo. Paul. Bob. Me . . . We all need second chances. And I'm so glad that God gives them. I wouldn't be here otherwise."

"Me either."

"He also gives third and fourth and fifth chances, and I think we should too. That's why we've got to be quick to forgive. Not hold grudges. That sort of thing."

I sighed. "Do you realize you're practically perfect in every way?"

"No, but I do realize you must be blind to think so."

I laughed. "Not blind. I guess I just see your good traits first. If you have any bad ones, they're hidden underneath the good."

Stephen chuckled. "I only wish my nona had lived long enough to hear you say that. There are plenty of bad ones, trust me. And God isn't finished with me yet. I've got a long way to go—as a father, a man, and a writer. I hope you realize that."

"You think *you're* flawed?" I started to tell him about my physical imperfections but stopped short. There would be plenty of time for my flaws to reveal themselves later. Right now I'd rather bask in the glow of our love.

Bask in the glow of our love? How cheesy was that? It seemed the deeper I fell in love with this man, the goofier my writing got. Oh well. Maybe that's the way it was meant to be. Maybe those romance writers had it right all along. The tingles. The buckling knees. The heaving bosoms. Maybe it was all meant to be.

Or maybe I just needed to stop thinking so much and let love lead the way.

21

Happy Days

I jumped into wedding-planning mode with a fury. With so much to do in so little time, how could I pull this off? Mama, of course, wanted me to have a traditional Greek wedding. The fact that we attended a contemporary, non–Greek Orthodox church didn't stop her from wanting the usual Greek fanfare.

Babbas didn't seem to care, as long as he could give me away. Kat was already looking for a maternity bridesmaid's dress, and Brooke had pegged herself as a junior bridesmaid. My phone rang off the wall as she shared her enthusiasm with me. Not that I minded. Every day I fell a little more in love with that darling girl. She'd captured me on every conceivable level.

The wedding plans were such a blissful distraction that I almost forgot about the Golden Globe nomination. As the evening drew near, however, Paul and Bob—both nervous wrecks—reminded me on a daily, if not hourly, basis.

"We get extra tickets for the Golden Globes," Bob said. "So you can bring a date, or what have you."

"Fine," Paul said. "I'll bring my 'what have you.'"

We all laughed at that. I knew, though, that his "what have you" was his ex-wife, and I'd been dying to meet her. Likely she would soon be part of the family too.

Kat, whose blossoming belly made me smile every time I saw it, helped me pick out a dress for the event. We had far too much fun shopping.

"Just think," she said. "The next dress we'll be picking out is your wedding dress."

"One event at a time," I said. "Let's get through the Golden Globes and then we'll talk wedding."

I chose an olive-green satin dress with a beautiful neckline and fitted waist. Underneath several yards of satin, no one would see my cellulite-covered thighs. I wished I could put them out of my mind altogether, but with my honeymoon night looming in the not-too-distant future, I felt compelled to somehow make them go away. I also wished I could get rid of my love handles. And that embarrassing mole. Ack.

Oh well. Stephen had agreed to marry me. Surely he could learn to live with those things. Right? And who knew—maybe he had a few imperfections too. I hoped.

On the night of the Golden Globes, I forgot all about my cellulite. In fact, the evening flew by at such a whirlwind pace that it felt like a dream. I vaguely remembered the look on Stephen's face when he saw me descending the stairs in that green dress. I heard the whistle that followed. I remembered how handsome he looked in his tuxedo, and how nervous he seemed as we drove to the theater. I laughed at Bob's antics on the red carpet and stumbled my way through a mini-interview with the gal from *Entertainment Tonight*. And I definitely remembered the feeling that gripped me when *Stars Collide* was listed as one of the nominees.

What stood out most, however, was the moment the shout went up. As the announcer opened the envelope and shared the news that *Stars Collide* had won Best Television Series for a Comedy or Musical, my insides turned to mush. I couldn't stand. I couldn't speak. I couldn't stop shaking. In short, I became a Greek statue. Frozen in place.

My co-workers all flew to their feet in joyous celebration. Stephen took my hand and pulled me out of my seat, dragging me along beside him to the stage, where I found myself huddled together with Rex, Lenora, Tia, Kat, Scott, and the whole writing crew. Rex spoke a few tearful words on behalf of the cast and crew, and we headed back to our seats.

The rest of the night was a blur. After the ceremony ended, we climbed into the limo to ride to the after party, and I turned into a quivering mess. Thankfully, everyone else was still chattering about the night, so Stephen and I managed to have a private conversation. My eyes filled with tears, and I choked out a few words about how happy I was, and yet how terrifying it had all been.

"We're in a limo, pulling away from the Golden Globes, where we won. We actually won." I shook my head. "This is so . . . surreal. If we'd written it as a scene in the sitcom, no one would have believed it."

"Truth is always stranger than fiction," Stephen said. He slipped his arm over my shoulder and drew me close. "Haven't you heard that?"

"I've heard it and I've lived it. After everything we've been through in the past few months, I'd have to say that the truth in my own life is definitely stranger than fiction. What happened to my normal, stable life?"

"Stable?" He laughed.

"Right. Stable. All I've ever known is stability. I've had a stable home environment. Stable family life. Stable love from my parents and siblings and other relatives. I'm stable Athena." *Makes me sound like a horse.*

"See?" he said. "You are a plotter. I knew it all along. You think things through."

"Maybe, but not on purpose. These last few weeks have been filled with a lot of things that I never knew would end up in my story. The news about Aunt Athena's estate. Milo and Melina's wedding. Our engagement." I turned to him and smiled. "I certainly never plotted any of that. And I never added in a scene at the Golden Globes."

"And I never imagined how God could bless me by allowing me to win a Comedy Award. But none of these awards even begin to compare with how I feel about you, Athena." He gazed at me tenderly. "Still, we're a mess, aren't we?" He flashed a smile. "I have to wonder if all writers are like this. I guess you need to loosen up a little in your real life. Don't worry about everything being so calculated."

"It's your fault." I punched him in the arm. "You're the one who kept bringing up that stupid twelve-step plotter. Before that I just went with the flow. Now I find myself wanting to plot out our wedding plans. Isn't that stupid?"

"Nah. It's funny." He kissed me on the forehead. "Go ahead and plot the wedding. Make your plans. Make them as elaborate or as plain as you like. Doesn't matter to me, just as long as you include Brooke. She's dying to be a bridesmaid. Or junior bridesmaid. Or whatever that's called." He laughed. "Can you tell I don't know much about this?"

"I'm not really up on weddings either," I said. "But don't worry. My mother's been planning my wedding since I was three. I have it on good authority that she's already rented the church and a hall for the reception."

"Of course she has."

"And I'm sure a band has been hired. Greek, of course."

"Of course."

"And Babbas will want to bring sandwiches. You can count on it."

"I wouldn't have it any other way. What's a wedding without a Super-Gyro?"

I paused to think about his words. Yes, indeed. What was a wedding without a superhero?

"Frankly, I'm not as concerned about the wedding as I am about the life," Stephen said. "Hope you're okay with that."

"Totally okay with that. I only plan to get married once."

My words were followed by silence, and I could see the pained look in his eyes. I suddenly realized what I'd said and how it must have affected him.

"Oh, man. I'm sorry, Stephen."

"No, nothing to apologize for. I never planned for things to go the way they did with Brooke's mom. When she took off with that guy, it broke my heart. I never pictured myself divorced. Not ever. And you can only imagine what all of that did to Brooke. But now that so much time has passed, I can honestly say that I'm grateful to be where I am now. I'm at a stronger place spiritually, and I'm a much better dad to Brooke." He grinned. "I think you're getting a better man."

"You are a great man, that's for sure." I gave him a gentle kiss. "And I pray you're okay with this completely imperfect woman you're ending up with. I'm a mess. You do know that, right?"

"You? A mess?"

Would this be a good time to tell him about the cellulite? About the love handles? No, maybe not.

I leaned back against the seat and released a happy sigh. "I still can't believe we're going to Greece for our honeymoon."

"Yep. We're going back to the land of our ancestors," he whispered. "Where the people are friendly and the culture is rich in history. Where the water is as blue as the sky and the food is sure to pack on the pounds."

Ugh. An image of my chubby thighs once again rose to the surface, but I pushed it away. No point in thinking about the negatives when the positives were staring me in the face. Greece! I was going to Greece. I could hardly believe it. All my life I'd dreamed of this.

Stephen took my hand in his and gave it a squeeze. "I keep forgetting to tell you, we've been given the run of the estate."

"I still can't believe Mama owns it. Crazy."

"Yes. We can stay as long as we like. And from what I hear, it's pretty amazing. Your uncle Milo showed me a ton of pictures. There are a couple of cars there too, but he doesn't have any idea what sort of shape they're in."

"Who cares? It's going to be the best two weeks of our lives."

"I can't wait."

"Me either." He gave me a tender kiss. Well, tender at first. As the kiss deepened, I gave myself a friendly reminder: *Better slow down. We're not on our honeymoon yet.*

I leaned back and smiled at my husband-to-be. "That was just a sample of things to come," I said with a wink. "You'll have to wait for the rest."

"I'm a very patient man." He gave me a knowing look, then smiled. "Once we're married, there won't be any inter-ruptions."

"Unless one of us comes up with a brilliant-beyond-brilliant idea for the show or something," I said. "Then you know what's going to happen. We're going to stop everything to write it down."

"Oh no we're not. No writing on this trip."

"Seriously? You really think we can go two whole weeks without writing? Impossible."

"The only story we're writing is our own," he said. "In fact, I've already started it. If you're a good girl, I might let you read what I've already written."

"Wait a minute . . . you're scripting our honeymoon?" I felt my cheeks grow warm as I thought about that. "Not sure that one will be PG."

"No, it won't be PG, but it will make you smile." He quirked a brow. "Trust me on this. You can read it later. After we're married."

"I might just have to do a version of my own," I said. "We'll compare and see whose is better."

"Enough with competition. From now on, we're on the same team."

"Oooh," I said as something occurred to me. "How can we lay down our competitive spirits when we've never had our baklava contest?"

"What?"

"Remember? We were going to have a contest to decide who was better at baking baklava."

Stephen shook his head. "Let me ask you a question."

"Okay."

"Does it really matter?"

"What do you mean?"

"I mean, in the grand scheme of things, does it really matter who's better at what? Does it matter who comes up with a better idea for a script or who bakes a better baklava?" When I shook my head, he said, "Okay then. Let's skip the contest. Declare a truce."

"You've got it." *But my baklava's still better than yours.*

"Thanks." He gave me a kiss so sweet it almost made me forget my competitive spirit. With this guy on my team, I could go a long, long way.

And I would, as soon as we boarded that plane for Greece.

"Stephen, promise me you won't tell me where we are on the plotline when we're honeymooning," I said. "I don't think I could take it."

He laughed. "I promise. We'll be seat-of-the-pants honeymooners. No plans." His brow wrinkled. "Oh, well, except one. I had to book one thing in advance. Couldn't be avoided."

"What's that?"

"I've been dying to tell you. You're going to love this." He gave my hands a squeeze. "We're going on a deep-sea-fishing cruise when we're in Greece. Perfect, right?"

"Deep-sea fishing? Why in the world would you sign us up to do something like that?"

He gave me a curious look. "Because you're into fishing. Isn't that right?"

"I am?"

"Well, yeah." He shrugged. "At least, that's what Kat told me. She said you were looking for a guy who loves to fish. Did I get that wrong?"

Oh no! A giggle arose. "Well, let's just say that was a test. That whole 'must love fishing' thing, I mean."

"It was for me too." As he gazed at me, I noticed a shimmer of tears in his eyes. "It's been a secret desire of mine since I was a kid. I never had a dad to fish with, and my nona wasn't interested, so you have no idea how much it means to me that you love to fish. I've waited all my life for a woman who wants to get her hands dirty. Bait a hook. Drag in a great catch." He gave me a little wink and then kissed me on each cheek.

I'd dragged in a great catch, all right. He continued to ramble on about the deep-sea-fishing expedition he'd booked for us, and I felt joy bubbling up from inside.

Should I tell him the truth about my so-called love for fishing, though? Nah. That could wait for another day. One thing was for sure—the Lord certainly had a great sense of humor. I could almost see him rocking back and forth on his throne in heaven, shouting, "Gotcha!"

I chuckled, thinking of that image. Yep. He was definitely a better writer than I'd ever dream of being. And his punch lines were out of this world.

Stephen continued to talk, oblivious to my thoughts. "Just wait till you see the waters in Greece. If they're half as great as the pictures on the internet, we're going to have the experience of a lifetime. We're going to catch all sorts of fish." He went off on another tangent, talking about the countless varieties of fish he hoped to snag.

Me? I'd already caught the one I'd been hoping for. And he could try for the rest of his life . . . but I wasn't letting this one get away.

Special Feature

"HONEYMOON IN GREECE"

WRITTEN BY
Athena Pappas Cosse

EDITED BY
Stephen Cosse

REWRITTEN BY
Athena Pappas Cosse

REEDITED BY
Stephen Cosse

A PLAZA in Athens at midday. Wide shot of two
STATUES in the middle of the square. Close-up
of a Greek statue of ADONIS (STEPHEN). Handsome male face. Camera pulls back to reveal
broad shoulders and ripped abs, covered par-
tially by an off-the-shoulder toga. GREEK
MUSIC BEGINS.

A tight shot to Adonis's left reveals a statue of ATHENA, virgin patron saint of Athens. She's smiling—until the camera zooms in on the cellulite on the backs of her thighs. Her smile turns to a frown and she shifts her position to hide her backside. MUSIC INTENSIFIES.

A TOURIST with a camera notices the change in ATHENA'S expression and position. He calls his wife over to witness it. ATHENA freezes as if she's never moved. The man takes a picture. ATHENA sneezes.

Camera zooms in on a statue of a small Greek DOG to the woman's right. Statue of DOG comes to life and leaps from the podium, startling tourists. ATHENA'S statue slowly begins to morph as well, and she steps off the podium, a smile on her face.

The TOURIST goes crazy with his camera, snapping pictures right and left. By now a crowd is approaching. Voices overlap.

WIDE SHOT on PLAZA, which is filled with vendors. DOG approaches a sandwich vendor, unties his apron with his teeth, and carries it to ATHENA. She ties it around STEPHEN'S neck, turning it into a superhero cape. He slowly comes to life, reaching over to grab a couple of sandwiches. He hands one to ATHENA. She takes it with a smile.

Just as the crowd goes crazy, STEPHEN adjusts his cape and takes hold of ATHENA'S right hand with his left. He sets his sights on the sky.

A resounding "Up, up, and away!" rings out from STEPHEN as his feet leave the ground. The crowd begins to cheer.

Tight shot on STEPHEN as he lifts off. The shot moves to ATHENA as she takes to flight as well. She can't stop smiling. At the last minute, she releases her hold on her sandwich and it tumbles to the ground. She extends her free hand to the DOG. DOG looks back and forth between sandwich on the ground and ATHENA'S extended hand. As the music swells, the DOG snags the sandwich in his teeth, then leaps into the air. Athena catches him.

Tight shot on the trio as they fly off into sunny skies.

FADE TO CIRCLE. DOG PEEKS THROUGH CIRCLE, EAT-ING SANDWICH. FADE TO BLACK.

Acknowledgments

As a writer, I connect with Athena on so many levels. I'm always wondering what stage of the plotline I'm at! I'd like to thank so many people who poured into me as a writer, including my good friend Patti Lee, who took me to my first writers' conference. Patti, you saw something in me long before I recognized it myself. Bless you for stirring up that gift in me.

Many thanks to sweet Janetta, who read every word of this manuscript, sticking with me till the very end. There's nothing like the eleventh-hour rush. Right, Janetta?

To my proofing buddies, Heather and Wendy. God bless you! Thanks for skimming over the manuscript to check for errors. I'm so grateful.

To my editor, Jennifer Leep. I still remember the day you called me to talk about this book. I thought I was in trouble! Turned out you just wanted me to add a dog to the story. Go figure! As a dog lover, I pounced on that idea! What fun coming up with the character of Zeus.

Many thanks to my copy editor, Jessica Miles. Girl, I sing

your praises from shore to shore. You are truly the best copy editor I've ever worked with, providing the perfect balance of polish and encouragement. Thanks for your kindness and your expertise.

To my marketing gurus, Michele, Donna, and the others who spend so much time marketing and promoting my books. Bless you! Oh, what fun to work alongside you.

To Chip MacGregor, my faithful agent. We are quite the team, aren't we? You will never know how grateful I am for your presence in my life. If not for you, these stories wouldn't exist.

And finally, to my dad. I know you're smiling down from heaven on this particular project. I remember that summer of '78 when you moved our family to L.A. so you could get into the movie biz. I cried my eyes out when you asked me to write that first script for you. Didn't have a clue what I was doing, and the idea of writing it terrified me. I think about that afternoon now and just smile. I might not have known what I was doing, but God sure did. He was opening up a Pandora's box (don'tcha love the Greek reference?) and planting seeds for the writing life that was to come. Thank you so much for seeing that gift in me, Dad, and for stirring it up. I miss you, but I know we'll pound out stories together in heaven one day. They'll be out of this world—literally!

Janice Thompson is a Christian freelance author and a native Texan. She has four grown daughters, four beautiful granddaughters, and two grandsons. She resides in the greater Houston area, where the heat and humidity tend to reign.

Janice started penning books at a young age and was blessed to have a screenplay produced in the early eighties, after living in the Los Angeles area for a time. From there she went on to write several large-scale musical comedies for a Houston school of the arts. Currently, she has published over sixty novels and nonfiction books for the Christian market, most of them lighthearted.

Working with quirky characters and story ideas suits this fun-loving author. She particularly enjoys contemporary, first-person romantic comedies. Janice loves sharing her faith with readers and hopes they will catch a glimpse of the real happily ever after in the pages of her books.

Come meet

JANICE THOMPSON

at www.JaniceAThompson.com

Read her blog, more interesting facts
about her books, and other fun trivia.

Follow Janice on Twitter

 booksbyJanice

"I hope you enjoy this romantic getaway as much as I did."

—Kristin Billerbeck, author of *Perfectly Dateless* and *What a Girl Wants*

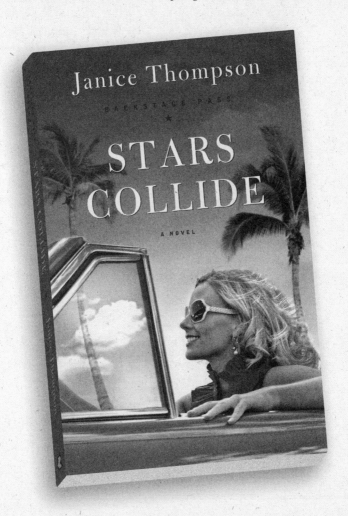

Catch the start of Janice Thompson's hilarious new series, Backstage Pass.

A Romantic Comedy That Will Have You Laughing All Day

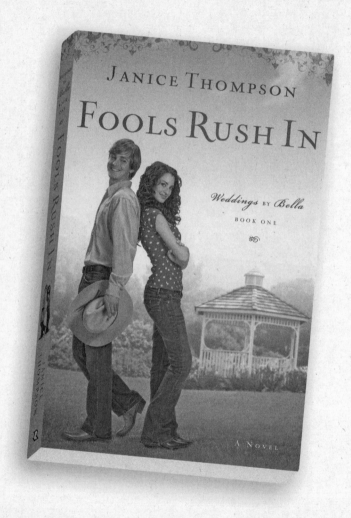

Don't miss book 1 in the Weddings by Bella series!

When *Hollywood's* most eligible
bachelor sweeps into town,
will he cause trouble for *Bella*?

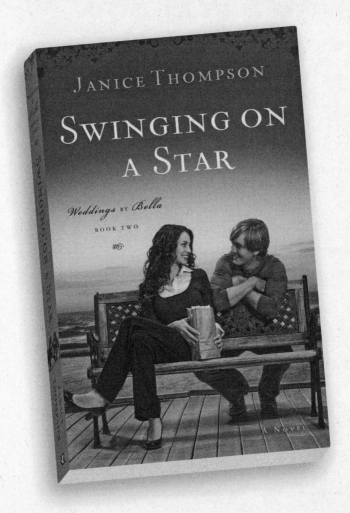

Don't miss book 2 in the Weddings by Bella series!

Get ready for a double dose of wedding frenzy!

Don't miss book 3 in the Weddings by Bella series!

Can this hometown hero sweep his girl off her feet?

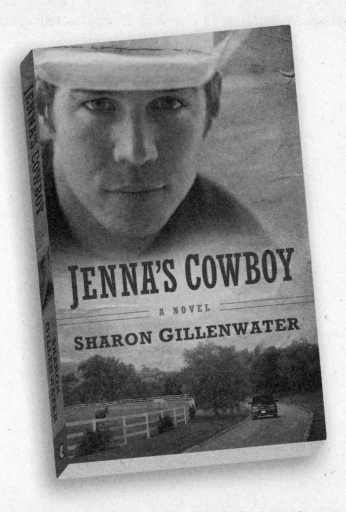

Jenna returns to her family's ranch to heal a broken heart. She never expected to see Nate Langley back in town—the first guy she was attracted to, the one her father sent away all those years ago. Can he heal her broken heart?

"Filled with Texas charm and the healing power of love."

—Debbie Macomber, #1 *New York Times* bestselling author

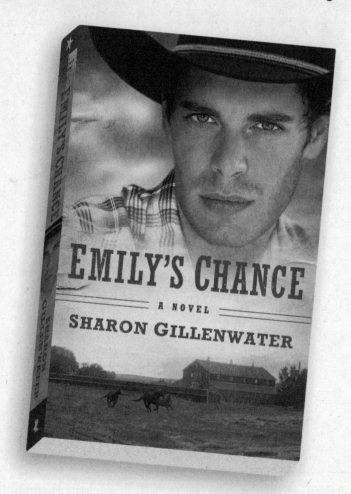

Emily's Chance is a heartwarming story of letting love take the lead that will have you wishing you lived in Callahan Crossing, Texas.

Can love truly heal the past?

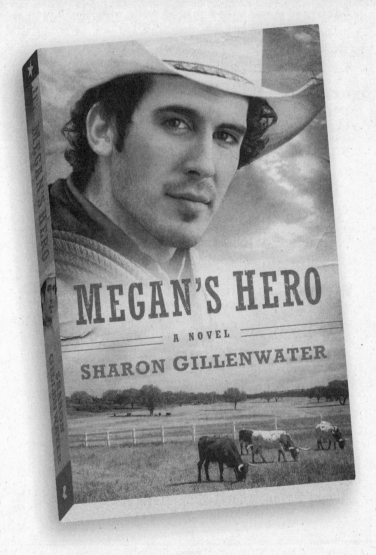

Filled with the easy charm and warmth of Texas,
Megan's Hero will have you believing in the power of love and forgiveness.

 Revell
a division of Baker Publishing Group
www.RevellBooks.com

Available at your local bookstore.